ORGANIC LOVE

A NOVEL

M. E. WEYERBACHER

To Nancy
Steph's Aunt

Cover designer: Oh So Novel.

Editor: Elisabeth Nelson

For the ones who didn't get to say goodbye

CHAPTER 1

Reese ignored the burning in her eyes and pressed forward, editing the manuscript on her laptop. All was peaceful in her downstairs writing nook, except for the yearning inside her chest. The sting of missing her family hovered, and she knew it was affecting her work. Irritation shot her bangs upward as she nudged her glasses back in place. Reese tried refocusing by stretching her back. *Ten more minutes.*

A light rap came from the front door. One glance at the computer's clock told her she'd been sitting too long: 7:15. She could hear her mom's rebuke launching straight from the nearby family photo. Reese crossed her arms tight. "I know, I know, take a vacation." *Still seven months away.* Another rap on the front door. Reese's neck tightened but she surrendered to the interruption.

Sliding into the kitchen, she set the timer for three minutes. Who could possibly need something on a Sunday evening in her quiet little town? Eastwood was about as exciting as watching paint dry, unless it was a holiday, when the town council ramped up the festivities. *I just checked on Lila and Stan. Who could it be?*

Reese caught her breath. A guy at the door stood patiently, kind eyes and warm smile. A deep stirring grabbed her stomach. Was it anxiety? She braced herself.

"Are you all right, ma'am?" He reached out his hands as if he were going to prevent a tragedy.

"Yes, sorry." *Just a little stressed is all.*

A grin replaced the man's worried expression. "Do you have an egg I could borrow—I mean have?" A short laugh escaped from his mouth as he ran his fingers through his chocolate-brown hair.

"Sure, just give me one sec. And no need to call me ma'am."

She left the door ajar, her mind reeling. *Who is he?* At least she remembered to smile. Her therapist, Dayl, wanted her to become more self-aware. Smiling more wasn't something she regularly thought about while living alone. The thought of practicing such a thing considering her despondent life almost seemed a little fake. Her best friend lost his life and her parents were off trying to change the world. The house was chronically quiet, and her favorite paperbacks refused to carry their weight in conversation. Was smiling more such a big deal? Brooding seemed acceptable.

Reese's toe caught the lip of the only raised floorboard in the house. She froze. The egg was safe. Her favorite shirt was still clean, and the guy hadn't witnessed her near-debacle. *Thank God.*

Reese smiled, gently setting the egg in the man's palms.

"I appreciate it, uh…"

"Reese," she finished.

"Reese. I like that." The handsome stranger turned the

egg over in his hand silently, as if he were in some deep thought.

"I haven't seen you around our neighborhood before. What did you say your name was?"

"Elliot. I just rec—"

The beep of the timer sounded from behind Reese. She tried not to smirk. "Uh…sorry. It was nice to meet you, Elliot."

"Yeah—no problem. Probably see you around." He made his way down the steps and looked back with a nod.

Her eyes followed him across the lawn, into the house next door. *New neighbor? And why do I freak out so easily?*

Reese shut the timer off. 7:20. Her stomach growled.

Guess I should cook something now.

REESE HUMMED WITH THE BIRDS AS SHE TUGGED THE WEEDS upward, tossing them into a pile behind her. She took her garden gloves off so she could move a hair out of her face and took a sip of water from her over-sized thermos. *This is where I need to be. Not hunkered down inside.* Being outdoors always seemed to help her spirits, but she'd let work take over her life these past few years and had forgotten how to have fun.

She put the gloves back on, then yanked at the next weed. *Invigorating.*

Editing manuscripts used to energize her, but over the last twelve months, the work began to lose its luster with the frequency of panic attacks. They sprang up about the time her family started packing for a long-term trip and got worse after they left.

Reese wiped her brow and replaced the mulch she'd shifted over.

Quitting wasn't an option, though. Not until she had another plan set in place. Her current position was rare, at least so she'd been told. She'd grandfathered in after the company changed CEOs and shifted its vision towards creating an alternative publishing option for writers. The flip side gave emerging editors a chance to gain experience. The combination of the two created a booming online business.

Reese rolled her neck and popped her fingers. The roots were coming out much easier today. The more she thought about it, the less she wanted to be indoors for hours at a time. She wasn't the best at making herself stop to take a break. She'd been known to edit for hours at a time, even scarfing a can of something down just to get back at it. At least the degree she got six years ago was paying off.

Reese felt the morning wind against her face.

Sure, her employer gave her the freedom to work remotely, but the panic attacks were getting worse. After months of struggling alone, Reese was glad to have reached out to her doctor about the inner stress.

The sun poked through the clouds. Reese reached for her sunhat. How wonderful would it be if her sister could sit out here with her? But her sister wasn't one to sit still. None of her family was for that matter.

She never pegged herself as one to suffer from loneliness. After all, she used to thrive on coffee and books for days. *Maybe smiling more and talking to an actual human really will help.*

At the thought, Reese pulled out her cell phone. *Not even a text.* She'd hoped to hear from her mom by now about if they'd be back in time for Thanksgiving or Christmas, but it had been a week since they last exchanged words.

Shoving the phone back into her pocket, she moved further down her neighbor's landscaping.

Reese thought back to her second therapy session after her family left. She was encouraged to revive an old passion. At the time, she didn't see the point, but was willing to try anything to help curb the anxiety. Over the next few weeks, she sifted through her childhood hope chest, filled with memories and musty smells. There it was, nestled under the turtleneck her mom couldn't convince her to donate: her teal art folder. Stacks of drawings of their neighbor's garden produce were wedged in the pockets. Some were stuck together by who knew what.

She remembered the swelling emotion and made up her mind gardening would be her passion revival of choice.

Dayl seemed hopeful and even proud. It would have been something to share with her family had she been honest about the whole ordeal. Her mom, dad, and sister were finishing up their current clean-water mission with a non-profit organization they were heavily involved with, and she couldn't bring herself to tell them about the shortness of breath.

Worrying her mom right before a long trip felt cruel and wrong. Reese wiped a tear and snapped back to the job at hand when she heard the front door swing open.

"Well you're out awful early, dear!" Miss Lila shouted as she wheeled her husband Stan out onto the front deck. The rectangular cabin was set south of Reese's house, their front yard partially forming her back yard. The elderly neighbors had built the cabin before Reese was even born. They'd been like grandparents to her all these years, and it was the least she could do to help them keep up the landscaping.

She heard a bark and turned to pet their boisterous dachshund. Just as quick as he'd come, he darted back up the deck steps.

Reese cleared her throat and replied using her I'm-too-far-away-to-carry-on-a-conversation holler. "Yeah, I know. Wanted to do your weeding while the ground's still damp!"

Miss Lila put Stan's brakes on and tossed Redford a treat. "Smart thinking!"

Reese wiped her brow and glanced at her watch. She had enough time to finish here, edit more of the manuscript, make a few phone calls, and go to the store before her appointment with Dayl.

Redford bounded back down the steps toward her, pawing at the wood chips.

"Leave her alone!" Miss Lila said, following close behind. She scooped Redford up in her arms as a moving truck pulled in. Reese jumped to her feet trying to make out who it was. Her heart picked up its pace, but she stepped forward as the driver put the truck in park then rolled down the window.

"Can I help you?"

"This isn't the Jacobson residence is it?" The driver reached beside him, fumbling through papers.

"Never heard the name. But if they've bought Grand's ol' place right there, you're not far." Miss Lila pointed toward Reese's back yard which conjoined with Grand's. All three properties had lovely, flat back yards unfolding to the edge of Reese's favorite childhood adventure spot: the woods.

Reese's upper lip tightened. She'd forgotten to tell Miss Lila about the guy she'd met the day before. She'd noticed what appeared to be his Jeep in the driveway, but the whole egg-borrowing ordeal threw her off. She pictured Grand sitting on his porch watching the sun go down. So many memories were made at that house. He'd been like another father to her growing up. And then there was his son.

Reese pushed Jett's face from her mind and tossed her

gloves in her work bag. She tried not to look emotional, but it was too late.

Miss Lila put her arm around Reese. “We all miss Grand. And Jett. How are you, really?”

“Life goes on, right?”

Miss Lila began to stroke Redford who was starting to wiggle out of her firm, one-armed grip. The truck driver’s presence was setting him off. “Have you heard from your parents? Sister?”

Reese looked down and shook her head. “Not since last week.”

“That’s hard, Reese. You know we’re always here for you.”

Reese forced a smile. She knew it was true. Deep down, she wished she could’ve opened up to her family about the reality of her pain. Especially her dad. Before he took on more hours at the organization, they’d talk at night while everyone else was getting ready for bed. Going from a close-knit family to zero was hitting her hard.

“Your parents love you, Reese.” Miss Lila added.

Her dad was caring and kind, but his mission-focused heart sucked him away into a vortex neither of them saw coming. At first, he’d stay up with her to do their usual chats, but over time they became less frequent until finally, they stopped.

“I know.” Reese replied. They were doing a good thing in the world, drilling wells for clean water.

Redford scampered back up the steps the moment Miss Lila set him down. Right back to barking he went. Miss Lila rolled her eyes, causing Reese to laugh. She was glad to be surrounded by love and pure hilarity, but how did one get on with life when everyday felt like a rerun?

Grand and Jett had been as close as family and losing

them both in a three-year span had left her dented. *When you're young, you feel like time is on your side. You put off hugs and questions, put off going out of your way. You think, tomorrow. But then someone gets taken away, and you wish rewind existed.*

Only, it doesn't.

Grand had lived next door as long as Miss Lila and Stan had lived on the other side. He'd always been there for Reese, reminding her of his open-door policy. Though there was much she couldn't talk to Grand about growing up, she did confide in him about many things. She wished she could turn back time. Be a free little girl again—but it was time grow up.

The driver of the moving truck answered his phone and held up a finger for them to hold on.

Miss Lila looked at Reese and smiled. "Not sure how you can get lost in our town. It's only three miles wide."

I should have confided in Miss Lila this whole time. But Reese knew they were aging fast, and she didn't want to put any extra worry on her sweet elderly neighbor. She told Miss Lila the truth but cut out a lot. Mainly, her family had been so busy over the last few years that the only way to get through Jett's death was to distract herself with her own work. What other option did she have?

Even being surrounded by people who watched her grow up, she couldn't find the courage to share with them the truth about the state of her heart. That she hadn't made time to mourn her best friend's death. That almost three years later, she still couldn't wrap her brain around the fact he was never coming back.

The truck driver rolled his window back down and laughed. "Sorry for taking up your time. Mr. Jacobson called to check on me. He's on his way here with more boxes. I guess I turned one driveway too late."

Miss Lila smiled and waved as the man backed slowly down the drive. Reese wondered what her parents would think about someone finally moving into Grand's. It'd been six months since he passed, and her parents were left the estate with full permission to do with it as they pleased. They'd taken a few months to auction off many of the items and finally decided to sell the house, agreeing the proceeds would go to the clean-water project they were heading up.

Everything had changed too fast for Reese. She longed for slow. She longed for togetherness. But that wasn't happening. Best to toughen up—right?

Miss Lila crossed her arms and turned toward Grand's. "Figured it would sell quick."

They had grown into one big family, more so after Grand's wife's passing a decade ago. Reese's mom would go over and make him dinner. Some nights they'd all cram around his oak table for supper, but not his son—her lifelong friend, Jett.

After their awkward kiss, he spent more time avoiding her than anything else.

"I miss the dinners." Reese said.

Miss Lila pressed her lips and gave Reese another squeeze. "Pie night won't ever replace it, but we sure love having you over."

Reese wiped her face with the back of her sleeve. "Tonight?"

Miss Lila winked. "You know it."

"Sure thing." Reese grabbed her garden bag and waved up to Stan, but he'd fallen asleep. "See ya later."

Reese made her way across the lawn, watching from afar as the truck driver backed into Grand's old driveway. He set the ramp and began unloading. She could see a few pieces of furniture tucked away in the back and figured the Elliot guy had to be the new homeowner. *I mean, he asked for an egg. Who else would it be?*

The truck driver struggled to move one of the boxes.

Reese set her bag down on the back patio and wondered if she should offer to help. Did moving etiquette exist?

He finally managed to slide the box atop a dolly. Reese let out a breath. She was glad he hadn't hurt himself but equally glad she could escape into her house for a shower. She smelled of weeds and sweat.

Just as Reese turned to walk into the house, she heard a familiar voice. Shading her eyes for a better look—she spotted the same burnt-orange Jeep from the day before, pulled up behind the moving truck.

A series of high-pitched barks startled her.

"Really, Redford?" Reese picked up the pooch and headed back across the yard toward Lila and Stan's. He wasn't supposed to be out unless someone was with him. Redford liked his adventures, but Miss Lila was picky about his cleanliness.

The familiar voice hollered something from behind her and Redford leapt, leaving a scratch on her arm.

"No, you brat, get back here!"

Fully aware of the dog's stubborn streak, she sprang toward her house and flung the mudroom door open, grabbing a few stashed dog treats. *Your little dachshund attitude won't stand a chance.*

Reese ran around the side where she saw Redford trot off. He was like a statue, staring at all the commotion next door.

"Redford! Here boy!" she called. He turned to face her, giving her a stare down. It looked like a single treat wasn't going to be enough this time.

"It'll be worth your while, mister." Reese tossed multiple treats out across the lawn, making a trail to her front porch. "Five dollars' worth!"

Just as Redford conceded, a young man wearing sunglasses came into view. He was carrying a few boxes, stacked meticulously, forcing his face sideways to see. Her eyes followed his movement as he set the boxes down to stretch. Walking to the Jeep, he took his glasses off, and appeared to tuck them away.

Reese took stock of the man, only able to see his back side, and tiny portion of the side.

Tall, dark, handsome. Athletic pants, tee, tan skin, and a hair style that says he's particular.

He turned around and met Reese's gaze. *Elliot.*

Grand's had looked the same for twenty-eight years, but not today.

CHAPTER 2

Chopin blared at six a.m. Reese smacked the phone's alarm. It wouldn't hush.

Swipe, Reese, don't slap.

Rubbing her swollen eyes, she stepped over the wad of tissues on the floor and splashed her face with cold water. If Grand knew she was crying over him, over Jett, he'd tell her to cheer up and find the positive note. *Positive note: I made it through my therapy session yesterday.*

Grand had a strong spirit. Even after Jett's passing, he kept his faith.

Reese shuffled down the wooden stairs to pour herself a cup of coffee. She peeled back the sticky plastic wrap hugging Miss Lila's leftover peach pie from the night before. Running her pinky through the gooey center, she licked the cinnamon-infused dessert, thankful for new mornings.

Reese shuffled outside, coffee in tow. Even among pain and questions, miracles existed—right? She always thought the birds proved it. No matter the storms, they still spread their wings. Eventually. Did they wait until the storm passed to fly? Wings. *Tattered wings.*

If Reese had wings they'd be tattered for sure. *No flying for me.*

She longed for inner peace, which meant she needed predictable and steady—right? Her family didn't think so, but she wasn't built like them. She was just fine in her one-stop-light town. *But am I fine?*

She shuffled onto the front porch with her morning essentials and glanced over her daily list.

- EDIT MANUSCRIPT
- CALL COLLEGE
- WATER FLOWERS
- FARMER'S MARKET
- FINISH GARDEN LAYOUT
- READ

A door slammed shut. She saw the Elliot guy retrieve something from his Jeep. He stopped short to look her way and gave a wave. Reese willed herself to be polite and added a smile to the gesture. She wasn't a people person, but at least he was ruggedly handsome and so far, well mannered.

Okay—now to get started on my list.

He stretched a few times, and Reese tried not to stare. She fidgeted with her coffee mug but looked back. *Look at those calves.*

She focused on something new. Her robe had a few stitches coming loose. She tugged, but they didn't break free. She looked up. He rolled his neck back and forth. *Dude—your shirt is glued to your chest.*

Reese swallowed. Why did she feel so weird?

She brought the mug up to her face for a drink, trying to distract herself.

Lukewarm. *I should reheat this.* She set it aside and

looked for Elliot, but he was just disappearing around the bend. *Just as well.*

She pressed her face into her palms. She hadn't realized her own chest would feel cut open the moment someone new bought her childhood best friend's home. Jett may have cut himself off from her for those last nine years, but she'd loved him anyway. *You can experience some level of love at sixteen —right?*

She'd held out hope that maybe someday he'd call her on the phone and tell her how illogically he'd acted. That the quick kiss didn't have to determine their relationship. The call never came.

She rubbed her temples, and realized her mind was going back down the familiar road to nowhere. Redford barked in the distance, signaling it was time to get to work. She was thankful for his annoying little yelp this time.

Stuffing the thoughts aside, she mentally went over the affirmations Dayl suggested.

Today is not chained to yesterday. Today is fresh, ready, and waiting. Waiting just for me.

"Hello? Yes, I was returning a call from your office." Reese fiddled with her hair as she paced the room, hoping to hear good news about the gardening class. "Okay. Oh, I see."

She found her keys and tossed her gear into the pickup, darting back into the house to scribble something down. "Sure, I'll get them turned in right away."

She circled Monday on the wall calendar and doodled a flower for good measure. *Intro to Vegetable Gardening here I come.* "Really wish I would have taken notes from Grand when I had the chance."

"There you are, my Reesey!" Miss Rosa's face beamed, her large arms squeezing tight. There was no escape. Her brightly adorned rebozo flapped around them both, cocooning Reese beyond her will.

"Heeey…"

Reese really did love her. Miss Rosa moved from the South to the Northern Kentucky region when Reese was just seven. She'd been like an aunt to her, filling her life with humor and drama. The kind Reese's mom almost disapproved of but would only shake her finger at and walk away. Miss Rosa was a caring widow with a keen sense of self and others. She said things out loud that no one else was brave enough to say. Maybe it was why Reese had always felt so drawn to her.

In a way, she wanted to be more like her. To just holler at life's mess, laugh at the funny parts, and throw herself into community living. Reese was trying—the last one, at least.

She set her bag down by the produce stand and scoped out the scene at the local farmer's market. It wasn't too busy today. She preferred to help during the week when it was less crowded.

Lately, their small town seemed to have an influx of travelers passing through on the weekends. Reese never imagined that three years into volunteering she'd still be trying to dodge the crowds, but personal bubbles had never been a thing for most of Eastwood's residents, let alone happy and energetic visitors.

"Did you hear back from the college yet?" Miss Rosa asked, eyebrows accusing Reese of holding out.

"I promise I will let you know as soon as I know. Transcripts come first."

"Okay, okay. But I know you'll get in. How could they not let you in? You've already got a master's degree, for crying out loud." Miss Rosa planted a gentle pat onto her head, bangles clashing. "This'll be a cake walk for you, Reesey."

"I don't know about that. Been a long time since I dabbled in planting."

Miss Rosa gave her a look. "I still think I could have taught you just as much."

"You know me. Always taking the long route."

"You are somewhat stubborn. More like me than your own mom." Miss Rosa curled her lips.

"And I really like books."

"True, honey. But just remember when you get billed—I could have schooled you free."

Reese couldn't help but laugh. She was right. Maybe taking a college class was going overboard, but it made her feel legit. It'd also stretch over the course of the year, helping her to stay busy until her family's return.

"Here. You're at this table today." Miss Rosa tossed Reese an asparagus bundle and a grin simultaneously.

Reese barely made the catch when she saw who pulled up. Small town parking wasn't exactly a buffet. The only orange Jeep she'd ever laid eyes on was now a short fifty feet away from the produce stand.

"Are you okay, niña?" Miss Rosa took the wrapped greens back from Reese and put her hands on her hips. "I knew there was something you weren't telling me. You've been too quiet lately."

"What? Oh no, that's just my new neighbor."

Miss Rosa got a better look. Her dimples deepened.

"Oh, put away that cheesy grin!" Reese rolled her eyes.

Please don't come over here. Please don't come over here.

"Reesey, sooner or later you're going to have to talk to a man. You can't avoid them forever."

Reese rocked on her heels. Did Miss Rosa known more about her than she'd let on?

"Give life a chance. A little risk is good for the soul." Miss Rosa hung a fresh wedge of paper sacks on a nearby hook.

Reese tried to soften her growing scowl.

"Charming…" Miss Rosa muttered with a twisted smile.

Elliot shut the Jeep's door and finished his phone conversation.

Reese rubbed her sweaty palms on her pants, pivoting into the bookshop a handful of feet away. Skimming the shelves, she grabbed at the first book her finger grazed. *Scary Close: Dropping the Act and Finding True Intimacy* by Don Miller.

Really? Out of all the books?

Anette, the bookshop owner, grinned wide. "May I help you—oh hey, Reese. Can I help you find something today?"

"No, thanks. I think I found it." Reese shook her head and opened the book down the middle. Using it as a mask, she peeked over the pages and peered through the front window.

Gorgeous Elliot was at the table talking to Miss Rosa.

CHAPTER 3

Seven days into gaining a new neighbor, and Reese had successfully dodged Elliot for each one. Every time she saw him, her nerves danced, and it wasn't pretty. One day, she'd almost worked up the courage to apologize for darting off at the produce stand, but at the last minute she became flushed and went the opposite direction.

She felt like a teen all over again. It was ridiculous. Even more ridiculous was the new habit forming. She'd watch him from her upper window. He'd go on a long run every morning at six, change, and reappear at his mailbox at seven. She'd wait until he was out of sight and then sit in her thinking chair, shifting while trying to focus her thoughts.

Today was no different. Normally by now, she'd at least have a few notes scribbled. A fresh thought. A doodle. Anything.

Right now, all she had was her white pad of paper, pen, and Elliot's tan muscles flexing in her mind. *Who am I? Some sort of creeper?*

The wind rustled the curtain's edge. Reese peered out the window. Her pulse quickened. It was 6:57 a.m.

"I am such a child. I should just go say hello already."

She thundered down the steps and straight out the front door. Flipping open her mail box, she shrieked as a hornet came rushing straight at her. Reese bit her nails while crouching for a better look.

"You lose something in there?"

Reese felt faint hearing his voice. "Oh…hi."

"How have you been?"

"Good, good. Except, well—this box of hornets—" Reese backed away as another came zipping out. "Every year these guys are an issue."

He stepped over. "Hmm, yeah I see they have a nest." He was bent over eyeing the bottom where it connected to the stand.

"Not sure why they chose mine. It's boring compared to your barn mailbox." Reese snickered, feeling her nerves ease. *See? You can talk to people.*

He laughed and shook his head. "I'll get your mail tonight and set it on your porch. Think I have spray somewhere."

"Wow, thanks. I'd appreciate that."

He nodded and gave a side smile as he walked away, tucking his own mail in his back pocket.

Reese straightened, unsure what to say next.

He adjusted his sunglasses atop his head and looked up at the trees. "Nice neighborhood."

"Sure is." Her eyes carried to his bright-red front door. She pictured Grand and the way he'd open it, yelling after her and Jett. "Don't stay out too long! You and Reese be careful near that pond!" Reese tried to shake the memory.

"Still unpacking. Fun, fun." He laughed, tilting his eyes toward his new house.

"Ah, yeah. Fun times."

"Well, have a nice day, Reese." Elliot turned to walk

away, waving two fingers. The way the edge of his hair met the corner of his eye was perfect.

He really is nice.

"See ya," Reese waved. She watched him go inside, the red door shutting behind him.

The familiar pain gnawed.

Jett.

THE WAFT OF APPLE PIE SCENT INFILTRATED THE LOG CABIN. "Miss Lila, you seriously need to sell these over at the stand."

She lifted a finger. "Oh, no. This was my mama's recipe, and it will remain a gift. I'd much rather enjoy passing them around for free."

"But you could have a booming business!" Reese said, sliding the last bite into her mouth.

"Stan, are you going to move or not?" Miss Lila tapped the chess board.

Reese laughed. "I'd better go; it's getting late." Part of Reese had always wanted to ask Miss Lila if she'd ever experienced loss in her younger years. Every time she worked up the courage, she talked herself out of it. *You're here to help them—to keep them company.*

Reese wedged the box holding her take-home pie piece into her purse and didn't mind the dew against her bare feet as she crossed the lawn.

Her phone beeped, revealing a message from her mom.

The text read: "Break tomorrow. Will call at 10 p.m. your time."

She slipped the phone back into her purse and remembered the pie. Instead of walking home, she kept going.

The rear of Elliot's house glowed.

Her foot found the back patio. She tiptoed toward the back door as if she were a spy. *Am I spying?* A hand on the pie, hand on the glass, she withheld her knock. So many times, she'd barged through this door, and now she couldn't. She hadn't been in the house since the day they put it up for sale. Even then, she hadn't wanted to.

Reese eyed the dessert. *It's too late. He'll be weirded out. Go home.*

She ducked and headed for home, feeling the sting of sinuses before a good cry. She set the fresh pie on the counter next to the older one and flipped the lid open for one more bite. The fragile homemade crust crumbled to the touch.

She glanced at a photo of her sister, Dana, on the fridge. "You calling me flaky?"

Too much pie, too much pain.

CHAPTER 4

"Aaaand, send!" Reese breathed a sigh of relief. "One manuscript down, one to go."

A loud banging interrupted her celebration. She swallowed the last of her cold muffin and shoved the chair under the desk. She tied the white kitchen curtain to the side to get a better look. Someone was making a lot of racket out back; her guess was Elliot. Sure enough, he was building something in his yard. She pressed her lips together, watching intently. Butterflies zipped through her stomach.

The phone rang.

"Hello? Oh, hello…Yes? I see." Reese held her breath.

After a few minutes of conversation, she set her phone down in frustration. The guidance counselor said the class was full. *Great. Back to square one.*

Reese watched as Elliot worked with his hands. *Maybe he wants a drink?* She wanted to get better at this hello thing. This conversation-with-a-stranger thing.

She poured two cups of coffee and awkwardly made her way out the back door.

In his yard, he was hunched over, measuring. There were several boards stacked in rows. He didn't seem to notice her.

Reese cleared her throat.

"Oh, hey there, Reese." Elliot tucked the pencil behind his ear, looking up at her with smile. He shielded his eyes from the sun. "What do you have there?"

"Coffee?" She held it out as an offering.

"Sorry—don't drink coffee," he said apologetically.

"Really? Wow. I live on it." She stepped back and set the extra mug in the grass for the time being.

"I prefer tea. But thanks," he said—turning back to his project.

"You don't strike me as the tea-drinking type."

He set the tools down and blew the dust from the slab he was focused on. His eyes followed its length as he gently ran a hand atop the edge of the smooth wood. His jaw muscle flinched. She wondered what he was thinking.

Elliot looked up at her. "You have a hobby?"

Reese thought about the garden she wanted to start. "Does it count if you aren't too good at it?"

He pulled the pencil from behind his ear, darkening a mark he'd made and laughed. "Sure it does."

Reese smiled and began walking back to her house, both mugs now in hand.

"Reese?"

She spun around. "Yeah?" she replied, glad for an excuse to see his face again.

"I know we just met, but I was wondering…"

Reese bit her lip and adjusted her glasses.

"You eat dinner?"

"Uh—yeah." Reese tried ignoring the pangs in her chest, but the thought of going into Jett's made her wish she'd kept quiet. Her face must have changed because Elliot stood, brushing off his hands.

"Too soon?"

Reese glanced at his new house. The home she'd run in and out of her entire life. *You have no idea.*

Elliot turned to look over his shoulder, probably trying to decipher her blank expression. His gaze fell to the project. "How about a backyard picnic then?"

Oh. That's different. It was a brilliant idea. *You should.*

He raised his eyebrows, waiting on her reply, but he finally broke the silence himself. "Never mind. Hey—maybe another time?"

Reese drank the last of her coffee to buy a few more seconds. "I can't make any promises—but it does sound like fun."

He moved his hair out of his face and grinned. "I'll take that."

Reese just smiled.

She watched his hair fall back over his eyes as he bent over, combining his tools into one neat line next to the wood slabs. He pulled a baseball cap from his back pocket and plopped it on his head.

"Have a good day there, Reese." He gave a wink and a nod and walked toward his Jeep.

At home, Reese pulled up her work in progress on her laptop. *I have three hours to get this done.*

Instead of editing, Reese closed her eyes and let herself fall backward onto the chaise, in the corner of her downstairs work nook. The sun peeked through the blinds, creating warmth on her arms.

Jett appeared in her mind.

She sat up and reached for the nearby filing cabinet,

quickly shuffling past less-important folders. "There you are."

She pulled out the teal folder she'd tucked away in a more accessible area.

Reese lay it open on her lap and began going through the papers one by one.

A crinkled paper full of notes and dreams peeked out among the rest. This paper was unique. Her entire childhood could be summed up and turned over with the flip of a wrist.

She scanned the drawings and signatures.

She and Jett got so dirty helping Grand with his backyard garden when they were small. They'd play for hours, pretending to be grownups in charge of their own land. One time, Reese took a single orange sock from her mom's drawer and stuffed it with uncooked beans, tying the end off with green yarn. Jett had made fun of her until he realized it was as close to a carrot as they were going to get on their own.

A few years later, with Grand's help they managed to grow a row of real carrots. The first time she yanked one out of the soil, Grand and Jett whooped and hollered.

She missed the sound of Jett's voice. His pale skin surrounded by tousled, blond hair. The last time she'd seen him was three years ago right before he left for a ski trip. He never came back. The funeral was hard on the whole community. Grand had shown strength around everyone, but Reese believed that when he was alone, he let the tears flow.

Reese's heart jumped.

At the bottom of the paper, Jett had penned his name next to Reese's inside a crooked heart. She remembered they were ten when he quickly scribbled the gesture and ran back across the lawn. They were sixteen when the line between best friends and something more became a blur. The quick kiss ruined everything. After that day, he tried to pretend it hadn't happened.

Reese reached out. She still wanted to be friends, but he stopped talking to her. Grand was strong but not so much that Reese couldn't see a glint of sorrow behind his glasses.

Like Miss Rosa, Grand had probably known more than he let on.

Reese tucked the papers back into the folder, putting the special one in front. It was true. The town got a double blow. Triple really, because Grand's wife had passed from cancer. *So much death.*

She barely had time to gather herself after Grand's funeral before her family announced they were leaving on the long-term assignment overseas.

She flipped her notepad open. *This is important.*

Dayl put emphasis on sharing anything surrounding her family's departure and events leading up to it. Maybe answers to the panic attacks were closer than she realized.

Just then, her phone lit up.

It was her mom calling several hours early.

Reese held her breath as she answered. Something told her this may be the night the truth would come gushing out. The truth about the anxiety. The truth about her hidden pain all these years.

CHAPTER 5

The screen door squealed, and Reese felt the opportunity greeting her. Her galoshes told stories of the past where mud remained jammed into the crevices of her soles. Pushing through unused tools, she found the gem. It was Grand's old garden bag, still sitting there in the mudroom right where she'd left it.

"It's yours," her mom had said, holding it out. With trembling hands, she'd taken it from her and wedged it into the corner of the mudroom. Out of sight, out of mind.

She let her hands glide across the surfaces. Its brown leather smelled of dirt, rain, and dandelions. She touched the indigo seam and wondered if she could pull off a basic garden without the college class. Surely, she could research enough to get her going.

During the previous night's conversation, her mom encouraged her to go for it but not to be afraid to ask for help.

Reese opened the bag and peered in. *Why do I wait to talk about my problems until I feel like I'm going to explode?*

Her mom had listened as she poured out frustration about Jett all those years before. She listened when Reese vented about Grand and how come the man had to endure such pain when he didn't deserve it. And her mom listened when she sobbed—admitting she was lonely and just wanted to know where her life was going.

Strolling outside, she saw Elliot's ever-growing tarp covered project. She hadn't told her mom about him. She couldn't believe she confessed as much as she did—but there was no way she was about to bring up another guy.

Rain clouds were off in the distance, but Reese set her bag and tiller down anyway. She traipsed through the edge of the woods bordering the back of her property. The skinny trees loomed overhead, creating a Spring canopy. "Ah, that'll work." She dragged an old log across the floor of the woods, to use it as a seat for rest breaks. She stopped short of the yard's edge.

A vehicle's rumble grabbed her attention. She looked up. Through the blooming buds draped across the branches, she could see Elliot's Jeep pulling into his drive. He got out, a gorgeous young woman accompanying him. They were laughing and disappeared into the front.

"Ouch!" Reese slapped her arm, killing a bug trying to eat her for lunch. She dropped the log and refused to set her eyes toward Elliot's property. *Who needs a break?*

REESE GAVE THE CANOE A GENTLE PUSH AND LEAPT IN. ALL was quiet except for the sound of a family of frogs and the summer bugs humming to the tune the birds started. The water was extra blue, and the sun wasn't shy at all. Every ray found its way down, bouncing off the lake as if it were a mirror.

This was Reed's Pond, but she'd always thought it a lake.

It was large, after all. Here, she'd come to think. Her thinking chair didn't always do the trick. Nature's powerful effect had acted as a reset button for so many years. It was hard to believe she'd avoided it for so long.

She glanced upward at the sound of faraway thunder. Maybe being at Reed's Pond in the middle of a thunderstorm was as adventurous as she would ever get. Maybe this *was* her life: avoiding pain, trudging alone.

No. Don't think like that. Mom cried, too, yesterday. Remember?

Lifting the paddle, setting it just inside the edge of the canoe, Reese adjusted her sunglasses and lay back, letting the sun bake her. She felt her wavy emotions settle. A gust of wind carried her boat. She fell asleep.

REESE COULD HEAR RUSTLING AT THE WATER'S EDGE. SHE paddled a bit closer to get a better look. It was probably a bunny. Reed's Pond could only be found on foot, so many animals found this space safe and inviting. As a youngster she walked the trails behind their house and discovered this magical place. Sticks and leaves, grass and wild onion. It was the stuff her world was made of—but she'd buried this child adventurer.

A frog jumped into the pond. Its edge formed a spade, bending out and back in. The top of the water sparkled, but Reese especially loved coming at night when the glow of the moon cast itself across the surface.

A sound made her jerk. *What is that?* It grew louder and more frequent, and finally Reese couldn't stand it. She found a pebble in the bottom of the canoe and tossed it toward land.

"Hey. Why'd you do that?"

Reese froze. Maybe if she sat still enough, the person would go away. She quietly dipped her paddle back into the water, moving the boat backwards.

"Don't leave—" and out of the tall, wild grass a face appeared.

No…

It was Jett.

Reese dropped the paddle and screamed, heart thudding wildly. Curly blonde hair and bright blue eyes revealed themselves past the brush.

"I thought—I thought—" She couldn't finish her sentence. Then she screamed again.

Elliot came up behind Jett.

Vegetables started popping up one by one, all over the bank. Reese's heart beat faster. She leaned over the edge of the canoe to retrieve the paddle. It had floated too far. She could feel the boat tipping, but she only needed to reach a little more—

SPLASH

REESE SAT UP, CLUTCHING THE SIDES OF THE CANOE. "Ahhhh!"

She looked around, but no one was there. Her heart slowed, and she regained her composure. Remembering the paddle, she glanced down. *Thank, God.* The water was quiet, and the sun was going down. She must have fallen asleep.

Wasting no time, Reese shoved the paddle into the pond and made her way back. She fastened both the bow and the stern lines, making sure the canoe was parallel to the dock. *No moonlit glow for me tonight.*

After practically running through the woods, Reese high

stepped it across her backyard so as not get the forming dew all over her shoes, and when she got closer she looked to Elliot's property. What was that? She could hear running water.

She got a closer look and noticed water spilling from a fountain on Elliot's back patio. He must have been hooking it up and wasn't finished—or it came loose. Either way, she was sure the overflowing water wasn't supposed to be a feature.

Momentarily brushing the image of the gorgeous blonde aside, she found the hose's knob and twisted it to off. The back door began to open only a few feet away. Out of pure surprise, she ran to the other side of his house. *Oh, my goodness! Really, Reese?!*

Someone stepped out.

"Hang on—let me shut my hose off—" There was silence for a moment and then Elliot's voice again. "Well—I guess I did turn it off. Okay—go ahead. Sorry about that." There was silence again, and Reese wasn't sure why she was still crouched by the other corner of the house when she could just get up and go around front.

He continued talking. "It's going to be okay—Amelia's in the house watching TV."

Reese felt heat rise in her chest. It was half guilt, half…what?

"We'll be in touch."

Her throat was dry. She tried swallowing, but it felt like sandpaper.

More silence, and then Elliot chuckled. His laugh was enchanting. Reese could feel the butterflies springing up again. She grabbed at her shirt. Her breathing sounded loud. *Am I loud?*

"I promise, everything's fine. She just needed to talk."

Silence.

Just go, Reese! Go!

She leaned forward and picked a blade of grass. She slowly shredded it to bits until there was nothing left.

"I realize that, but just give her some time."

Reese remained glued to the ground. It was as if she had no choice, her body—dead weight.

"Look, if it makes you feel better, I'll do it. Don't worry about the logistics. You know me. Problem? Bam, I'm there."

Reese smiled. Miss Rosa pegged him right. *Charming.*

She felt behind her. What was that? She looked over her should just in time to see a lawn ornament fall over. It was like slow motion, and Reese let out a light yelp. It hit the ground loud enough to cause a piece to chip off.

Her face twisted.

"Hey, I'll call you back—I think a racoon's in my trash can."

Crap!

Survival mode kicking in, Reese jumped to her feet and bounded to the front yard. She'd barely made it when Elliot's voice flew around the corner, but she couldn't make out what he said.

She took a second to catch her breath and ducked across the front lawn. She pushed through the front door, practically falling inside.

What a night.

CHAPTER 6

White walls gave a person time to think. Reese thought she might stare a hole into the one she was aimed at, feet up on the couch as her therapist, Dayl waited for her response.

"Just say it as it comes. Don't overthink it."

She swallowed hard. "He avoided me. He died. His dad died. They left. I hurt. I suck at talking to people. I do weird things. School-girl tendencies."

Last night's escapade replayed in her mind.

Reese opened the folder she brought, handing her therapist the paper with Jett's name. Dayl was quiet and looked it over, tapping her pen against her rosy cheek. "Anything else?"

Reese leaned her head back, closing her eyes. *Is there? Is there hope? Will I ever change?* "I told Mom. About everything but Elliot moving in."

Dayl laid her paper on the desk and scribbled something on a white pad. "That's a start." She scribbled something else and pushed her glasses up. "And the pains?"

Reese wished she'd reply with something besides another

question. "Yes. And sweaty palms. And the heartbeat of a hummingbird. Is this normal?"

Dayl wrote on the pad.

Just tell me!

Reese turned on her side but forgot there was no clock in the room.

"How's your passion project coming along?"

Reese let out a laugh. "Uh—trying. The class was full, but I started tilling up the dirt. Figured doing anything was better than nothing."

"Bypass the class if need be. Ask around, research—find something different. Just make sure you get outdoors, since you said it helps. Make time for it like you would a doctor's appointment."

Reese nodded. "Will do."

Dayl smiled and shifted in her seat, marking something off. "Let's have you back in two weeks. You're doing great, Reese."

If she was doing so great, how come it felt like she had therapy amnesia? She forced a grin. "Thanks."

THE TINY LOCAL BOOKSTORE SMELLED MUSTY WITH A SIDE OF coffee beans. Two leather chairs paired in a corner, raised table in the other gave it a café feel. It was small but winning. Reese adjusted the messenger bag on her shoulder. Stacks of days had been spent in these aisles. Reese would never outgrow books. It was fate that led her to start editing manuscripts. She relished her job, but at the end of the day, it was isolating, so she liked to come here and read around people—or pretend to read and just plumb people-watch.

Her social awkwardness didn't seem to bother others as

much as it did her. Plenty of times while pretending to read, she'd been interrupted by an outgoing soul who apparently thought it was okay to banter in a bookstore. She only wished she could pick and choose who to talk to and what to talk about. Relationships and conversation made her uneasy. She wanted to know where everything was going to lead.

"What are ya looking for, Reese?" Anette had dimples the size of craters. Her spiral hair tumbled all over. She placed her armful of books on a table and then pushed up her frames.

"Gardening everything," Reese said in a quiet tone. She didn't want to be the annoying person.

Anette didn't have a bad bone in her. Only a few years younger than Reese, she kept the shop, handed down by her grandmother, in sparkling condition. It didn't matter that the outside wasn't as appealing, though Reese imagined the next generation braving some change. She stared at Reese as if she were studying. "Gardening, eh?"

"Yeah—worked the ground yesterday. Just feel rusty." Reese had known Anette as long as Jett. She wasn't sure why she'd never been as close to her. It wasn't that she didn't like her. Maybe even as a child Reese's inner adventurer was flaky. Was Jett her best friend simply because he had lived next door?

Anette beamed. She was naturally shy except with people she knew, so when she did meet a friend, it was like watching a morning lily wake up. "I understand and wish you well."

Reese always thought Anette dressed like she was in a different decade because she talked like it too. Maybe her grandmother handed more down to her than the bookshop. "Thanks," she replied.

Anette adjusted her polka dot skirt before loading back up with books and disappeared to the back.

Reese scanned the shelves sideways until she found the

gardening section. She found three books and tucked them under her arm, but she caught the neighboring section and couldn't help herself: *FICTION*

The smell of what was probably Anette's snack break floated by.

Reese checked the time on her phone. A few more free minutes, then she had to go.

Her brows knit together. There, a few rows above her, were four copies of a book. The spine read*: E. L. JACOBSON*

"Jacobson," she muttered. Elliot was a Jacobson. Gardening would have to wait. She flipped open the cover and let her eyes fall to the contents. *Author bio here I come.*

Her phone rang.

"Hello?" What a surprise. It was her sister. She gathered up the books and set them on the counter.

"Are you ready?" Anette's lips curled up into a grin, her voice shushed so as not to interrupt Reese.

Reese put one hand over the phone but only nodded. "How are you? Hey, let me get out of the bookstore so I can hear you better. I think we have a bad signal or something."

Anette picked up her pace, completing the sale.

Reese hung the bag over her wrist and gave a wink, trying to be polite. The sun was hidden by dark clouds, and she could smell rain in the air. *Man, I was really hoping to get my seeds in the ground today.*

She decided to head for the town gazebo rather than walk home. "You there?" Reese looked at the phone screen and sighed. They'd been disconnected.

The phone rang again. Reese gently tossed her book bag onto the bench. "Hello?"

Her sister confessed the bad signal. "I know, I can tell."

Reese tried hard to consecrate and pushed the phone into

her face as if it would help. "It's cutting out bad, sis. I hope you're good, I'm fine too."

She waited to hear a reply but nothing. No, wait—something about not making it for—Christmas? Reese couldn't have heard her right.

"If you can hear me, tell mom and dad I love them." She tried to speed-talk in case it hung up again.

Nothing.

Reese growled under her breath. "If you can hear me, have mom call when the signal's better."

The phone screen went black.

Eight months. Eight months they'd been apart. No way were they going to miss Christmas.

Reese saw a familiar woman walking up the sidewalk. She wore jean cutoffs and a yellow halter top. Her cheekbones were stellar.

It's the lady. Amelia, Elliot had said?

Reese shoved back her eavesdropping memory and perked up. She slid her book bag back onto her wrist. The Amelia woman had a backpack on and disappeared into the bookstore.

Reese slid off the gazebo bench and nonchalantly strutted over to the book exchange box. She pretended to care about the contents but peered over the edge. It was placed just outside the shop on the curb.

She saw movement, but Reese was unsure it was even her. She looked down at her feet, feeling a twinge of awkwardness come over her. *Here I go again.*

Reese shut the box door and turned to head home. The flowers and leaves on the trees began to blow harder.

Thunder rolled in the distance.

Reese fast walked. She crossed the street but stopped.

She turned left instead of going her usual way. *This'll be quicker.*

There were three ways she could go from the town's center. The way the blocks were laid out, she usually took the more scenic route. *Now I remember why I don't like sidewalks*. A few cars whipped by. She hated feeling exposed.

Rain. Slow rain. More thunder. Orange. *Elliot?*

A Jeep went by opposite side, heading toward town.

She kept walking but caved to the urge to spin around, if only for a moment. She was still within sight of the shops. She saw the Jeep pull up to the bookstore curb.

I thought it was her.

Reese bit her lip as she walked along the puddling sidewalk. The rain was starting to come down harder now. She clutched the book bag tightly to her chest, hoping to keep her purchases dry.

A car sped by, sending a surge of water straight toward Reese. She didn't dodge it in time and really didn't care. Drenched, Reese slowed her pace. *No need to hurry now.*

With one mile to go, a honk from behind startled her, almost sending her tripping over the curb. She turned to see Elliot's orange Jeep ten feet behind her. His lights were on, and it was raining so hard now she could hardly see him through the windshield.

For a minute, Reese wanted to run. The other way. Remembering the books she'd slid under her shirt, she swallowed what was left of her pride and jumped in the back seat, careful to avoid eye contact.

She was drenched. *So embarrassing.*

"Thought that was you, Reese." Elliot let her shut the door before pulling back onto the road. "You headed home?"

"Yeah, thanks." Reese took the books out from under her shirt. She was shivering now. Elliot must have noticed. He held an arm out toward the woman in the front passenger seat.

"Hey, sis, pull off my cardigan."

Sis?

"Sure." The woman yanked, and he fidgeted to get his left arm out but finally tossed it back to Reese.

Elliot happened to look in the rear-view mirror, and Reese caught his gaze. His eyes were piercing. Her heart stopped.

"Thanks," She muttered through the vibration of her lips.

"Anytime."

Reese analyzed every detail of the side of Elliot's face. His bangs swept out to the right from under his hat. His jawline was sharp, and he must have not shaved in a few days. She shifted her eyes to her feet.

"Hey, I guess now's as good a time as any to introduce my sister, Amelia."

She popped her head around the front passenger seat, white teeth sparkling past ruby red lips. "Hi." Her top bun was so tall, Reese could see it past the head cushion.

"Nice to meet you." Reese cracked a smile. *Dry clothes, dry clothes!* She noticed Amelia gently elbow Elliot.

He said nothing, but shook his head, grinning slightly.

Reese bit her lip, unsure if she was missing something and tried to avoid the rear-view mirror. Her feet were boring. Instead, she focused on Elliot's arm. Muscles. *No, stop.* Thankfully, they were almost home.

Her eyes lifted, and there they were. His. *Those big brown eyes.*

"You're quiet back there," Elliot said softly. They turned the corner leading into their wooded neighborhood. Reese loved the way it looked like they were submerged in a thicket, but so close to the hustle and bustle of the little shops.

"Just cold," Reese answered, pulling his cardigan tighter.

"Almost there," Elliot replied, as if to help. He pulled into her drive a few minutes later.

She opened the door and grabbed her things. "Thanks again, Elliot. Bye, Amelia. Hope you like it here." Before they could reply she shut the door and ran through the downpour, trying not slip on the rocks.

Letting herself in, a sudden waft of cologne filled her nose. She looked around and then realized it was Elliot's cardigan. Her stomach fluttered. She pressed the fabric up to her face and drew in a deep breath. Her world tipped on its axis.

CHAPTER 7

Reese lingered at the mailbox. *I wonder where he's gone off too?* A week had gone by with no sign of her handsome neighbor. Not that she should care. Well—she should care because it was nice to care about people. But worry? She wasn't worried about him.

Her phone rang. It was the college. "Hello?"

After a few minutes of listening, she smiled. "Really?"

She couldn't believe this. "Thank you so much! I sure will."

She hung up and dialed Miss Rosa. She'd be up already. When Miss Rosa answered—she dove right in. "Someone dropped out of next semester's class. Gave me the slot."

In Miss Rosa fashion, she roared through the phone. Reese held it away from her ear. *Finally. Something's going right.*

THREE WEEKS WENT ROLLING BY WITH ZERO SIGN OF ELLIOT.

It shouldn't have been torturous. She didn't really know the man well, but his dimple-inducing laugh left her wanting to hear more.

Reese peeked every morning at six a.m. on the dot. She checked his mailbox. Nothing. She asked around town. Nothing.

Cupping her hands around her face, she peered in his back window. The lights were off all the time, no matter when she checked them. *Creeper. He probably just went on an extended vacation.*

Miss Rosa had asked about the guy who bought Grand's house, but Reese fumbled over her words, exposing her inner butterflies. Luckily, she'd dropped the subject, and Reese tried to focus on selling produce without picturing Elliot's face in the vegetables.

It was a couch kind of night, so Reese stretched out to study. She was probably getting a late start deciding what to plant for late summer—but better late than never. Or did people use that phrase with gardening? Maybe this wasn't the best idea.

She flipped the pages, bookmarking her areas of interest. Pesticide License Certification? *No thanks.*

She wasn't sure how long she lay there reading. Her eyes began to get heavy. Finally, she closed the book and curled into a ball, yanking a throw over her body.

A LOUD NOISE WOKE REESE. SHE GOT OFF THE COUCH AND rubbed her eyes. Who was here this late? She peered out the front window. *Elliot.* The orange Jeep sat there as if it'd never left.

She went to the kitchen for a drink of cold water to help curb the burning sensation inside her chest. It didn't work, but the big bowl of juicy red apples did look appetizing. *I wonder how hard it would be to plant my own apple tree?*

She took one from the bowl and bit.

CHAPTER 8

Journal entry–July 14, 2018

Is it normal to crush on your neighbor? Again? This wasn't supposed to happen.

Reese squirmed. She shifted positions until the twinge in her back subsided. She yanked weeds from the third row of the garden and contemplated Elliot's reaction if she were to go strike up a conversation. But what would she say? Was there anything *to* say? Not really. And she made small talk ten times more awkward than it already was.

Something had to give. She either had to get past her fear of making new friends or pack up and move, because living next door to Elliot was driving her bananas. All the mailbox-view window lurking was starting to weird even her out.

She moved to the fourth row but rotated her view to keep Elliot in her line of sight. He lay next to his back patio working on something. From where she was planted, his backside was facing her. *Why do you intrigue me, Mr. Jacobson?*

Reese wiped her brow. The heat was intense. So were her nerves. They slammed into one another, begging her to brave up and go talk to the man, but she still didn't know what to say. *Just go ask how his trip went—or tell him you thought he'd sold the house and moved on. That'll make him laugh —right?*

She took a sip of water from her thermos. *Maybe I could give him information about the town's holiday festivities?*

She moved to the fifth row.

Elliot stood, brushing his shorts off.

Reese plucked a weed and kept an eye on him.

He walked to a table next to his grill, and she heard the radio grow louder. He went inside and came out with a notebook in hand. He kicked back in a lawn chair with his feet propped and began writing.

He looked up.

Is he looking at me?

He smiled and waved.

She did the same.

And this went on for weeks.

What does he do for a living? He's always home—except for the extended vacation or whatever it was.

If she could ever have more than a mailbox conversation with him, it would help. It seemed like he wanted to, as well, because he'd linger until there was no small talk left—which Reese was getting a little better at with practice. But she was pretty sure he was waiting for her to initiate something. He had, after all, asked her about a picnic, and she'd put it off, almost as if it never happened. He probably thought she didn't really like him.

Dayl told her sometimes you had to get to a point of hating staying in the same place more than you hated change, first. She was starting to understand what she meant.

This whole avoidance thing was ridiculous.

"I'M NERVOUS," SHE ADMITTED TO MISS ROSA.

Miss Rosa flared her nostrils and cocked her head. "Have you ever thought about just having dinner with him? He did ask, right?"

Reese's neck stiffened. "True."

"What could go wrong?"

Reese shrugged.

"He seems like a down-to-earth guy—not easily scared off. He did, after all, come and talk to me at the stand that day, remember?"

"I remember."

"He asked where you went, and I told him you had to run to the potty."

Reese's jaw dropped. "You what? Miss Rosa!"

"Hey, I was just trying to cover for ya. Next time stick around so I don't have to make excuses on the spot." She slapped her knee with a rolling laugh, echoing too far for Reese's liking. "Anyway, if a guy can stand a little humor, I think you'll be all right. If he wanted normal he could have moved to—" Miss Rosa put her finger on her chin, probably trying to think of a town, but a customer walked up to the booth. "We'll finish this later, Reesey," she winked.

Reese sneered and shook her head. "That's more than a little humor."

Wrapping her messenger bag around her shoulder, she gave Miss Rosa and the customer a wave as she headed back home on foot.

When she got there, Elliot was cutting his grass out back

in the scorching heat. Reese looked at hers. She really needed to cut her own, but she'd been spending more time at Miss Lila and Stan's, making sure their yard was kept up.

She walked out back to check the growth of her tomatoes.

Elliot had shut the mower off nearby and walked over, slapping a towel across his neck and face. "Hey, how are ya?"

"I can't believe I haven't killed them yet."

He tilted his head. "First time?"

"Doing it on my own, yes."

"Didn't know. Sure looks like you know what you're doing," he said, grin spreading across his face. "I was wondering if you wanted me to mow for ya. Not trying to overstep or anything—just wanted to help if you were too busy to get to it."

"You sure? I mean—it needs it, but I was going to soon—just hadn't gotten around to mine yet."

"You help the older couple over there a lot?" He gestured toward Miss Lila and Stan's.

She nodded. "Yeah—we're pretty close and they're getting up there in age."

"That's kind of you."

"Hey, you want a drink?"

"Sure."

"I won't bring coffee this time," she laughed.

"Not in this heat," he replied, making a face.

She laughed. "Be right back."

She jogged to the house, heart beating wildly. *Drink, drink—water, yes, water would be good.*

She filled a glass with ice and water. When she returned to the yard, Elliot had already brought the mower over and was bent over cleaning it out.

"Thanks," he said, chugging the whole thing down. He

took the clippings in one big scoop and tossed them into the back woods on his side.

"So, where did you move from, if you don't mind me asking?"

He set the towel across the back of his neck. "Suwanee, Georgia—you ever heard of it?"

"Nope. What you brought you up here?"

He looked up a minute and then answered. "A lot of things—but I think I'm still trying to figure it out myself," he chuckled.

"Oh, okay—"

"Sorry if that was confusing. Long story."

"You work around here?"

"I work from home," he said, putting the key in the ignition as he readjusted himself on the seat.

"Oh, wow—okay. Me too."

"Ah, nice. You like your freedom then too, huh?"

"You could say that."

"If you ever need any help out here again, just ask."

"Thanks, appreciate that."

For the next month—Reese felt some inner walls break down. She had gone from fake conversations to real ones. The kind that made her feel good. Elliot seemed interested and not bothered at all—which just blew her mind, because she'd always assumed she wasn't capable of being friend material, other than with elderly people or dogs.

Over the course of those weeks, Reese recounted and stored away all the kind gestures and little instances where she'd catch Elliot looking her way as they crossed paths. When she looked at the red front door, she'd get a lump in her throat, but she couldn't bring herself to tell Elliot about the house's history. What if it weirded him out?

He began asking her if she needed anything from the store when he'd go, and one day, they walked together into town, since neither of them needed much. When Reese told Dayl, she thought it was wonderful progress, but Reese wasn't sure which was helping more, the garden or Elliot's friendship.

CHAPTER 9

Cars. Everywhere. Elliot's driveway was jam packed, and there seemed to be some confusion about the property line. *Oh well.*

Plopping her messenger bag down on the back patio, she unwound the hose and began walking it out to the garden but kept her head down. *So many people.*

"Reese!" It was Elliot. Reese had spotted him out of the corner of her eye but refused to make eye contact. Her heart banged against neighboring organs.

She threw him a grin but kept walking, then heard movement and turned.

He was jogging towards her with a broad smile plastered to his handsome face.

"What are you up to?" She said it a little louder, so he could hear her over the music they had playing.

He finally caught up to her and stooped to straighten a bend in the hose. "Why don't you come over? Some friends surprised me. I'd love to introduce you."

"Oh, I don't know—"

"No pressure. Just come over and hang out when you're

done?" He stooped to get a closer look at the garden. "Looking good."

"Thanks."

He stood but seemed closer now. His eyes. *Breathe, Reese.*

Elliot rubbed his hands together and pointed behind him. "If you come—I'll give you a kabob. I tried for sushi, but they wouldn't go for it."

"Are you bribing me?" she laughed.

"Maybe."

"I don't want to intrude."

"You won't be. Plus, you agreed to dinner and technically this is almost a picnic."

"Technically almost?" Reese made a face and fiddled with the hose settings before giving her garden a thorough soaking.

"Cut me some slack." The corners of his mouth slid upwards. "It's my birthday."

"What? Oh!"

They talked for a few minutes before one of the guys from Elliot's yard cranked the music up even louder, the others joining the apparent leader of the pack in his whooping. He finally gestured for Elliot to come back to the excitement.

"Looks like they're having fun."

They walked back toward the houses together, Reese pulling the hose.

"Old college friends," he said, looking their way.

Reese coiled the hose back up and dried her hands. "I'll get cleaned up and be over in a bit?"

Elliot's face beamed, and he threw his hands up. "Yes!"

She laughed and watched as he edged his property, gesturing toward the grill and giving her a thumbs up.

He's hilarious.

Reese went inside to clean up but stopped where his cardigan was draped over the foot of the bed. She wasn't going to keep it forever. It was supposed to serve as a backup conversation starter if he ever asked where it went, and then she just sort of forgot about even that excuse. Somehow, she felt like a different person than she'd been on that soggy day.

Was hope that powerful? Could laughter really heal?

She felt the fibers of the sweater between her fingertips.

Picking it up, she breathed in the sandalwood scent of Elliot's cologne.

This is more than friendship, isn't it?

REESE HUNCHED OVER THE TOILET FOR A FEW MINUTES before *s*liding onto the couch.

She wrapped herself in a throw.

No kabobs. No sushi. Ever. Yuck.

The cupcakes she'd whipped up for Elliot sat on the counter, but she couldn't move.

Her eyes heavy, head on fire, all she could do was lie down.

Sleep.

A KNOCK AT THE DOOR STARTLED REESE.

Exhausted and sore, she tried to get up but realized she was immobile. "Come in," she attempted to raise her voice.

The door opened. "Leftovers for ya—" It was Elliot, and he quickly frowned. "Reese?"

She clutched her stomach. *Oh, God, not now.*

She tried to get up to make it to the bathroom but fell, tripping over the blanket.

Elliot was already by her side helping her down the hall into the bathroom. She guessed he'd backed away, but all she could make out was the inside of the toilet bowl. Again.

Ten minutes later, Reese emerged and untangled herself, looking a hot mess. "Sorry you had to witness that--and thank you."

Without a word, he strode to the kitchen. "Where're the dish rags?"

"Top right drawer." Reese lay back on the couch, lifting her feet up, eyes sliding shut. She felt Elliot place a cold rag on her forehead a few moments later.

"Any more blankets?"

"Hallway closet."

Her body was heavy but cold. She felt the weight of another blanket.

"Cupcakes?"

Reese tried to laugh, but it didn't quite come out right. "Made 'em for you earlier. Was going to bring them by."

Did he reply? Her head was throbbing.

She murmured and drifted off.

REESE COULD SMELL SOMETHING. SHE BREATHED IN, RUBBING her eyes. It was dark except for the light above the stove.

She tried peering over the end of the couch. Her head was closest to the kitchen. The last she remembered was something about cupcakes. *Oh, Elliot was asking about them.*

She rubbed her head and sat up slowly.

Something moved in the corner.

"Reese?"

He stayed?

She let her body relax. "Hey."

"I must have fallen asleep."

Her eyes adjusted in the dark.

Elliot sat up slowly where he leaned against the wall, closer to her feet than her head.

Poor guy. Wow.

He stretched and disappeared into the kitchen.

"I ate a cupcake," he snickered.

Reese moved the mangled mess of hair out of her face, hoping he hadn't noticed. "Oh, good."

He came back with a bowl of steaming something in hand. "Dad's chicken soup recipe."

"I feel so weak."

"May I?" he asked as he held a spoonful up.

Reese nodded, and he held it up to her mouth, except—her stomach churned. Reluctant, she pressed her lips together.

"It's good, trust me."

"I just hope this ends well," she attempted to joke, voice low and scratchy.

He gave her a bite and waited to see her reply before offering another.

"Mmm. Mmmhmm."

"Told ya." His eyes looked tired but kind and gentle and all the fitting adjectives that described such a man as Elliot.

"This isn't at all awkward for you?" She didn't have the energy to beat around the bush.

He shook his head. "I cooked a lot for my sister growing up, while Mom was at work and Dad was off flying the skies. It kinda became my thing for a while until Mom hired someone to cook for us. They shooed me out of the kitchen."

"Hire?"

"Long story."

"Your dad's a pilot?"

"We haven't really talked about our families have we?" he grinned. "And yes, by the way."

Reese swallowed. The soup was helping the queasiness go away.

Elliot set the bowl aside and wrapped his arms around his knees.

Reese smiled and shrank deeper into the covers.

"Still cold?"

She nodded.

"Can I look through your medicine cabinet?"

"Sure. I should have taken something, just so tired."

He came back with a fresh cup of water, sizzling from the tab he'd dropped in.

"So where did she go?"

"Who? Amelia?"

Reese nodded.

He helped her sit back up and handed her the cup of medicine. "I drove her back to Mom's in Georgia. That's why I was gone for a while. Another long story."

"It was weird. I mean, without you here."

Elliot stood with his arms crossed, leaning against the wall. "I should have told you—neighbors look out for each other, right?" He ran his fingers though his hair and rubbed his eyes. "Amelia insisted I take her back the next day. Didn't want to make matters worse."

"So, she's okay?"

"Yeah, just a lot of drama. Needed to talk. She and Mom don't see eye to eye. She has a lot of growing up to do for sure, but I understand where her frustration is coming from. Mom's just…" he trailed off before continuing. "Mom's hard to live with."

Reese felt a wave of exhaustion creep over her. Elliot

must have noticed.

"Here, lie down. No more family drama for you tonight." He bent over, pulling another blanket up from her feet. The front part of his hair hung over his eyes, and she wished she could brush it out of the way.

He stooped down to face her and checked her forehead with the back of his hand. "I hope I'm not being too forward. Just used to helping Mom and sis, like I said."

He caught her stare, and her heart kicked up a thousand beats per second.

He moved the trashcan next to the couch.

"Thank you."

"I'll be back in the morning to check on you, if you're okay with that."

She dug into her pounding brain for something. *Don't go.*

His hand on the doorknob, he added, "You want it locked?"

Reese shook her head. "It'll be fine."

He stood in the doorway, lingering.

"Elliot." She loved to say his name.

He looked back. "Yeah?"

"Happy birthday."

CHAPTER 10

The clouds dotted Kentucky's blue sky. It was August, but Reese had Thanksgiving on her mind. It was hard not to. She pictured her garden's harvest in its final state spread across her mom's fine china. Normally, her whole family would pile dinner helpings in a heap and sit around sharing funny stories. This yield wouldn't make it that long unless she cut and froze everything.

I could try canning.

Reese pulled her phone calendar up. Thanksgiving was over three months away. There'd be plenty of time to ask Elliot about his own holiday plans. He seemed like the kind of guy who could enjoy a big meal during a round of cards.

Redford barked as he bounded toward her.

"Hey, boy!"

He climbed into her lap and licked.

"You better behave. No digging up my soil, you hear?"

So far, she hadn't had issues with him, but Miss Rosa said she and her neighbor had lost a few tomatoes. The coons were practiced thieves in these parts, mainly coming out after dark.

Redford's ears perked up. He surveyed the woods a couple hundred feet behind the garden. Even if the coons—or Redford for that matter—got hold of the harvest, Reese still believed she'd be proud of her accomplishment. To bury something and watch it multiply over time was nothing short of a miracle—especially with her rusty skills, pre-college class.

Shielding her eyes, she saw Elliot atop his roof, ladder leaning close by. Her stomach flip-flopped.

Always the butterflies.

Only God knew what was going on between them.

As little as two weeks ago, he'd practically tripped into her door making sure she was all right after catching that 48-hour bug. When she recovered, Elliot made himself scarce. She'd gotten behind on her work and at the time, hadn't given it much thought. Slowing down revealed the reality—Elliot *had* backed off, but why?

He wasn't as chipper. Something was off.

What's going on in that beautiful head of yours, Elliot?

REESE SUBMITTED THE LAST ROUND OF EDITS SHE'D GOTTEN A jumpstart on for the next day and headed for the porch to enjoy the evening. The sun would be down soon; her favorite time to sit and gaze, listening to the summer bugs.

"Elliot. Hey."

He walked up as she shut the front door.

"Hey, Reese."

"How are you?"

He was quiet for a moment then replied, "I've been better, but I'll be fine."

Reese tilted her head. "You sure?"

“Yeah—no. I mean, I have a weird favor to ask,” he laughed.

Reese inwardly questioned his response but didn’t want to make a fuss.

“Oh?”

“Well, I’m putting this piece of awning up over my back patio, and I was wondering if you could stand back a ways and let me know if it’s centered?”

“Sure, no problem.”

He looked off in the distance before saying anymore.

She set her book on the porch table and fought the urge to throw her arms around him.

He popped his knuckles. “I’d appreciate it. And, if you can’t get to it right now, that’s fine, just let me know.”

“No, I’m free. Now, I mean,” she laughed.

“Great.” He walked around back while she followed.

She stood back, trying to focus on where the center would be.

“Okay, go right just a hair! Eh—a little more!” Reese hoped she was telling him correctly as she gestured with one hand. “Okay, looks good there!”

Elliot went to work screwing it into place.

Reese joined him on the patio and sat in one of his chairs. She admired the nice touches he’d given the landscape. *Grand would love it.*

He climbed off the ladder and set his drill on the table. “Thanks.”

“My pleasure.”

“Crap!” He slapped his neck.

“What?”

He doubled over in laughter. “I felt something crawling on me, but it was just a lightning bug.”

“Yeah, they tickle.”

He paused and squinted, then rushed forward, clapping his cupped hands together.

Reese leaned forward. "What on earth?"

"Here, have one." He lay a firefly on her arm.

"Thanks?" She made a face and patted his arm, teasing him.

"Didn't you used to catch them as a kid?"

"Well yeah, but not so much anymore."

"I think sometimes we need to unleash our inner child more often."

Reese sat back in the chair again. "Oh, yeah?"

He crossed his arms and thought for a minute. "Yeah—I plan to. I need to."

Reese was quiet, pondering his words. Her elbows rested on her legs, chin in the palms of her hands.

He continued. "Just been so busy trying to finish—well, I write, and I'm trying to finish this book—"

Reese slung forward to her feet. "Have you published a novel?"

Elliot almost had to catch her from tripping into him. "Yeah, why?"

She put her hands on her face. "Does our bookshop have it in stock—or do you know?"

"You found it, didn't you?" he laughed.

"E. L. Jacobson."

He ran his fingers through his hair. "Yep. That's me. Unless there's another—which is probable." His mouth slid into a half-grin.

"I almost forgot I bought it—no offense—" she said. "But I've been so busy with work and skimming gardening books, and then got sick…"

"Anette said she'd stock a few."

"How neat. I need to read it. I don't even know the genre yet though," she laughed.

"Are you serious? How did you—"

"Your truck driver had mentioned your last name, and when I saw it—I just bought the book on a whim."

Elliot grabbed the broom and swept the patio. "Sweet. Well, I guess I should say—thank you for contributing to my bills."

She twirled a strand of hair around her finger, imagining Elliot writing with fury, wrapped up in one of his stories. So far, anytime she caught him writing outside, he'd been too far away. It seemed she was always in the garden when he came out. Wait—

"So, what will you do when it gets cold out? I mean—for fresh air—since gardening is seasonal?" Elliot searched her like Anette had months ago, as if trying to crack a code.

Reese hadn't really thought about it. For the most part, she stayed hunkered down indoors unless there was snow. Then all bets were off, and she'd just about challenge anyone to a snowball fight. Maybe even a stranger. Yes. She loved them that much.

"Snowball fights."

"Oh, now that sounds fun."

"Ever gone camping?"

"When I was little."

Elliot rubbed his chin.

"Why?"

"Just thinking."

Reese stuck her hand in the fountain water. "You making plans?"

"Maybe. I need adventure for each season. Fall means camping."

"I'd have to agree. I wouldn't mind going sometime. I'd bring books, though."

He just laughed.

"I've got to read yours—it's driving me crazy now. I can't believe I forgot about it. When I do, though, I may not come up for air for a few hours."

"Oh, you're that kind of reader." Elliot pulled up another chair across from Reese. "Want an IV drip during the journey?"

Reese grabbed her waist, bursting with laughter.

Elliot let her catch a breath. "Drink?"

"No—I probably need to head back soon."

Elliot folded his hands behind his head, almost ignoring her comment. "So, you work from home too. You never said what you do."

She raised her brow. "I didn't, did I?" She paused before going on. "I'm an editor."

A childlike sort of grin took over his face. "The irony."

Reese shrugged. "I know right? We could be a dynamic duo or something."

"Is that a business invitation?" he smirked.

Reese was in awe of how Elliot made her feel. He was familiar and safe, yet wildly exhilarating to be around.

MISS ROSA PASSED REESE THE STACK OF INVOICES. "WE DID good, kid. I'm hoping for beets next time around."

Reese's face twisted. "Beets?"

Miss Rosa ignored her. "How's Elliot? You two ever have that dinner?"

Reese looked down and fidgeted with the papers. The stack was thick. They had done well this year.

Miss Rosa gave her that get-on-with-it look.

There was a long pause while Reese pretended to be distracted by an older woman trying to get her dog to obey a command.

Miss Rosa waited.

"This is the first month I haven't had a weird dream with Jett in it."

Miss Rosa gave Reese a look of compassion.

"I'm starting to think dinner shouldn't be the goal."

"Oh?"

"Just being me should."

Miss Rosa smiled. "And?"

"And with Elliot, I can. Be me. I prefer it. Which is new for me."

"You like him a lot, don't you?" Miss Rosa had a hint of excitement in her voice.

"I haven't told him about Jett. The house…"

"It'll come in time. Can't force depth in a relationship."

She was right. Reese hadn't thought of that before.

"Sometimes we don't know the answers, Reesey—we just walk and find out."

CHAPTER 11

Reese scribbled her thoughts down in fourth grader-fashion because that's how fast her mind raced most days. *I hope Dayl can decipher this when she reads it. Maybe I should join Elliot and write a book. Ha.*

Her mind was on pie at Miss Lila's and the chance to ask Elliot if he wanted to join. This newfound bravery needed to be documented. Not only because Dayl had asked her to note any changes in her behavior, but for herself.

If someone had told her six months ago she'd be inviting a guy over to her friends' house for board games and dessert, Reese would have squinted and called them crazy. But if Elliot lived next door, pie night was inevitable. She was surprised Miss Lila hadn't gone knocking on his door already, pulling him into their cabin and flooding him with stories before he could get seated. For Reese to ask was a huge stepping stone.

Progress feels good.

When Elliot showed up in April, her heart was long overdue for connection. The raw kind where you stop skipping over the hard parts. Her family had never asked her to hide anything—she'd just gotten into the habit of keeping quiet over the years. After her dad pulled away to work more, she stopped sharing what was going on—on the inside.

Why did I stop? Was he the only one I felt I could trust? We did have a special connection.

All those times Dad asked me if I was okay with the changes, how I was doing—had I lied? Is this where the stuffing started?

Reese hopped out of her chair in bewilderment. "That's where it started." She scribbled her discoveries onto the pad. "I didn't want to be a burden."

Something clicked.

How did I not realize this?

REESE GAVE ELLIOT'S RED FRONT DOOR THREE KNOCKS, EVEN though it was ajar. She waited and knocked again. *I am actually doing this. I am here—knocking.* She poked her head in.

"Elliot? You busy?"

"Door's open, come in!" he said from somewhere in the house.

Reese stepped in, smelling the faint traces of musk and sandalwood. Music played in the background.

Catchy.

"Excuse the mess," Elliot said walking in, drying his hair with a towel.

Reese swallowed and stooped down to divert her gaze toward one of the many book-filled boxes lined up in the living room.

"Oh, sorry. Hang on." He grabbed a grey tee draped over the back of the couch.

Reese looked up, feeling flushed.

"It's clean," he winked.

"You've been busy, eh?"

"I need to categorize them. One for the library, one for Anette's, one for the bookstore cafe in Nashville."

"Way to go."

"Thanks."

Reese leaned against the wall, trying not notice how different everything looked. Or maybe the fact that it did was a good thing.

Elliot walked to the open-concept kitchen and filled a glass with water, gulping it all down in one breath.

"What's playing?"

Elliot turned his head. "Punch Brothers."

"Huh?"

"You asked," he chuckled. "Look them up later. So, what did you need?"

"Want to walk over to Miss Lila's with me? For pie? And chess?"

Elliot wiped his counter and gave her a look. "I'll skip dinner to have dessert first, sure."

"Oh, I didn't realize—"

"Reese. I'm messin' with you. It's fine—I want to go. Just give me one sec." He walked out and down the hall.

"You want me to meet you or walk together?" she called from the living room.

He stepped in rubbing something through his hair. "You initially said walk, so that's what I agreed to. You leave me alone, the deal's off." He smirked and walked back down the hall.

"Real funny, Jacobson."

He came back in looking around for something. "Oh, so now we're on a last name basis?"

"Maybe. Your sarcasm is pulling mine from the woodwork. What are you looking for? Need help?"

"My cardigan. I always hang it—" He met her wide eyes.

"Uh—yeah, I keep forgetting to bring that over."

"No biggie. It's more habit than necessity—although I haven't needed it until now. Glad for the fall weather."

Reese headed for the door. "I'm breaking your habits. Crap."

Elliot walked past her to a table by the front door. He opened a drawer and shoved a few things in his pockets. "It is my favorite one though."

"It's not far away, I promise. Want to get it now?"

"Now I want pie."

She made a face and proceeded him out the door.

They walked down the middle of their property, closer to the edge of the woods, the long strip of land looking a lot less summery.

Elliot plucked a twig and poked her side. "If it's pie and chess night, are we having chess pie?"

"Are sure you don't write comedy?"

"Okay, I'll stop," he grinned, dimples showing.

"So many memories in these parts."

Elliot turned his head toward her. "You'll have to tell me sometime."

Reese cocked her head toward him and smiled. *I just hope you don't regret saying that.*

CHAPTER 12

The professor slapped her hands together. "It's a great opportunity. If any of you are serious about taking your gardening skills a step further, I'd say this is your chance."

She tapped the papers on the desk, knocking them into an orderly stack.

Reese opened her phone calendar. She thumbed through and found May. *So far away.* A small group from the college would be traveling to the Emily Dickinson Museum. She marked the date with a new event.

"If you plan to attend, I'll need to know before this class ends. And I hope you enjoy Judith Farr's book. We'll discuss it next week, so be prepared."

Reese fastened her messenger bag and swung it around. She was thankful to get into the class this semester. Between learning to garden and having Elliot around, she was almost able to enjoy her work again, and now homework was helping to keep her busy as well. Even if her family couldn't come home until New Year's, she was sure she'd make it through just fine.

"You going?" a guy next to her stood up and adjusted his backpack.

Reese snapped back to the present. "Not sure yet."

"Me neither," he said, and turned out of the classroom.

The professor cleared her throat in a don't-leave-yet manner. "If you are able, download this app for identifying plants." She held her phone out as if everyone could see from where they were. "Try it out and let me know what you think. I'll write it on the board here."

A few students formed a line at her desk, and Reese jotted the note down. She glanced at the clock, and a few people walked out while the professor chatted with the ones up front.

She made her way to the door, slipping out without saying a word to anyone. She had Elliot on her mind, and they were meeting at the local deli for lunch. Walking back home from Miss Lila's the other night, they conspired to break up their work days by intentionally hanging out or pursuing some mini adventure.

Putting her truck into reverse, she cranked up the radio and rolled down the windows. She backed out but when she pulled forward to the stop sign—she forgot to look to the left.

CRUNCH.

"Hey!" Another driver hollered out his window.

Reese had slammed into his front right corner.

REESE PULLED INTO THE DELI PARKING LOT THIRTY MINUTES late. Elliot's Jeep was still there.

She huffed through the door, bell jingling.

The woman at the counter smiled. "Can I help you?"

Reese searched the tables. Elliot was in a booth sideways, chatting with an elderly gentleman at a neighboring table.

I feel awful.

She slid into the seat giving a slight wave to the older man.

"Well, now that she's here, I'll leave you two to your lunch."

Elliot nodded. "Have a good day, and nice to meet you." He took a sip of his tea. "What happened?"

"Sorry. I almost caused a fender-bender. Luckily there was no damage done."

He narrowed his eyes. "Oh man. Glad you're alright."

"Yeah, nothing major." She bent her neck side to side and flipped open a menu.

"I almost headed home. Thought maybe I heard the time wrong. We—uh—haven't exchanged numbers."

Reese looked over the menu. "We haven't. Right. We should—could, if you want."

He tucked his bottom lip and shook his head, grinning.

What?

"We don't have to. It's just—if we're going to plan things—it'd be smart."

"Yeah, I agree. Here—give me your phone."

He handed her his cell, and she punched the numbers in for him.

He just looked at her with the same grin. Seemed his eyes spoke louder than words most days.

She really just wanted to kiss him and get it over with. Not in an annoying way, but in a let's-cut-through-the-tension kind of way.

He pointed to a picture of cheddar and broccoli.

"Soup? We had that last time there was food involved."

"You did. I left the rest in your fridge remember?"

"Oh, right," she laughed. "I passed it on to Miss Lila to try. It was that good."

"Sure—trying to pawn your leftovers off on an elderly couple. I see." Elliot's phone was sitting on the table and lit up from a text message. He glanced over. "It's mom. Just a sec, sorry."

Reese needed to scan the menu but scanned Elliot's face instead.

He pecked away, rattling off a text and sighed as he set it back down.

"Everything okay?"

His neck tightened, and he popped his knuckles. "Mom's coming up for Thanksgiving."

CHAPTER 13

The September air was perfect. Mid-seventies.

Reese crouched as she tended to the troublesome weeds near her front steps. Elliot strolled up his drive, earbuds and ball cap in place. The little details made her feel like she knew a secret. Elliot said he only wore a hat when his hair was unfixed. She now knew he could only stand a certain brand of earbuds; the others got on his nerves. These things sounded petty, but to her they weren't. They let her into his world. And it was nice to know a world other than her own.

He shot her a wide grin and headed for the road.

Reese pulled a few more weeds and shifted her weight, watching him jog away.

A familiar drop.

I can't always be with him.

She brushed off her knees and went inside.

Clicking open the email from her professor, her eyes scanned the paragraph.

"Thank you for choosing to attend the Emily Dickinson museum with us. Attached is a list of everything you need to bring, the dates, our hotel with group discount. You may also bring one person to accompany you, but they must pay their own way."

Reese closed it and spun in her chair. By May, Amherst, Massachusetts, would be gorgeous. *I wonder if Elliot would want to go?*

She checked the time. She was forgetting something. What was it? She glanced at the calendar, but nothing was marked for today.

My appointment! She was going to be late.

Reese threw her bag over her neck leaving her email on the screen. She hopped in the pickup and turned the key over but there was only a loud, awful noise. She tried again. More grinding.

"What?" Her truck was old but what a time to have issues.

She tried it a few more times and sat in the seat, unsure. She dialed Dayl's office.

"Hello? Yes, I need to leave a message for Dayl—okay, thank you."

She bit her nail and waited to be transferred.

"Hello, Dayl, this is Reese Lockhart. My truck is having trouble this morning, and I was trying to find out if I could reschedule. Thank you."

Click.

Reese tossed her phone onto the passenger seat and tried the engine again. This time, nothing. *Great.*

She retrieved her phone and went to go work on a manuscript while she waited for Dayl to call back. It was almost lunch before her phone rang.

"Hello?" Reese answered. It was time for a break anyway. "That's fine—I'll find a ride if it doesn't run by then."

She microwaved the last few swallows of her coffee for the fifth time.

"Okay, thanks, Dayl."

Click.

Reese chugged the last of the coffee and regretted doing so. What a day this was turning out to be. At least she was having dinner with Elliot tonight. He was supposed to walk over and let her know when it was finished, but that wouldn't be until seven o'clock.

She spent the remainder of the afternoon reading Judith Farr's *The Gardens of Emily Dickinson* and used the rest of her time before dinner to take care of her own patch. A few of the veggies hadn't turned out—a couple rotted underneath which she'd learned too late could have been prevented—and the racoons had been stealing some of the yield. At least she could say she did the thing. She had a garden in 2018.

If her mom were here, she'd probably be proud of how far Reese had come. Though Reese missed her family, she was finally beginning to experience peace with their continued absence. She wasn't sure exactly the moment this peace started seeping into her bones, but this much was true: Elliot refreshed her.

Having another person to celebrate small victories with made life more enjoyable.

I've missed closeness.

Reese felt a lump form in her throat.

CHAPTER 14

Blush? Lip gloss? *Just pick one.*

Six o'clock arrived, but Reese couldn't wait for seven. She'd already waited for this night long enough—the last week of October was here. Where had the year gone?

Elliot would come get her when dinner was ready, but she figured heading over early to help him cook was the better option. Better than pacing the floor questioning her choice of jeans for the hundredth time.

The butterflies were back. She swallowed and applied a clear coat of lip gloss. She pinned her hair up on the side and slid on some mascara. *Forget the blush.*

She was overthinking. Again. But what else could she do?

A question began to bubble in her mind. She wondered how long she should go on pretending she didn't feel strongly for Elliot. They were just friends, right? When was it appropriate to mention anything else? She wasn't sure anymore and she sure as heck hadn't planned to feel this way. What was she supposed to do? Just spring it up on him? How hilarious would that be? *Elliot, I'm sorry, we can't be friends—because*

I might be in love with you. It's all or nothing. Okay never mind—it sounded more depressing than hilarious.

Reese's neck tightened. *It'll be all right. Chill. Just be natural.*

She slid the contents of her purse into a handbag and jogged to Elliot's back door. It was cracked, and she let herself in. "Elliot?"

She saw the boxes first and then books strewn about. Then the leg—

"Oh, God what happened?"

Elliot moaned at the foot of the stairs, holding his calf, eyes closed. Something didn't look right.

"Elliot, what happened?"

He put up a finger so she stopped, holding in a breath. From the surface, she couldn't tell what happened. Her eyes scanned his horizontal body.

Elliot tried to move but moaned and lay back down.

"We need to take you to the hospital; do you want me to call an ambulance?"

He tried sitting up again and grunted through the pain.

Reese felt her heart thud. She sat still, rubbing his arm.

The oven beeped.

Elliot finally managed to sit further up and scooted against the corner where the last step and the wall joined. He leaned his head back, bracing himself with one hand.

Eyes closed, he felt for Reese's hand. "I was carrying books down the steps and yeah…"

"Are you sure you don't want me to call?"

The oven beeped again. Reese dashed into the kitchen to turn it off and cancel the timer, then returned to Elliot's side. He hadn't moved.

"I know something's not right. I just don't think I need an ambulance. Here, help me up."

Reese braced herself with her left hand against the wall adjoining the kitchen and living room and helped pull him up with the right.

He used the wall to help himself up. Reese noticed how he kept his left foot from pressing down.

"Careful. Care if I drive your Jeep? I'll fill you in on the way."

He nodded and pulled his keys from his jeans pocket, eyes closed.

"Okay, ready?"

Elliot hobbled out the front door to the passenger side, letting Reese act as a human crutch. She helped him in and they both took a breath as he buckled.

When he opened his eyes, he looked at Reese, and she could tell it was a forced grin.

Please let him be okay.

CHAPTER 15

Tuesday night at the local hospital wasn't exactly what Reese and Elliot had in mind for a casual respite, but at least the waiting room wasn't cramped.

Replaying the scene over, she was thankful she'd gone to Elliot's when she did. Her feet dangled from the waiting room chair, and she bit into a candy bar, giving it all the grief she could muster.

Good news, please.

Nothing else mattered.

A couple nearby held each other close. One old man sat in the corner, nodding off, paper slipping off his lap.

Her phone lit up, revealing a text message from Miss Rosa.

Reese sent a few short, rapid-fire text messages in return, letting Miss Rosa know she still hadn't heard from the doctor. She'd already flown through three magazines and couldn't remember a thing.

All my nails will be gone before midnight.

Reese glanced at the time. It was 8:26. She slipped her

phone into her back pocket and paced the floor, counting the squares to pass time.

Between the drive to the hospital and the time it took to get Elliot registered, an hour passed. Hopefully by now they'd gotten his X-ray results.

The low hum of the large overhead lights matched the annoying hum inside her head.

He should be out soon, right?

The doctor came around the corner.

She let out her clenched fists.

The doctor's face was unreadable, but he flipped a few papers around his board and put his pen to the corner of his mouth. "You're Reese, I presume?"

She nodded.

"The X-rays confirmed Mr. Jacobson has broken his fibula."

He adjusted his glasses and continued. "They also revealed a slight twist in the break. Though this isn't good, it could have been worse."

He stepped forward, handing Reese the papers. "We've given him a removable cast and set of crutches. The cast will help keep his knee straight since it broke right here."

He pointed to his own leg right under the knee to demonstrate, and Reese tried not to tap her toe too fast.

"He can take the cast off when at home but needs to keep full weight off it. We'll probably see him back in about a month to find out if it's healing right. He will probably need to be off work until then, if not longer."

Oh, I'm sure even a broken hand wouldn't stop Elliot from writing.

"Sometimes it can take up to six weeks for this kind of break to heal. Mr. Jacobson will be just fine though."

Reese smiled politely and nodded, hands folded tight, squeezing her armpits.

A nurse walked over and handed the doctor another set of papers. He looked them over and gestured, "Right this way."

As they walked down the hall, the doctor reassured Reese. "He has pain medication and will be able to refill it once before his next appointment."

Her phone buzzed but she ignored it.

"He's going to need a hand getting around." The doctor and nurse stopped outside a door. "Here we are."

"Thanks."

She pushed the ajar door and moved the curtain to the side, heart beating wildly.

Elliot was laying, head back. "Hey."

Reese puffed her cheeks out. "Crap, huh?"

He laughed. "My own fault."

She shook her head, unsure what to say.

"Books of death," he laughed.

"I could have helped."

"If I would have known I was going for a tumble, I would have asked, trust me."

She made a sad face.

"It's going to suck not being able to run."

Another sad face.

Reese studied the awkward contraption around his leg, thick black foam with lots of Velcro. "Not very trendy is it?"

Elliot shook his finger. "Don't judge my style."

"What were you doing with the books?"

"Getting them organized for my next signing. Have time to be a chauffeur?"

Reese scrunched her nose. "Tonight was only my test run?"

He shrugged. "You're hired then."

She set her handbag on the foot of his bed and gave his hand a squeeze. "I'll help with whatever you need."

He closed his eyes. "Thanks. I'll be all right, just bummed."

Reese sat on the edge of the bed, eyeing him. "Waiting on the nurse to discharge you. Then we can leave."

Her stomach growled.

Elliot laughed, eyes still shut.

"We did miss dinner."

"Well chauffeur—prepare to take us somewhere unless you want cold ribollita. Should have used the crock pot."

CHAPTER 16

The white clock read nine-thirty, and the hospital halls were eerily quiet. Where was the nurse? Reese was about to peek her head out the door to find someone, but Elliot's phone cut through the silence.

He tossed it to her.

"I don't know what to say!" she snorted.

"Just tell her not to worry, that I'm okay, and you're helping me."

"No, you do it! She's your mom!" Reese tossed it gently back to Elliot.

He slid over and pushed the call button, tossing the phone back to Reese. "Sorry, I have to use the bathroom," he smirked. "No, really."

She scowled and caught the device. "What's up with you and your mom?"

He switched expressions, but she didn't have time to further investigate. "Hello?" She walked out of the room looking for the nurse.

His mom was irate on the other end of the phone. Elliot had told her she could be a little overbearing.

"Yes, it's Reese."

Then his mom went into a spiel about how Elliot should have called her rather than texted.

Reese bit her lip and paced. "I understand. It all happened so fast, Miss—" and then she cut her off, so Reese piped down and peeked into Elliot's room. He must have been in the bathroom. *You're going to get it.*

"Yes. He probably just sent a quick message while I drove him here. He didn't mean anything negative by—"

Reese flared her nose and listened.

"Oh, yes, I have insurance. It's okay, we—"

She poked her head back in the room as Elliot shuffled to the bed.

He gave her a two-finger wave with a dopey grin, and she rolled her eyes.

"I'll let him know and have him call you back."

Elliot was balancing the remote on his head.

Are his meds getting to him?

She covered up the mouthpiece. "What are you doing?"

"It's fun to watch someone else talk to her. I'm just enjoying the moment."

Reese flicked his good leg and walked back out. "He's looking forward to your visit, I'm sure."

The nurse walked over to Reese, jotting something down on a paper. *Thank God.* "Okay, yes—he'll call you back—the nurse wants to talk to us."

She could feel the heat radiate from Elliot's cell phone.

Click.

Reese came in and adjusted the curtains. "She was not happy."

Elliot winced. "She rarely is. I love her, but I need a minute."

Reese knew from a few stories he'd shared that his mom

wasn't the easiest to get along with, but she was starting to wonder what else he might be dealing with. She looked at the nurse who followed her in.

She finished searching the document in her hand. "Here you go, Mrs. Jacobson. Now Mr. Jacobson—you call if you need anything, hear?"

Reese and Elliot both shot each other a glance.

Elliot's mouth slid upward, revealing his dimples.

"Oh, I'm—" Reese began.

Elliot started talking at the same time. "Sure thing, and yes—Mrs. Jacobson—just hold onto those for me. You know how I am. I lose everything." He winked.

The nurse paid Elliot's banter no mind. "The doc's number is on the paper. Have a good night and try not to fall down anymore stairs."

"Thank you." Reese said, still feeling flushed.

She turned back to Elliot and grabbed her hips.

He just wore the same cheesy grin.

CHAPTER 17

"This is going to get old fast." Elliot made his way slowly from the Jeep to the first step while Reese unlocked his door and propped it open. "I feel gross."

"Showers help with that," she joked.

"My sister broke her leg years ago."

"Oh?" Reese said, helping him in.

"She fractured something. Don't remember."

Reese shut the door.

Elliot looked tired.

"You want to shower or sleep first?"

Elliot sat slowly on the couch and let the crutches fall to the floor next to him. He pulled his casted leg up first, then the other.

Reese set her bag on the table and checked the oven. "Smells like it was good. Still warm."

He laughed from the other room. "Foil's in the drawer."

She opened three before she found it. "I'm glad we ate on the way back, but I do want to try this tomorrow."

Elliot didn't respond.

Reese set the dish in the fridge with the edge of the foil lifted and went to check on him. His eyes were closed.

She pulled a nearby blanket up over his lap.

His phone rang, and he jerked. “Too tired.”

Your mama needs to talk. Reese stooped next to him. His hair was a mess, but she wanted to run her fingers through it. *One day?* “Maybe you can fill her in tomorrow.”

“Mmmhmm.” He was falling asleep.

“I’ll be back in the morning. You be okay?”

He didn’t answer. His chest was moving.

He’s out.

She watched him for a moment. *If I could just—a peck—wouldn’t hurt, right?*

She stalled time by moving the chaotic mess of boxes. They’d left everything earlier, but other than the books on the floor, Elliot’s house was pristine.

Reese took a long look at the man she was pretty sure was becoming more than a friend. *He should be asleep now, for sure.*

Feeling fifteen again, she leaned in to plant a small kiss on his right cheek.

Her heart almost stopped.

He turned toward her—her kiss landed on his lips.

His eyes popped open, and she pulled back quick.

“You caught me.”

His eyes heavy, he took her hands into his and pulled her back down, face level. It looked like he might say something, but he stopped and smiled instead.

He kissed her cheek and turned back over.

She wasn’t sure whether she wanted to run or scream but either way she had to will her feet to move. Crossing the lawn back to her house seemed to take forever. Everything was in slow motion—including falling asleep.

CHAPTER 18

Reese jolted out of bed, sweat covering her neck. *I hate bad dreams.*

She stumbled to the bathroom and splashed her face and lay back down. It was only three o'clock in the morning, but now she felt wide awake. *Elliot. Is he okay?*

She gathered her laptop and notebooks and stuffed them into her messenger bag. *Clothes, Reese. Clothes.*

She added a sweater and a pair of leggings to the mix and tossed her toiletry bag on top, but it fell out. After fumbling around a few minutes longer, she left her house toting two bags.

Elliot's back door was the way she'd left it—patio light on, main door cracked.

He was still asleep, but the blanket lay crumpled on the floor.

Reese shook the olive-green velvet and pulled it over him. She stretched out on the sectional opposite Elliot and edited until she became torpid. She pulled Elliot's extra blanket over her bottom half, then curled into a fetal position, using her arm as a pillow. She thought coming here would be a help to him—but it went both ways.

Good dreams. Good dreams.

Reese rubbed her eyes and felt for her glasses. First came the sizzle followed by a savory scent of bacon. She sat up blinking. Blankets were strewn about, the curtains pulled open—a bright autumn day, revealed by the colorful lone tree in Elliot's front yard.

"Good morning, not-so-stranger."

She turned, arm on the back of the couch which faced the kitchen area. Elliot was cooking, and boy was it a sight. In a good way.

"Hey," she replied calmly.

"Here," he scooped up a helping of eggs from a bowl and added three strips of bacon to a plate. Using only one crutch, he carried her plate with the other hand.

"You don't have to—"

He set it on the coffee table and went to get his. "I wanted to."

"It smells amazing."

They ate breakfast together on the couch while Elliot scrolled through his favorite Spotify playlists, quizzing her knowledge of artists. It wasn't what Reese pictured as being her favorite chill moment, but every time she was with him, time seemed to stop.

"Thanks for cooking—and sorry to crash your couch. I've been having these nightmares for a while now…"

He swallowed his bite and turned the volume down on the music. "Oh?"

She nodded. "Yeah, they were getting better, so it threw

me for a loop last night when I had another one. And—I wanted to check on you…"

He grinned and set his plate on the table. "Honestly? I'm glad you did—but I was taken aback a little when I awoke to a woman on my couch." He adjusted his leg, wincing slightly.

"Again, sorry." She pressed her lips together.

"No, don't be. If you hadn't come over to begin with, I'd probably still be stretched out horizontally—remember?" he winked.

She smiled and got up to head for the bathroom, but he reached for her and pulled her closer, back down next to him.

"You remember?"

"I remember."

Heat washed over her from the chest up.

"Are you okay with this? Us being more than friends?"

She could hear the thump of her own heartbeat inside her head. She couldn't get the words out but took his hand in hers. Despite life's curveball--hadn't she wanted this? Now that it was here, she thought she just might fall over, useless to the world.

She guessed he could see right through her, because he wrapped his arms around her, gently kissing her forehead. "Since your truck's down again, you can use the Jeep."

Reese's insides turned to mush. She rested her head on his chest and didn't want to talk. If she talked, it would mean moving a part of her body which meant she might tamper with the moment. *Can I live in this, right here—forever?*

"Thank you."

CHAPTER 19

Reese put the Jeep into park. Her heart still hadn't slowed from the frantic oscillation of the morning. Whatever happened since Elliot's hospital visit until now had pretty much elbowed them into a new lane. Elated was an understatement, but Reese bit the whites of her thumb nail as she watched cars go by.

Forty-eight hours ago, Elliot was a friend she cared deeply for—her mind rocking on the edges of something more. Now? What was this? *Is this how love plays out? Taking hearts by storm—giving people whiplash in the process?* Or maybe it was just her. She wasn't sure. *Are we moving too fast?*

They couldn't go back. Not now, without pretending—and Reese was finished with pretending. It was just a kiss on the forehead—but it represented a door. To what?

A knock on the Jeep window startled her.

"Hey!"

She rolled down the window.

"You all right, Reesey?" Miss Rosa crossed her arms.

"You forgot to let me know how your Mr. Jacobson is doing—don't leave me hanging like that."

Reese slapped the steering wheel, trying to be funny but unsuccessfully hiding her anxiousness. "You're right. I'm so sorry."

Miss Rosa's eyes narrowed, and she pulled her arms into a tighter knot. "Reesey."

Reese swallowed and looked up at the Jeep ceiling. "He's all right. Casted and crutched. I'm helping him, but really he doesn't need me—except for driving him around, maybe."

Miss Rosa pursed her lips and opened the Jeep door. "Stay a while."

"Actually, is Ron home? My truck broke down again—but I think for good this time."

Miss Rosa gave the Jeep a once over. "Oh, duh—this isn't yours. What's going on?"

Reese hopped out and filled her in on the issues her truck had been having. How Ron had been coming over to mess with it—only for some other problem to arise shortly after.

Fat drops of rain came out of nowhere.

Miss Rosa gently grabbed Reese's arm. "C'mon, honey."

They sat on her covered porch, but Reese was quiet.

"How's the family?"

Reese scratched her head. "Not really sure. They don't reach out much."

"I have a care package almost finished for them—you want to add anything?"

Reese grabbed her chin. "Why haven't I done that before?"

"It's okay. You've had a lot on your plate."

"Have I?"

Miss Rosa adjusted the pendant around her neck.

"They have stuff going on too, and I've been stuck in my own head."

The rain was loud now.

"And you're talking to someone about it. Reesey, have mercy on yourself."

Reese pushed her glasses up and rolled her neck. "Yeah—I've never been good at that."

"So what's really going on?"

"Mmm?"

Miss Rosa took a sip of her drink, which had been on the table between the chairs. Reese knew Miss Rosa would eventually press the answer out of her. She gave a person the space to breathe, but when she suspected drama or someone in need, she was like a P.I. with a degree in psychology.

Maybe I should have hired her.

"Dad's old truck was a piece of him I had with me every day."

"You miss him. It's normal, Reesey."

"Some relationships I want to see change in—others I wish I could freeze frame, ya know?"

"Has your relationship with your dad changed that much?"

"Sort of. He's been busy for so long. I just miss the way it used to be between us."

Miss Rosa swirled the drink in her glass. "He loves you."

"I don't hear it anymore though."

"You need to hear it. Or see it."

"Or feel it."

The rain let up just as quick as it had come.

"Is there anything else you need to talk about?"

Reese looked down.

Ron walked up to the porch, wrinkles defining his smile.

"Reese. Well I'll be. Rosie told me you were heading over today."

Miss Rosa rolled her eyes. "Ron."

He winked at Miss Rosa, and she pulled her lips in, hand on hip.

"Anyway—Reese, so the truck finally rolled over, huh?"

"Well, you did your best." She shrugged and stood. "Thanks again."

"I see you're driving a Jeep. You didn't come to me for a new car?"

"This isn't hers you ol' fart." Miss Rosa boomed.

"In that case--you got a soft spot for them foreign cars?"

Reese folded her arms, shocked Ron didn't jump at the chance to drive over and tinker with the old pickup one last time. She glanced at Miss Rosa to see what her response was. All she got was a shrug.

"Don't look at me. Ron's been getting these catalogs in. I think they're making his eyes bigger than his pocketbook if you ask me."

Ron gave her a funny look. "Don't go causing trouble, Rosie."

Miss Rosa threw her hands up. "I'll leave you two be. Reesey, call me later if you want."

Reese nodded.

Ron gestured for her to follow him behind the shop.

The rusted building gave the wrong impression of the vehicles he had for sale in the lot. Lower-end sedan models, a few trucks, and a few crossovers. They seemed well maintained from outer appearances. But what was this?

He pointed to a very new hunter-green Nissan Pathfinder and pulled two black keys from his jeans pocket, placing them in her hand.

"What is this?"

"I was just told to give you these and tell you to look on the seat."

Reese wrinkled her nose and looked down.

"Watch the mud back here."

She walked to the vehicle's door and swung it open. Arching her head inside, she noticed a white envelope in the passenger seat. *What's going on?*

She turned it over.

From DAD.

CHAPTER 20

Miss Rosa climbed into the new vehicle. "Nice."

Reese shook her head. "Thanks for driving it to the house. See you there."

She walked back to the Jeep and drove home gripping the wheel the whole way.

A few minutes after pulling into Elliot's drive, Miss Rosa pulled into hers.

Reese jumped out of the Jeep. "Be right back to drive you home. Checkin' on Elliot real quick."

Miss Rosa gave a thumbs up with a sly grin.

Reese went to open the front door, but Elliot was already opening it.

"Hey, how'd it go—" He saw the green vehicle in her drive.

"Um—I'm not sure yet." She laughed.

"You went and test drove a brand new car without me?" He joked.

"No, no—um—I have to take Miss Rosa back though. You doing okay?" She had a hand on the door frame.

"I'm okay, but you don't look so good." He tucked a hair behind her ear, summoning the faithful butterflies.

Reese took a deep breath, feeling the blunt weight of the morning's shift. A faintness crept over her.

"What's up, Reese? You need to sit down?"

Reese looked at the cast around Elliot's leg. He was always thinking of others first. "No, I mean eventually—but I have to go. Can we talk later?"

Elliot's eyebrows pressed together. "Sure." He stepped backward into the house carefully.

Reese swallowed and closed the screen door. She looked at Elliot one more time before jogging to the other car.

He smiled and gave her a nod.

"Well, what a surprise, right?" Miss Rosa said, trying to lighten the vibe Reese was apparently giving off.

Reese switched gears. She had to ask. It was now or never. "So, what do you think?"

"About?"

"Elliot and I."

"Oh."

"We've only known each other for six months."

"Almost seven." Miss Rosa corrected.

"Is it too soon to be more than just friends?"

Miss Rosa made a face. She let out a sigh and folded her arms. "Reesey—pinpoint this stress. Is it really from the fear of moving too fast, or is it from the risk of the relationship in general?"

Reese was quiet.

"When we stay frozen in place only to keep ourselves safe, it's no better than moving into unknown territory a little unprepared. In my opinion, anyway."

Reese thought about her words. They hit the back of her rib cage.

"I think if you cut the fear out and set it aside, you'll know what's right when you study what's left on the table. What do you want? What does he want?"

"Yeah…but is it really that easy? What if something happens?"

She already knew what Miss Rosa was going to say, and her friend's next words proved her right.

"*What if* are the two biggest idiots to climb out of our mouths. Using them as a scapegoat to not follow the convictions in our hearts is the same as blatantly running from what we know is right to do."

Reese rubbed her knee with her free hand, making it hot to the touch. "I—I want to be with him—if that's where this is headed. But I never planned—"

Miss Rosa laid a hand on her shoulder. "Sometimes the best things in life aren't planned."

"I don't want to let the past run my life."

"Everyone's not Jett. He was young. You both were so young, Reese."

Reese shot her a look, lips quivering. She pulled into Miss Rosa's drive right on time because now, she couldn't see through the tears.

"Oh, come here, honey." Miss Rosa pulled her close, and Reese cried into her silky shawl.

CHAPTER 21

The red front door was chipped in the same spot. Jett's face flashed in her mind. She tried to shake it.

Then Elliot opened the door.

Do I even know Elliot?

"Reese?"

She drew in a breath. "I don't know if I can do this."

He shook his head. "What? I don't understand."

"Can I get my things from in here?" Her heart thudded a zillion miles an hour. Ironically, she felt like she was making the biggest mistake of her life—but there was a force inside bullying her to pull the plug.

Elliot moved to the side and swallowed. "Um…sure."

She saw him look down then forced her gaze the other direction.

Here comes the current. The tears were hot, sliding down her cheeks as she collected the few remaining items not already in her bags. She didn't look at Elliot's face or pay attention to where he was. She couldn't handle looking him in the eye again. At this rate she probably would have to move.

Wait—what was she doing? *Acting on impulse—that's what. You've been here before. Panic doesn't have to run your life.*

Elliot remained quiet. *God, I want to look at you. I don't want to do this.*

"Reese—"

"You have my number…" She trailed off without looking up. Jett's kiss flashed in her mind—then Elliot's—the cheek, the forehead. She put her fingers to her temples.

"I'm sorry—"

"I just need some time." She threw her bags around her shoulder, and her heart ripped in two as she jerked the knob of the back door and fast-walked home.

CHAPTER 22

Reese shoved the ear buds in, stretching up—then down. Downward dog. Plank. Plop. *Ugh.* She lay on her stomach and let the tears flow into the boards beneath her.

I thought these days were behind me.

A few minutes later she peeled herself off the floor in time to see her phone ringing on silent. It was Dayl calling her back.

She pulled the ear buds out without pausing the music and slung them across her bed.

"Hello?" she sniffled.

She listened as Dayl spoke regarding the emotional voicemail. An opening had popped up on Dayl's calendar, so she was bumping Reese's appointment up days early. Like in a few hours, early.

"Yes, and I have a new car now—won't be a problem. Thank you so much." Reese hung up feeling the familiar sting of guilt's slender trip wire. If she only had the skills to overcome the emotion of the moment. But she didn't—and blast it all—the freaking self-sabotaging was getting old.

Reese ran the white envelope from her dad between her fingers. She hadn't had the guts to open it yet. She was going to ask Elliot if he could sit with her while she read it. She didn't plan on running. And was it really running when she was right there? Yeah—felt like it. He'd looked like a sad puppy the afternoon before.

Trying to sleep last night sucked. Why did she do this to herself? Would Elliot even give her another chance? She felt like the unsafe friend they warned people about. They being people who didn't have to deal with people like her, who boarded themselves up safely from her kind. At least she thought. And that's why she also never felt the urge to pour her guts out to people--until Dayl.

Fake or falling. Was there any other way? Had she imagined the hope not so long ago? Did panic have that strong of a grip on the mind that it could trick her into thinking everything was nothing—and that nothing was everything?

Steady had come for a short time. Now it was gone. She had come such a long way and now—*I hate myself.*

Reese tossed her purse in the new vehicle and set her messenger bag gently next to it. She added the bag with the change of clothes she hadn't taken out. *Just in case.*

She had made sure the house doors were locked while diverted her eyes from Elliot's. She was good to go. Backing up, all she could think about was getting help before she did more damage.

THE ROOM FELT WARMER THAN ALL THE TIMES BEFORE. REESE wasn't shivering to death and immediately settled down as she let the couch squish beneath her.

Dayl looked over her glasses, but then uncharacteristically took them off and rolled her wheeled chair closer. "Reese, this is a safe place. You have nothing to worry about."

Safe. That word. And she pictured Elliot's arms holding her, then ripping them off of her once he knew the inner struggles she fought too frequently.

"I'm scared of trying. I'm scared to let myself be loved. I'm tainted and feel like I will damage whoever I get close to —so I pull back. I did it with my family—I did it with my friends in town by not telling them everything…"

Dayl scribbled it down, or whatever it was she did, and lifted her face to look into Reese's eyes.

"I opened up—mostly—to Miss Rosa, but when I go into panic mode—I get scared to admit it and wind up going downhill. Usually I just cry into my pillow and it's over by morning."

Dayl nodded.

"The voicemail I left you about the car, Dad and Elliot. It was all a big mess at the time, in my mind. It's like I can't make decisions when I am emotionally charged. I go berserk."

Reese wiped the tears, and Dayl yanked a handful of tissues from the box on her desk.

"And the envelope?"

Reese shook her head. "No. Not yet."

"When your dad left on this trip, your mom, sister—all that—how did you end? On a good note? Bad note? Describe the relationship."

Reese popped her neck and thought for a moment. Had she thought of this before? After a few minutes she sat up. "I faked my way through it. Friction on my end—don't know if they felt it."

Dayl straightened. "Anything else come to mind?"

Reese cleared her throat. "They had sprung this on me with hardly any notice, shortly after Grand's funeral. Which was already hard because, like I said, I hadn't gotten over Jett and then Grand passed. So—my family didn't know the pain inside—and when they finally shut the trunk and we said our goodbyes, it was fake."

She stopped and took her glasses off, rubbing her eyes. She looked up at Dayl. "I just don't want to lose someone I love—again."

Dayl was wiping her eye.

"Dayl?"

Dayl drew her lips in and nodded. "You are protecting yourself. You are also trying to protect others because you think the truth will hurt them. Panic can send us into fight or flight modes. You've experienced the latter many times. May I share something with you?"

Reese chewed her lip.

"My dad left when I was a kid. I spent most of my adulthood trying to prove my worth to my stepdad. No matter what I did—it wasn't ever good enough. Not for him, no. He never said those words. It was me. I was my own worst enemy."

Reese didn't know what to say. "I'm so sorry."

She put up a hand. "No, Reese—don't be sorry. I'm here for *you*. I could lose my license saying this—boundary violations—but your voicemail had me worried. You see, I became who I am today because of the pain I walked through. You need to know there's hope no matter how dark it seems in the moment. And keeping the lines of communication open are important. As soon as you cut yourself off from what's good for you—it's that much easier to slip into despair, go numb, and make poor decisions alone without any accountability."

Dayl stood and searched the white walls with her gaze.

"Never feel like a coward for calling for help. Never believe the lie that if you reach out or just get gut honest with people, you are weak. And don't feel obligated to share your wounds and scars with just anyone. Healing doesn't come about from pressure. It comes in the natural process as we release the pain and refill with newness and life. We all deserve to be loved, and we are all capable of loving. First—it starts in here," she pointed to her chest.

Reese widened her eyes.

A knock on the door startled them.

Dayl wiped her eyes and straightened her skirt. "Just one sec."

She walked to the door, opened it only a crack, and nodded.

She shut it and turned back to Reese. "Listen, as far as the white envelope. Don't do it alone. Sometimes you can't trust your gut. If your gut tells you to do this alone because you don't want to get anyone else involved—remember you are on the edge of a rocky cliff right now. When our inner child is hurting, we treat them as they are: a child. And a responsible adult doesn't let a small child make big decisions alone, right? They guide them onto the right path because the child doesn't really know what's necessarily right for them. Do yourself a service and invite Miss Rosa, your mom, sister, or Elliot into this with you."

"What about Dad?"

"I truly believe whatever's in the envelope will tell you the answer—but I could be wrong. The point is, open it with someone you love and trust. Don't walk this alone. I am here, but you need someone in your daily life too. Don't shut them out. Don't give in to the nonsense that you don't deserve that much. And chances are, they want to. Give them a chance."

She handed Reese a folder.

"What's this?"

"You need proof of hope. Take this home. Look it over. See for yourself how far you've come, Reese. Progress doesn't always look how we think it should."

"Thank you. So much."

CHAPTER 23

The pine trees passed by like shadows of a bad dream Reese was leaving behind. It wasn't as fast as she wished, but Dayl gave her hope that forward motion at all was still the right direction, no matter the speed of it.

The white envelope sat in the seat next to her, and she was planning how to open it. No matter what scene she imagined playing out, she couldn't get Elliot out of her head.

She knew he was the right person to walk this road with her—*but will he forgive me?*

She pulled into the park. It was just past lunch, but she wasn't hungry. She pulled her phone out and composed a new message to her mom and sister, individually.

"I love you. I am sorry for being distant. I thought this whole time it was you—but it's been me. I see that now. Forgive me."

Reese really had assumed they'd pulled back, and maybe they had—but it wasn't the way Reese's mind was making it look. Most of the time her mom and sister tried reaching out to her, she'd made excuses of being too busy, "I'm fine," or whatever she could muster up at the time. Slowly over time, they reached out less and less. Not because they wanted to—Reese had given them no choice.

What were they supposed to do?

She sent the messages and felt another weight lift. And now to figure out this Dad problem. But she wasn't going to do it alone. Dayl's tears had been genuine.

She composed another message.

"Elliot, I'm so sorry. I'm broken. I panicked. Please forgive me?"

She let her head rest against the seat. What to do now? There was too much daylight left to drive home and curl up in bed. That probably wouldn't help anyway.

She got out of the car and walked down the sidewalk that led to the lake's beach.

All my life I've been running from what's real, because real is scary. Real is messy.

She let the warm sand from the autumn day filter between her bare toes. "I have to accept life is short, risky, and sometimes gets scuffed up. I have to accept that not only am I broken and on a journey—but that it's okay to admit it."

A tear slid down her cheek.

Reese looked up. "I'm not alone. I know I'm not."

She saw a white boat go by.

Her phone buzzed in her pocket, and her heart skipped.

She pulled it out just enough to see who it was from.

Elliot.

CHAPTER 24

I can do this. I can accept what he has to say. No matter what he says, I can do this.

Reese opened the message.

She shut her eyes and remembered why she felt drawn to Elliot in the first place. His nature warmed her heart. So many times, he showed care when he didn't have to. She wanted to picture him as he really was—no matter his human response. He deserved that much.

"Reese, I'm broken too. I didn't want to say this in a text: Can I please just love you?"

Reese let the phone drop to the sand.

And then fell to her knees.

Please. Yes. Please.

CHAPTER 25

Thunder filled the evening sky and a cool wind tailed Reese as she came around the last third of the trail that looped around the lake. She reread Elliot's message fifty times.

He loves me.

He loves me.

He loves me.

He loves me?

Me?

He actually loves me.

He looooves me.

He loves…me?

Me?

Me. Yes—me.

Every way Reese flipped it—her heart felt unworthy.

Why do I feel unworthy? Because Jett rejected me? Because I felt distant from my family all these years? Because I didn't like myself?

Jett, we were so young.

"Elliot wants to love me."
As is?
As me?
As is.
As me.

CHAPTER 26

Reese pulled into the driveway behind Elliot's Jeep.

"I want this. I want to let you in, Elliot."

It was time to fly out of the cage. Or fall out. Whichever—it didn't matter. The cage had to go.

Reese met the chipped red door. Face to face, they stared before her knuckles made hard contact.

It opened.

Elliot's dark hair swooped over his eye. The way he'd looked the first day she saw him. This side of a door was vulnerable. *I can't believe I timed him with the oven the first day we met.*

His eyes pierced deep.

He stepped forward, searching her.

"Elliot—" Her eyes descended, tears following.

He lifted her chin before pulling her into an embrace. They stood in silence.

Reese gripped his shirt, buried her head in his chest, and sobbed until she couldn't.

"It's going to be okay."

Her eyes danced with his. "Elliot—I'm sorry. You didn't deserve to be treated that way. I'm such a mess."

Elliot's eyes narrowed. He put a hand behind each of Reese's ears, letting her long hair fall over them. "You are more than your issues. I am more than mine."

She wanted to believe it. She had to. And if she believed it was true for him…she had to believe it was true for her.

He leaned in, forehead on hers. "When I moved here, I was trying to escape from something, Reese. There's so much I haven't told you. Not because I didn't want to. The opportunity just hadn't presented itself."

Reese looked at his bare feet.

He adjusted his leg. "We all have a past. Some aren't too far behind."

His dark brown eyes stared into hers. "Life back in Georgia filed me down. I left desperate for anything but family drama—in search of peace and solitude, really. I never imagined finding more than I hoped for—you."

The lights in the house flickered. Reese and Elliot looked around and then back to each other.

"You've reminded me laughter is worth the investment."

Thunder rumbled. The entryway became darker.

Reese lifted her gaze.

"After my runs, I'd shower and sit at the kitchen table to pound out a few chapters. Do you know what happened?"

Reese shook her head.

"Day after day after day I saw this wonderful person outside, enjoying life—pushing past self-doubt, trying to enjoy life in the moment. I found myself making excuses to be near you. Like more than usual," he laughed softly.

She didn't know what to say.

"A lasting friendship is priceless, Reese."

She pursed her lips and nodded.

Elliot closed his eyes. "I feel like you're the friend I've always prayed for." He opened his eyes, tears forming. "The kind who reminds me who I really am."

"I like who you are."

"Thanks," he laughed through the tears.

"So—we're friends?" she asked.

"I know what I want to say—"

"Say it."

"Friends first—always. But when you leave, I count down the minutes until I see you again."

Reese pictured him sitting at the kitchen table, trying to concentrate on his book. All the times she wondered how he felt. Now she knew. Any frozen tundra left in her heart puddled. "You were crushing on me. I saw it at the hospital—and in your dimples. Yep."

He slipped his fingers through hers. "Guilty."

Reese could feel her mouth curve.

"I've never felt this way with anyone else, Reese. You don't picture yourself growing old with all your friends—do you?"

Reese felt the prickles of his unshaven face.

"You can live your life, and I can live mine. We don't have to be together. I think I can survive—but I don't want to. When you're around, I—"

Reese finished. "Feel alive again."

His eyes were serious now. "I don't know everything about you, but I want to be a part of your life. Don't ask me to explain it. Seven months…"

Reese ran her fingers through his hair, titling his head toward hers, and kissed his forehead this time.

He smiled and pulled her closer. "Will you be my best friend? Will you let me love you? Am I selfish to want both?"

The lights flickered again. The thunder was getting closer.

Elliot's hands grasped her petite head, her hair woven between his fingers.

"No. You're not selfish. I've never thought that, Elliot. I've wanted both, too—but didn't know if it was right—normal—whatever…"

"I don't have all the answers."

"I know."

"I may let you down."

"I know I will."

He laughed. "See? You are so wonderful and funny and smart and beautiful. Reese, you are—"

She put a finger to his lips. "You can kiss me now. I won't run—I promise."

He leaned in, and her world spun. The force of his lips on hers took her breath away.

Thunder cracked, and lightning lit up the room. Wind thrashed through the branches of the tree out front, causing a scraping against the siding. Her feet went numb, and she was pretty sure not even a tornado could have pried them apart.

CHAPTER 27

The room went black.

"Guess we better shut the doors," Elliot said.

Another streak of lightning lit up the room. He went to the back and shut the door, locking it in place.

Reese felt her way past the couch and ran her fingers across the edge of the counter and felt for the drawers. "Candles?"

"Garage."

She slid her hands across the counter again, following its length to the end, putting her near the hallway. Then she walked the length of the hallway until she felt the garage door. She gripped the knob and turned. Elliot could probably find everything in the dark since it was his house. "Where?"

"I'm coming."

His crutches clanked against each other, and she felt the cold metal touch her. "I'm not going down the stairs with those things."

"I don't blame you. Be careful."

She followed him into the dark space.

"Watch out for—"

"Ow!"

"My tool bench."

Thunder shook the house. Reese covered her mouth.

"Did you just squeak?"

"Maybe."

"That's a first."

"Won't be the last."

"Here, found some. Hold out your hands."

They felt for each other.

Reese heard a drawer open, followed by shuffling and then a scratch.

Elliot had lit a match and touched it to the wick of the candle she held. "There."

"Okay, now what."

"Should you try and call Lila and Stan? See if they're okay?"

"Good idea." She pulled out her phone. "I never thought to use the screen for a light."

"Me neither."

She gave them a call, and Miss Lila said they were okay.

"It's dark out—when the storm passes, we can go over and check on them in person."

She loved his caring heart. The next time doubt showed its ugly face, she needed to remember the truth. To focus on the good nature of people. *Practice makes…better, right?*

REESE FELT SOMEONE SHAKE HER.

"Reese."

"Huh?"

"You fell asleep on my bed."

She looked around and saw a light from the hallway.

"The power came back on about thirty minutes ago. Thought you'd want to know."

She sat up and touched her hair, swinging her legs to the left to face Elliot's dresser mirror. "Oh my—"

"I took a nap on the couch."

"Oh, that's right. We played cards in the candlelight."

"Yep—and we talked until you drifted off. Made me sleepy."

"Storms do that."

"Reese?"

"Yes?"

"Before you fell asleep, we were talking about the envelope."

She straightened and turned to face him. "I haven't opened it yet."

"You said you were scared of what it would say, but I want you to know—whatever your dad has written—I'm here for you."

Reese sighed. "I know. I wasn't ready until now."

"Like, now-now?"

"No," she laughed. "Metaphorically."

"Let's assess the outside damage first then, although—I hope there isn't any."

"I just hope the garden isn't completely wrecked."

CHAPTER 28

The gray sky loomed over the soggy ground. Twigs and leaves formed chaotic piles of randomness across the adjoining yards.

"Make a good burn pile," Elliot said.

"Yeah—once it dries out," Reese folded her arms, eyeing the downed branches.

"Who's that?" Elliot asked, peering at a vehicle pulling into Reese's drive.

She squinted. "Oh, it's Miss Rosa. I didn't recognize the car. Ron probably let her use one of his. She's always test-driving them."

"Ron?"

"Remember the car guy I told you about?"

Elliot shook his head. "Right."

Reese turned back to her garden, her hands shoved deep into her pockets. At least it was the end of the season—not much more left to harvest anyway.

Elliot's arm wrapped around her. "You rocked this. That's what counts."

Miss Rosa walked up, clutching her chest. "I see you two

are fine. That's good. When you didn't answer, I got worried."

Reese held her phone out. "When did you call?"

"An hour or so ago, but when I got out to check on my neighbors—check on the shops—I thought I'd drive over."

"I have a signal now. Sorry."

"It's fine, honey." Miss Rosa rubbed her chin. "Sorry to see the remains of your garden go."

Elliot tried to crouch but stopped.

"Want to come with us to check on Miss Lila and Stan?" Reese decided it was better not to mourn the last yield. She was so tired of mourning. Rehearsing issues the right way, had their upside she'd discovered with Dayl. But this mess? Not worth it.

"I'll leave them to you for now—heading back to help Anette. When you get ready to pull out your decorations for the festival, let me know and I'll meet you at the gazebo for our yearly tradition."

Of course, Miss Rosa was all about the festivities. Thanksgiving and Christmas were her babies. Not even a storm could wreck her inspiration.

"Sure thing," Reese said as she watched Miss Rosa walk away.

Elliot yanked his sinking crutches out of the mud and they walked the back way to Miss Lila and Stan's.

Reese was behind him and for the first time, it hit her that her parents hadn't called in a while. Or had they and she'd ignored it? It was possible. In the dark moments, she often flung her phone onto a soft surface to avoid the world and bury herself in a book. Then she'd forget to go back and check.

Elliot trudged carefully through the wet yard. One of his crutches sank deep, and it broke up the monotony in her head.

"Here—let me help," she laughed.

He carried one above his head, and her the other—just for fun. Because sometimes when the mud pulls downward and the foggy atmosphere envelopes the body, the best thing to do is goof off and remind oneself that even storm aftermaths are only for a time.

She poked his backside with the end of the crutch.

"Hey!"

See? It's worth it. So remember it, Reese.

CHAPTER 29

Seeing the handwriting made her heart jump. *Dad.*

Reese swallowed hard, but there was nothing to swallow. She wasn't sure if she wanted to know the truth or not. Would the truth reveal more of him or more of her?

Elliot sat with his back against her bedroom wall; Reese sat in front, leaning against him. She tugged the white paper the rest of the way out, revealing the words. Not too short, not too long.

"Reese,

I am writing this note months before we leave on our trip. All I can think about is leaving you behind. I hope you will come, but from the way you talk lately, your plans are to stay home hunkered at your desk. If this is to be your decision I respect that—but I will miss you terribly.

Having said that, this gift is in case you do stay. This car is not to suck up. Please, understand...I know the pickup won't go on forever, and last week when you sped off to help Miss Rosa, it echoed a familiar sound I heard from my own pickup right before it went out. Maybe I'm wrong. We'll see.

Your mom and I talked it over and decided to get you this and have Ron store it as a surprise if the other dies while we're gone. I hope you like it.

I hope you know I love you. We all do. We haven't been great at showing it lately. So caught up in helping the world that we sometimes forget who's right in front of us. And that's no excuse. This is me kissing your forehead, tucking you in burrito style.

Keep positive. You make me proud, sweetie. —DAD"

Reese dropped the paper.

Fat tears fell, pooling half on her dad's words, half on her lap. She missed the nights he'd tuck her in. She missed their late-night talks before he took on more hours at work. Almost two decades of pain had been internalized—but he hadn't changed.

Sometimes life dealt a different hand. Sometimes life threw curve balls. She needed a new lens to filter pain through.

Elliot kissed the top of her head and put his hands on her arms.

Neither of them said a word.

CHAPTER 30

The damp autumn air bit Reese's chin.

Neighboring farmers were beginning to break out the combines, and like most everyone else in the area, Reese was on a mission. She dug through the shed, found the right boxes her mom had labeled with giant black font, and carried them two at a time into Elliot's house.

The smell of Miss Lila's crisp apple pie and Stan's cigar —back when he still smoked them—were some of her best childhood memories. The Thanksgiving festivities were just some of the joys Reese hoped to share with Elliot.

Eastwood's traditions weren't at all unique, but they'd become a staple of the season. Decorating for the Fall Festival, watching the elders argue over who would take home which pie, and bobbing for apples were on the list of things Elliot had to witness. It was a riot having the toddlers elbow to elbow with seniors. A few teens would usually participate, and Miss Rosa always tried to talk Reese into the mess, but she'd mosey behind the corn stalk photo booth. Her hideout worked every time because Miss Rosa wouldn't dare walk away from the fun.

Reese glanced at Elliot—feet propped while his laptop's noisy keys revealed he'd thought of the next chapter of his latest book. "You think you'll be up for stringing some lights?"

Elliot raised his brow. "Lights? In November?"

"Welcome to Eastwood. We don't like hanging them for December alone. We make it worthwhile."

He set his laptop aside and stretched. "A little late for a welcome—but sure—give me three more hours." He peeled a banana from the fruit bowl. "Book signing's coming up, and I want to be finished with the draft by then."

"Is that the real reason?"

He looked up. "Well—I really want to be done by Christmas."

"Ah, so you *are* looking forward to the holidays."

"I never said I wasn't."

"The other day—"

Elliot's phone rang. He wrapped his arms around Reese, kissing the top of her head as she fished through an open box. "Hold that thought."

"Sure. It's not like I don't have anything to keep me buuusssy," she teased.

She peered into the box stuffed with pine cones, fake pumpkins, and packing popcorn. *Nope.* She shoved it to the side and opened another. It was full of table cloths, random decor, and a stack of cookbooks on how to properly cook turkey. *Nope.*

She shoved it aside too and went for a third.

The sound of Elliot's serious tone reverberated from down the hall. Probably his mom on the line. He called her back five days after the hospital visit. She was rather irritated, but he convinced her of the truth: He'd been overwhelmed.

"Oh, my favorite candle," Reese sniffed. "From Mom."

She drank in the rich aroma of pumpkin and spice. *Mmmm.* Scents had a way of taking a person back. If Reese hadn't been such an emotional train wreck—inwardly speaking—the past few major holidays, she may want to visit old times. Not today.

I'm ready for some new memories.

After Elliot's doorway confession the other day, she wasn't about to rake up dead leaves.

She spied something. Something useful. *Finally.*

Ribbon that wasn't plaid. And clear jars.

Elliot walked in with a twisted look on his face.

"What's wrong?"

"Mom. Something's not right. I can hear it in her voice, but she won't say."

Reese spun the loose ribbon around the spool. "Is she still coming for Thanksgiving?"

"Yeah, from what I gather. Still, her voice was off."

"Maybe she wants to tell you in person. I wouldn't worry about it."

"Probably right. What's all this?"

Reese shrugged. "My measly attempt at creating baskets to raffle off. Miss Rosa insists I be in charge every year, though she knows it's not my strong suit."

Elliot laughed. "Have fun with that."

"Three thousand pounds of ribbon later—I might." She tossed a spool at his back.

"You just made more work for yourself."

"I need a break. If I don't get out of here, I'm going to mummify you with this blasted bling."

"Thought you loved the holidays?"

"I do, but I'm not the best crafter on the planet. These things need to be worth the cost of a ticket, and Miss Rosa didn't set the price too low. I don't do flashy. Look at my garden—or what's left of it—my house and my yard. I don't even do lawn ornaments."

Her eyes grew.

"What?" Elliot looked at her sideways.

"Oh, my gosh." She burst into laughter. "Remember that lawn ornament that fell over a few months ago?"

"Think so."

She got up and slowly backed away from Elliot.

His eyes narrowed. "Wait."

"My bad. You were just so addictive to be around, so I stalked you for a millisecond—then I bumped into it and down she went."

He set his crutches aside and strode toward her, careful not to hurt his left leg. "Oh, really?"

She threw her hands up. "Since I confessed, you're going to cut me a deal, right?"

Elliot caught her as she came around the other side.

He pulled her into a playful hold. "I can't believe you made my gnome creepier than it already was. All this time I blamed Redford. I owe him now."

"He'll forgive you."

Elliot kissed Reese on the cheek and sat down, bring her down with him.

Reese was quiet.

"What are you thinking?"

She poked the cleft in his chin. "Are you going to save me from the evil clutches of cornucopias or what?"

"I can't drive. Guess not."

"Fine—I'll save myself and you can tag along."

Elliot looked at his watch. "Three hours."

She flared her nose. "Three hours it is."

CHAPTER 31

Elliot's upstairs study was of the industrial variety. The simple wooden desk beneath the window hosted a clip-on lamp, a single pencil to the right. The iron bars connected across the bottom reminded Reese of a jail cell. A clean one at least.

"Okay, Dayl—what do you have for me?"

She opened the folder that held months of treatment notes, daily regimens, triggers, and changes in behaviors. It was filled with words like irritability, social anxiety, grief, and cognitive dissonance.

"Reese?"

"Yeah?" she said loud enough for Elliot to hear.

"It's your dad," he called from downstairs.

The jagged edges of crunchy oak leaves slid across the top of Reese's head as she walked under the tree to the Jeep. Elliot talked her into taking a camping trip and they were loading the last of their stuff. "He called. Finally."

Elliot set the cooler by Reese's feet. He flipped it open. "Looks good."

She slammed a bag of ice on the ground and ripped a hole in the plastic. "It's just surreal. He's been busy for ages."

"I'm happy for you. I know his letter had you nervous."

"It'd just been so long since we talked about more than the weather in passing…"

"It's great you connected again."

"Baby steps—for all of us."

Elliot wiped his face with the bottom of his red tee.

"I don't think any of us realized that living together didn't equal connection. You have to make it happen—can't live on autopilot with each other."

"Sounds like a billboard."

Reese knew he was joking. "Speaking of steps—I bet you can't wait to hit the ground running."

"Two more weeks, and I should be good," Elliot said, fixing a strap on his cast.

"Are you sure you don't want to wait until it's completely healed to do this?" Reese said, dumping the ice over the drinks and food.

"No, I'm sure. I want to do it now before it gets too cold. And you don't want Mom trying to sneak into the tent to cuddle at night, do you?"

"Would she try?"

Elliot gave her a look.

"Oh, dear."

"This is long overdue," Elliot said as he shoved the tent into the designated spot.

"I'm feeling it too. Glad to wrap up my class soon. Feel like I'll be ready for a completely new adventure then."

Elliot suddenly had an intriguing look come over him, but Reese didn't pry. "Are you disappointed?"

Reese grunted as she attempted to stuff a bag under the back seat. "I mean, a little—but a flattened garden sorta' makes me want to move on."

"You don't think you'll garden next year?"

"Don't know. I love it but—"

Elliot helped her finish shoving the bag in place.

"I feel like it was a gateway more than a lifelong commitment for me."

"Deep."

Reese opened the other back door and set her duffel and backpack on the floor. "Served as a jump start."

He nodded. "After you told me what Dayl said about your progress, I would agree that getting outside helped—helps—will keep helping…"

"You're funny."

"Running helps me re-center. If gardening wasn't it for you—you'll find your thing."

Reese pulled Elliot's hood over his head and tied the strings into a bow.

"—or, you've already found it," he smirked.

Amused, Reese gave him a peck on the lips and crossed her arms. "Maybe so."

CHAPTER 32

Reese pulled up in front of the bookstore.

It looked like Miss Rosa got a head start. The awnings of the first three businesses were strung with lights, and a few other residents were working on the gazebo near the playground.

"Can't wait for you to see this place at night for the next two months. You'll fall in love if you haven't already."

Elliot's phone lit up.

"I'm gonna hop out and drop this stuff off—see if they need any help before we head out," she said.

"Amelia, what did you do now?" Elliot glared at the text on his phone screen.

"Hope everything's okay."

Elliot kissed her cheek. "I'll join you in a few."

Miss Rosa came over to the Jeep as Reese shut the door. "I'll take those for you, Reesey." She peered into the flapless box.

"Hope they work."

"Oh, I'm sure they're fine. Thanks, honey."

"We have more lights for you, but I need to test them first. Just ran out of time."

"Where are you two love birds off to?"

Reese fixed the hem of her shirt.

Miss Rosa pulled a leaf out of Reese's hair.

Reese turned to face Elliot in the Jeep. He looked like he was now in an intense phone conversation. He was even more handsome when focused.

"See?" Miss Rosa said.

"What?"

"You're already off in another world. Next year I'll be decorating everything alone, won't I?"

"No. I'll make Elliot," she laughed.

"He is something special, huh?"

She guessed Elliot figured they were talking about him. He pointed to the phone and shrugged but blew her a kiss.

"He is—and thanks for helping me sort through my mess lately."

"We're all born messy—into a mess, Reesey."

"You, Dayl, and Elliot have said the same thing in different ways."

Miss Rosa squeezed Reese. "Here, take this and hold it while I tack this end up."

"Hey, Ron," Reese said.

He was carrying a giant inflatable cornucopia. "Look what I found."

Reese rolled her eyes. "Thought I buried that thing far enough down—darn."

He shook his head. "Shame, shame. You know this was voted the town's favorite for three years in a row."

"Elliot's really about to find out how excited y'all get for Thanksgiving."

"Y'all? We. We, honey," Miss Rosa corrected.

"*We* may need to wait on puttin' it up," Ron said, eyeing the sky.

"You and your radar," Miss Rosa said throwing her hand out.

"Said we're supposed to be gettin' another storm in a few days."

"Well, why on earth am I putting all this up?"

Reese's arms were starting to burn. She was pretty sure Miss Rosa forgot about her.

"Oh, the lights'll be fine, darlin'. Just hold up on all this. I's just checkin' to see if there were any holes. Looks like we're going for four years."

Miss Rosa grimaced. "Storms in November ruining my plans."

"Miss Rosa?"

"Oh shucks, honey, I'm sorry." She walked over and took the strand from Reese. "Ron, toss down your trophy and help me—Reese has to go."

"Off so soon? We haven't seen you around as much lately."

"Yeah, camping. And Elliot broke his leg so—"

Miss Rosa interrupted. "So she's been home taking care of him."

"Somewhat. He's really fine—I'm just driving and stuff."

"Well y'all be careful out there camping with a broken leg." He shook his head.

"It's really not that bad. See ya around soon."

Ron piped up before Reese got to the Jeep. "You got a flashlight, blankets, and a radio with batteries?"

"Yes, sir."

"Okay, just checkin'. Have fun, doll." He and Miss Rosa waved as she got in the Jeep.

"Hey," Reese said, eyeing Elliot, who was now off the phone.

"They good?"

Reese pulled out onto Main. "They got it. Did you see the dreadful blowup?"

"I think it's fun."

"Fun? Not my word of choice. How's Amelia?"

"I'd rather not talk about it right now."

Reese glanced over and back to the road. He did look a little flustered. "Sure thing. You still want to go?"

"You bet."

FOR EVERY TREE THEY PASSED, REESE HAD A THOUGHT ABOUT her future. What would it look like a year from now, if things had already changed so much this year?

Elliot was asleep, seat leaned back. They were now in Buchanan, Tennessee.

Reese played with his arm hair and eyed the GPS. "Yes!" They were getting close.

She followed the directions and turned into Paris Landing. The sun was slipping over the horizon. "You pitched a tent in the near dark before?"

Elliot shifted in his seat.

"Hey, sleepy head."

She put the Jeep in park. The trees loomed overhead, creating a glorious canopy beneath the evening sky.

"This spot looks perfect." She turned to Elliot, who had his hands behind his head, and kissed his cheek. "We're here."

His eyes peeled open.

"You pitched a tent in the dark before?"

"Oh—yeah, well I brought a spotlight."

When they finished, they admired their quick teamwork.

"A yellow tent."

"It's not like we're hunting."

"You hunt?"

"No—that's beside the point."

"I can't believe you hid a piece of the tent from me!"

Elliot had laughed when she'd thought they'd left a vital component back in Kentucky. "I had to get you at least once."

Reese pulled her gear from the duffel and squished it up against the side of the tent, opposite Elliot. The tent's interior boasted more room than it appeared to have from the outside. She flopped her sleeping bag out, set the radio near the foot area, and put her bathroom bag in the pouch attached to the wall.

"There." She stretched out on her sleeping bag and watched Elliot.

He carefully unrolled his green and gray sleeping bag, flattening out any wrinkle he noticed.

I love every detail about you.

Reese checked the time. "Want to take a dip?"

"It's too cold to swim!"

Reese squinted. "You chicken?"

"Hold old are you?"

"You wanted adventure, right?"

"Yeah—but…"

"C'mon. We don't have to stay in long. Just to say we did it."

"I thought it was closed after dark."

"No one's going to care. We're here during the week—it's dead." Reese already had her bikini on under her clothes, so she slung her backpack around her arms and climbed out.

He threw her a worried look. "Just give me one sec."

Reese went back to the Jeep to grab the towels. She hung one around her shoulders and hung the other around Elliot as he climbed out and zipped the tent back up.

They strolled down to the river's beach, the only light coming from a dusk-to-dawn lamp and the moon.

The cool grass felt good under her feet. She dropped her towel and bag and found the water's edge. "I'm going to regret this."

"Can't back out now."

Reese stepped down into the water where an entrance made of concrete steps led to the shallow bottom. The light from the moon reflected on the water's surface. The only sound came from traffic on the bridge above the river.

"So cold!"

"Don't make me give you a boost," he laughed.

"Here goes—" And she jumped in.

She came up for air and slung her hair back. Okay, bad idea. It was like swimming in ice. Where was Elliot? "Hey!"

Elliot was still standing there. "It's cold!"

Reese swam up to him, teeth chattering and pulled his hand.

"You wouldn't."

"I would."

He grimaced and lowered himself into the cold water.

Reese swam out where the water deepened, and he followed. "Bet I can beat you to the wall."

"I have a broken leg and now I'm frozen. You can win. Go ahead."

"Excuses, excuses," she said, taking off. She swam to the wall and pivoted back to where Elliot was—but he wasn't there.

"Elliot?" She swam around for a few seconds and called

again. "Elliot?" She squinted and looked up onto the bank. He wasn't there either.

The chill was starting to become a bit too much, but she didn't want to admit it to him, wherever he was. She felt something grab her from under the water.

Elliot's head poked up.

"You scared the crap out of me!"

"It worked then," he laughed, chin quivering.

She flicked his arm.

"Ow. Can we go yet?"

"Hey, look."

The water was moving, small waves hitting the side of the wall.

Reese grabbed her arms. "I was okay when I was moving."

"Let's go. At least we got to have fun for a few. If you call that fun."

"I conceed."

The water's movement became stronger.

Elliot looked across the water. "Uh oh."

A light shone from a patrol boat speeding across the river. It was nearing the beach area.

"Go under or head for the bank?"

"Can you hold your breath for a few minutes? Who knows how long it will take."

With that, Reese swam for the steps--Elliot behind. They wrapped in towels, lips looking a bit dark in the dim light and laugh-chattered as they headed back to the tent.

"Swimming in freezing water is now crossed off my bucket list," Elliot said from outside the tent as Reese changed.

"It was on your list?" She carefully wiped wet grass clippings off her feet and rolled the towel at the foot of her sleeping bag. Elliot was quiet. "You there?"

"Yeah. And no. I was joking."

She put her wet clothes in a bag and tied it off, still trying to catch her breath.

Elliot grumbled.

"What?"

"My sister…"

"You never told me."

"Uh—yeah. I'll fill you in when I know more."

She slid the tent zipper down and poked her head through. "Okay, handsome."

Elliot looked down, water dripping from his shorts. "Who? Me?" He looked around sarcastically.

"Yes, you—but you are not coming in here with those on."

His eyes got big. "I'm not stripping out here."

She shook her head and threw him a dry towel from her gear. "Here, use this, and I'll go out while you come in. And hurry. Your lips really are purple."

"Oh," he laughed. "That I can do."

After they were both dry, Reese nestled against his chest. He wrapped his arms around her.

"You're still shaking."

"I know. My worst idea ever."

"Braver than I was." He rubbed her arms fast, trying to create warmth.

She looked into his eyes.

"You ready for bed?"

"I guess."

"Just wanted to warm you up enough."

Reese rolled over and they both climbed into their sleeping bags.

She turned to look at Elliot, but he was studying the cooler. "What?"

He pulled the cooler between them from the waist down.

"What are you doing?"

He laid on his side facing her and grinned big. "Now we're good."

She could feel one of her hysterical laughs brewing. "You are one of a kind."

CHAPTER 33

Bacon. Bacon. *Bacon?*

The sun's warmth turned the tent into a mini oven. Camping in November was a risk. They could have had the perfect weather—or rain—or an early snow. This area's weather was always up in the air.

Reese sat up and looked around. Scraping sounds came from outside the tent. The aroma of breakfast filled the yellow dome.

She threw a blanket over her shoulders and climbed out of the tent. "Breakfast—I'm starving," she said, grabbing a finished piece of bacon from a plate.

Elliot spun around, revealing his rugged face and messy hair. "You're one of those people. I knew it."

"What?" She asked, chowing down.

"Who eats all the bacon before it's finished. Before the cook gets any."

She laughed. "I'll share, I promise."

"Good morning, by the way," he said, kissing the top of her head.

He flipped the last of the pancakes and set them on a plate. "Here."

The picnic table was already set. The sun was peeking through the many trees around them. It was a perfect scene.

"This looks amazing."

"I couldn't sleep in. I tried."

"Cooked instead?"

"Try this." He forked a bite of eggs into her mouth.

She closed her eyes and savored the flavor.

"You like?"

"Mmmm. Yes."

"You haven't lived until you've had my scrambled version."

"You have versions of eggs?"

He winked and took a bite of bacon.

Reese looked around. "It's so peaceful out here."

"The isolated riverfront was peaceful too."

"The beach?"

"Yeah—went there this morning before the sun came up. The view is much better than the temperature."

Reese wiggled her flip flop. "Okay, okay. I was wrong. I get it. Anyway—it's nothing fancy, but this is about the cheapest getaway a person can find."

Elliot took a sip of orange juice. "Fancy is overrated."

"So, what are we doing today?"

"On my walk this morning I found a nice trail over that way," he said, pointing.

"Sounds great. Your leg up for it?"

"Honestly, I think so. Only minor pain lately. And even then, it's not constant."

"Alright then, sounds like a plan."

Elliot brought the platter of food over and peeled back the foil. They both reached in and piled their plates. They made small talk until they were through, but once the table was clear, Reese thought Elliot seemed a little off.

"You okay?"

Elbows glued to the table, he raked his fingers across his face as if he were trying to wake himself up—but Reese knew it wasn't that. He was wide awake.

"Heading to the bathroom. Be right back."

He nodded and she turned to walk away. On her way back, she stopped to watch him before approaching their campsite. He was pacing back and forth, hands clasped behind his head.

Reese hoped he was alright, but standing here watching him wasn't going to make things better. She grabbed a stick and walked over to the fire pit, poking the smoky pile. "What's up?"

His eyes shot over to where she was, as if he'd been startled by her presence. "Oh—nothing. I'm good. Just thinking. You ready?" He asked, and stuffed his water bottle into the side of his backpack. He tossed Reese her backpack and slipped an energy bar into the side pouch before she could say anything else.

They started off on the shortest trail and decided to hit them all up, if his leg would permit.

Another couple passed them on the path, and Elliot nodded.

The combination of dirt, pebbles and dried leaves crunched beneath their feet, creating a rhythm as they walked.

Reese was behind Elliot, mind reeling. Elliot seemed disturbed—not in a bad way, just preoccupied. It wasn't like him, especially now that they were here. *Is he having fun? Is Amelia okay?*

They came to a clearing with a bench. Reese stopped and set her backpack down to take a drink but Elliot didn't notice and kept going. She twisted the cap back on and shoved it back into the holder.

Elliot finally turned around.

She caught up to him and gave his back a friendly pat. "Are you still glad we came?"

"What? Of course." He rubbed his hands together and they both continued. Elliot's sudden quietness was peaking Reese's curiosity though. She tried to focus on the moment. Where they were. The beauty of the towering trees. The almost echo of the breeze.

They hiked up an incline, and finally he spoke up. "What would you do if what you wanted to do was the opposite of what you'd always planned?"

Reese rolled the question over in her mind for a minute.

They came to the top of the incline, did a few stretches, and he watched for her reply.

"Things change. We change—right?"

He chugged his water and looked across the woods.

"Plans evolve. You've witnessed me—" she laughed. 'I'm prime example."

His arms crossed tight, he looked up. "True."

They continued down the far side of the slope.

"You're so quiet today."

"I hope I don't seem rude. Just been thinking."

"I'll say. I thought we'd talk each other's heads off this whole time."

"Sorry."

"No, don't apologize." She turned to him and cut him off, holding her arm out. "You know it goes both ways, right?"

"What?"

"You can tell me, if something heavy is on your mind."

His eyes narrowed. She searched his face for some clue. His jaw flinched. *There.*

"Reese—"

"Yes?"

"Help!" someone yelled.

Reese grabbed Elliot's arm tight. "What?"

Elliot cupped his mouth. "Hello?"

"Someone help us!" a woman's voice yelled.

They walked down the slope to the bottom but didn't see anyone. The woman yelled a few more times.

Reese's heart was banging through her chest now.

"Reese, someone could be hurt bad. We need to split up. I'll go back the way we came, you go that way. If you find her, yell for me because I'm not getting a signal out here."

Reese nodded and took off the way they'd been going while he ran back down the trail. "Be careful!" she hollered back to him.

The path went another hundred feet before it curved.

A woman ran into Reese. "Please, can you help? My son —" She was panting. "He needs sugar. He's hypoglycemic, and we left his tabs on the other end of the park. Stupid, stupid me."

"Where is he?"

"He's back there," she pointed in the direction Reese was heading. "With his brother, but passed out or something."

Reese took her hand. "Go back with him. Take this with you," she handed the woman the energy bar Elliot had put in her bag. "I'm going to get my friend. We have orange juice in our cooler not too far from here."

The woman took the bar and ran back.

Reese ran up the slope looking for Elliot. "Elliot!" She ran for a couple more minutes. "Elliot, I found her!"

As she topped the hill, he nearly bumped into her. "What's wrong?"

Reese stopped to catch her breath. "She needs sugar. Orange juice. Her son passed out."

He dropped his backpack. "Wait for me, I'm gonna run."

"Elliot—your leg."

He shook his head. "I don't care. Wait for me." He took off toward their campsite, and Reese watched him disappear.

CHAPTER 34

The ground felt hard. A steady ringing pierced through Reese's skull.

She tried to focus. They were almost there.

The woman looked up and ran to meet them. "He's still laying there," she said in a raspy voice.

The three of them ran to the spot.

Elliot stooped down to the young boy and felt his pulse. He sat him up against his chest. "Reese, here."

She threw the cap off the drink and slowly gave the boy a sip, trying not to spill it all over him.

"Sean, please swallow. Can you hear me? It's Mom. These people are helping."

Elliot gently slapped the boy's arms. "Ma'am, tap his feet please."

She did what he said until the boy moved.

"He's swallowing!" Reese didn't realize she had been digging her nails into her leg.

"Hey, buddy—you're doing great. Keep it up—you'll be good in no time."

The mom paced back and forth while the other sibling sat

cross-legged on the ground. He looked to be about twelve, while Sean looked about six.

"He'll be fine, ma'am. You'll be fine," Elliot said into the boy's ear.

Reese gave him another drink. The boy started to come to.

Elliot sat patiently waiting for the boy to sit up. His eyes met Reese's gaze.

The mom was now stooped in front of her son, who was still leaning against Elliot. "You all right? Mommy was so scared."

Reese turned to the woman. "You're not getting a signal either?"

The woman shook her head. The boy sat up.

"Oh, baby—I'm so sorry mommy left your tabs." She grabbed him up into a big hug. "Thank you all so much."

Elliot and Reese stood. The woman shook their hands.

Elliot turned to Sean and pulled an extra juice from his bag, along with a few snacks. "Here—keep these on you. Never go anywhere without something, okay?" He winked and rubbed the boy's head.

Sean smiled. "Thank you," and he dumped the goods into his mom's hands. "Can we play now?"

The adults laughed, and everyone parted ways, Reese and Elliot continuing forward on the path.

When they had walked a good way, Reese broke the silence. "That was nuts."

"Could have been worse."

They walked a bit slower than before.

Reese got closer.

Their hands touched as they walked, but Elliot still seemed distracted.

Reese flared her nostrils. It was as if she had passed through a screen of marvelous smells. The scent of grilled meat and possibly a vegetable or two taunted her stomach. "We didn't bring stuff to grill—did we?" She joked.

Elliot tossed her a pre-made sub from the cooler. "Nope."

"This'll work."

The sun beat down, but it was a cool 63 degrees according to the outdoor thermometer Elliot had on the Jeep.

She slammed down her sandwich and hopped in the driver's seat. "Tennis?"

Elliot rubbed his leg. "I don't know."

Reese made a face. "I knew that was going to happen."

"Had to be done."

"I know."

"Think I'm gonna' take a nap."

"Okay, I'm not tired, but I did bring a book."

Elliot was asleep before Reese finished the first chapter of his book. *This is really good.*

She'd been wanting to dive into the first of his series. *No wonder he's making a living on these.*

She saw chapter eight and didn't realize what time it was —Elliot had probably been asleep about an hour at her reading rate. Her eyes got heavy and she laid the book on her chest. And yes, the cooler was between them still.

Reese laughed and fell asleep.

CHAPTER 35

Flowers lined the wooded path. The breeze blew Reese's hair across her face. She peeled it away and put one foot in front of the other. *The path must lead somewhere.* The soil was cool on her feet, and the smell of the wild chickweed infiltrated her nose. Where was she? It didn't look like anywhere she'd been before. *Chickweed's native to England, right?* She fished through mental notes from class. Yeah—but England? And how could she tell it was chickweed?

The wind picked up and something caught her eye. People. They were watching from the woods. Reese swallowed and kept walking. *Should I turn around?*

Wait—was that her professor? Reese tried not to stare.

A rustling came from up ahead. Two torches set apart from each other looked to be at the end of the path. What was this?

She looked to her left, where jars were lined up, glowing from tea candles placed inside them.

She glanced to the right. The same.

Thunder cracked in the sky.

Reese wanted to run but couldn't. Her feet felt like they weighed a thousand tons.

Soft strings played.

I need a drink.

Her feet were cold, but her throat was hot. She looked down. An ivory gown hung over her petite body.

The sound of the strings grew louder.

So did the thunder.

The torches got closer.

Reese focused her eyes. "Elliot?"

It looked like he was wearing some sort of suit.

She tried to walk faster. "Elliot!" She wanted to ask him where they were.

The wind was now blowing so hard, her dress clung to one side of her legs. She reached out her hand as Elliot turned to face her. He was wearing a tux. And—he looked different.

"You grew a beard?"

His eyes were piercing, but he almost looked sad.

"What's wrong?"

Rain began to pour on them, but the torches didn't go out. Reese looked around, and everyone seemed to be waiting on her to say something.

"Elliot, what's wrong?"

Her hair was stuck to her neck, but Elliot reached to pull it off—putting his hands on her face, pulling her close.

"Are you going to answer him?"

Reese looked around. "Who?"

Elliot turned, and Reese saw a man in a suit next to them. He hadn't been there before. Or—she hadn't noticed?

Her heart beat wildly. Something sharp stabbed her hand. "What?" She looked down. She'd been clinging to a bouquet of flowers. She dropped them and looked into Elliot's eyes. "Answer what?" Her body was shaking.

"I said, 'I do,' but you didn't answer the man when he asked. Do you?"

Reese didn't understand. Then it hit her. *This is my wedding?*

"Why is everyone acting like this is normal? We're soaking!"

Elliot didn't respond. "Do you?"

The man walked closer. "Do you?"

Reese held her face, eyes closed.

Elliot moved her hands and put his forehead on hers.

She opened her eyes to see his.

"Don't be nervous. It's just me."

"But—"

Elliot leaned in and kissed her shaking body.

So cold.

"Reese!"

Her body was still shaking. "What is this?"

"You're dreaming, Reese. Wake up."

She sat up, hair matted to her face. "What?"

Elliot felt her head. "We need to get you some fresh air. You're burning up."

"Not again," she murmured.

Elliot unzipped the tent, and Reese could feel the cool breeze rush in.

She let herself fall back onto the ground. "I can't move."

He gave her a drink. "Sorry I was out for long. I see you like the book."

Reese snapped out of it. "It's great."

"You gonna be okay?"

She nodded.

"Sounded like a bad one."

"Shouldn't have been."

"What?"

Reese got on all fours and crawled out of the tent.

He looked at her from the door, waiting for her to reply.

When she didn't, he turned around to grab something. "Here—found these."

He had a handful of white flowers. "Picked them while you were sleeping. From over there—" He pointed toward the woods.

My imagination is on steroids.

"Lovely," she took them.

"The temperature is supposed to drop tonight—want to head back early?"

"Do you want to?"

"I'll be okay—just not sure about you."

"If the cooler wasn't in the way, we could keep warm." She smirked.

"Nice try."

Reese kicked a rock, and Elliot climbed out of the tent. "So, what's the plan?" she asked.

"Plan?"

"You said your plans were changing."

Elliot rolled his neck back and forth. "Did I?"

"Uh—kind of."

He squirted lighter fluid onto the wood in the metal firepit. "Think they are. Just not so sure of the timing."

He tossed in a match. The flames popped and cracked, rising higher. He wiped his hands.

Reese put a marshmallow on her rod and sat on the stump.

He sat across from her, now roasting his. "We started too soon."

"What?"

"We should have waited for coals to form. You like burnt ones?" He laughed and shook his rod. "Scorched."

"Nice."

He popped the black ball into his mouth and slid a fresh marshmallow onto his rod.

The afternoon was slipping away, and they really hadn't done much—but wasn't that the point?

Reese tossed the question in her mind before releasing it. "You hear from Amelia?"

"Nope."

"I'm not tired now."

"Curse of the nap." Elliot looked around. "You weren't kidding when you said this place was dead during the week."

"Yeah, it's not a well-known spot."

"Reese!"

She turned back. Her marshmallow caught fire. "I did that on purpose."

"Sure ya did."

"We should go boating tomorrow."

"We could."

Reese looked around. The area was so quiet. She pulled her burnt marshmallow off the rod and got up.

"What are you doing?"

"Here, open up."

"No."

"Open up."

"Look—mine's almost done and it's gonna be perfect." He slid the rod away from the flame, but Reese grabbed it and took off running.

"Oh—it's on!"

Reese stuffed the perfect marshmallow in her mouth.

"You didn't."

She taunted him with her eyebrows.

He almost caught her, but she pivoted to the right. "You're quick—I'll give you that."

She turned to the left, but he tricked her. He backed up, spun around, and enveloped her in his arms.

"Gotcha!" But as he said it—she shoved the burnt one in his mouth. His eyes got big.

Reese burst out laughing and he let go.

"You're ssslick, you know dat?" But his mouth was too full.

She ran backwards, trying to keep an eye on him, but he went to the cooler and pulled something out.

"Oh, no. Someone's going to get your special yogurt." He peeled the top off and stuck his finger in.

"That's my last one!"

"Mmmmm."

"I'm not falling for that trick!"

"Oh no? What about this?" He tossed it into the fire.

She jutted her head. "Elliot! That was perfectly good yogurt! Some kid somewhere could have eaten that!" A playful rage welled up, and she charged toward him.

"Some hot woman at a campground could have—but she rebelled and ate something she wasn't supposed to."

He ran toward the tent, unzipped it and dove in.

"Can't lock me out—haha!" She dove in after him and landed on top of him. Just as quick, he lifted her off. Reese tried to catch her breath.

"My plan worked. You came to me—ha."

Reese grabbed her stomach, laughing so hard. "How old are we?"

"Young enough."

Reese pulled a hard object out from under her. "Ow." She set the book aside and climbed out. She unzipped the top, so they could see the stars.

"I think I got my exercise for the day."

"All in five minutes."

They were both quiet for a long time, lying there on their backs.

Elliot rolled onto his side. The way he searched her, she knew he had something on his mind. More than burnt marshmallows.

"What is it?"

He turned back over and found the stars. "I just don't want to rush this—"

"Rush what?"

She rolled closer to him, propping herself up on her elbows.

He moved her bangs out of her eyes. "How committed do you want to be to us, Reese?"

She didn't respond right away—but she was pretty sure she knew what he meant. "You mean…"

He took her hands and felt her fingers. "We've already thrown it out there—a little. There's no going back—to just friends—right?"

She moved her finger over the edge of his jaw. "Right."

"Will you be my Mrs. Jacobson?"

CHAPTER 36

The smell of dry leaves wafted through the tent.

Reese felt weightless.

She shut her eyes and pictured a new dream. Miss Rosa's words, "Trust your gut," came to mind. Her gut said, "Say yes." Her gut screamed and threw confetti. Now she just had to decide how to respond. *Do people take this long to respond? Yes, Elliot—yes—a thousand times—yes!* Then how come it wouldn't come out? She swallowed the dry lump in her throat and rubbed her sweaty palms on her pants.

She reached out for Elliot. *There you are. You're still there. My eyes are shut, and you haven't left. You're not offended, are you? No, you aren't, because that's who you are. You are gentle and considerate. You are who I want with me for the rest of my life.*

"Yes," she said opening her eyes.

His grin spread wide, and he lunged into a giant bear hug before Reese had the chance to do or say anything else.

He wrapped his strong arms around her waist and pressed his lips into hers. "I love you so much."

Reese settled into his arms, and he held her there under the night sky, stars beaming bright.

It was the last day of their mini-getaway.

Elliot tossed the remaining gear into the back of the Jeep. "Now all we have to do when we get back to the dock, is leave."

"Awesome," Reese said, shutting the rear door.

They took one last look at the campsite before walking to the marina.

Elliot grabbed his pocket. "Shoot, I forgot my phone."

Reese made a face. "It'll be all right—I have mine."

"You're right, we just need one."

The man at the marina looked like Jack Nicholson, and Reese wondered if she should hide behind Elliot. "He looks like Jack Nicholson," she whispered.

"Reese, shhh." He gave her *the look* and shook the man's hand.

"How's it going?"

"Need a boat."

"All day?"

Elliot looked at Reese. "Three hours?" she said.

Elliot looked back at the man. "Three hours. You do that?"

"Sure. Here—sign this—but pay now."

He scribbled his name on the paper.

The man grabbed something off the wall and stuck it to the paper. "Here's the life vests; just pull into the dock by noon."

Reese went out onto the dock to wait for Elliot to finish up. Some of the boats were way old and some looked super new. One older man coasted into an empty slot after he shut the motor off. Other than that, there was no one else.

Elliot tapped her shoulder. “Ours is over here.”

Reese followed him to a newer pontoon. “Nice.”

He helped her on and untied the rope. “I’m glad we had a big breakfast.”

Reese shaded her eyes. “Let’s go over that way.”

Elliot backed the boat up and they took off down the river, heading for a dent in the woods Reese had pointed out.

“It’s so gorgeous out here!”

Elliot smiled.

I can’t believe I’m going to marry this man. It seems too good to be true. I need to tell Mom. Oh my gosh, I need to tell Mom.

The blue water sprayed Reese’s arms. She closed her eyes, letting the wind hit her face without a fight. The boat grew quieter; he was slowing down.

“What a rush.”

“I love these boats.”

“Look over there,” Reese pointed to a flock of geese.

“Heading south.”

“Sounds nice,” she laughed.

She watched the way Elliot handled the wheel. He’d done this before—although, how hard could it be to steer? Still, he was a natural. She watched his face—was that a smirk? *What is he thinking?*

The boat came to a stop, and he walked over to large black plastic tarp. Reese hadn’t really paid it much attention before. What was he doing?

He pulled it back, revealing a box, and he knelt to open it.

“What’s that?”

Elliot pulled out a bottle of wine and two glasses.

“When did you sneak that on?”

"I'm not telling."

"How did you know—"

Elliot handed her a glass. "I didn't. I brought it just in case."

She watched him pop the cork and pour the dark red liquid.

"I don't drink," he said.

"What?"

He smirked. "Until now. Just this."

"You crack me up."

He sat down beside her at the rear of the boat.

"Let's toast, as they say."

"You do it."

He nodded. "Okay. I want to make this toast to forever—you and I—to the rest of our lives together. May our days be full of life, joy, and laughter—and when they aren't—well, may we cry well and hug often. No matter what happens—let's not forget who we are and how we met."

Reese bit her lip. "I feel like I should say amen."

Elliot nudged her with his free hand.

"I love you, and I've known this in my core. Life has surprised me again—but in a way I never imagined."

They took a sip, feet resting in the cold water.

It was almost noon. By now, breakfast had worn off and they were both eager to get back to the Jeep and dig through the cooler before taking off toward Kentucky.

Elliot pulled the boat into the marina right on time and tied it off while Reese climbed out. There hadn't ever been a day like this one—Reese felt the urge to journal every detail. And these details brought her joy. Dayl had told her when you pour out the bad you have to pour in the good. These details were worth rehearsing. Maybe on a hard day, she could flip open to *these* pages—once she actually recorded the memories down—that is.

She shut her eyes, replaying their trip—hoping to remember every single piece, from the boy with the sugar problem to the hilarious time spent in the tent, to Elliot's unofficial proposal and now this.

Every moment was special, but not because it was perfect. And that's how Reese knew she was making the right decision. When things didn't make sense, just him being there was enough.

He climbed out of the pontoon, box in hand.

Reese followed while he turned the key in at the desk. "I'm so hungry."

The man wasn't there, but Elliot left the key where he was told.

Reese flung open the Jeep door, and he set the box inside.

"You want me to drive this time?"

"Your leg up for it?"

"I ran. I'll be fine," he laughed. "Give you a chance to lie back and relax."

Reese hopped in the passenger side. "Oh, I've had plenty. It was amazing."

"Bonus: You get a few more hours."

He got in and grabbed his phone, scrolling the screen. "Almost forgot I left it."

Reese reached behind them and pulled out two prewrapped sandwiches.

"Mmmm. Here's yours—"

Elliot's jaw was set. The vein in his neck twitched. He set the phone down and ran his fingers through his hair.

"What's wrong?"

"Mom's been trying to call all morning. Amelia took off in a huff, and she isn't answering her phone."

Reese swallowed her bite. "She's probably fine—just needs some air. We women can be angsty."

Elliot set the phone in the cup holder. He dropped his head.

Reese pushed her thumb and forefinger against his neck, hoping to relieve the tension.

"She does this. All the time."

"I can drive, Elliot."

"No, I'm okay—just can't catch a break. Wish she'd grow up already."

She could see the stress in the way his arm muscle flexed.

He gripped the wheel.

"Here—you need to relax. I have no problem driving." She unbuckled and put her hand on the door.

"No, really—it's fine. I just need to eat. Sorry."

Reese turned back to face him. "You're a wonderful brother. I hope you know that."

"I don't feel like it, but there's only so much I can do."

"I see it. And you're right. You are only human."

He leaned over and kissed the corner of her mouth.

CHAPTER 37

"Why is it that life tends to resemble a roller coaster and not a bubbling brook?" Reese wiggled her toes on the dash.

"That's a good line. I may use it."

Reese threw a piece of caramel popcorn at him.

"What?"

She turned the radio knob.

Elliot's phone buzzed in the cup holder. They both reached but Reese beat him to it.

"What's it say?"

She squinted and scrolled. "It's from your mom."

Elliot rolled his neck around.

Reese read to herself first. "She says Amelia's been life-flighted to Piedmont."

He sped up.

"Elliot."

"We're almost back. I'll drop you off, grab the rest of my stuff and catch a flight."

She raked her finger nails across the top of her jeans. "I hope she's all right."

Elliot shook his head. “I knew this was going to happen one day. I knew it—” He slapped the wheel.

Reese swallowed.

“She doesn’t listen.”

They passed the sign telling them they were entering their county. Elliot stopped at a red light and looked out his window.

“I’m sorry.”

The light turned green, and he floored the pedal.

Reese rechecked his phone. She texted back on his behalf. “Driving—will call asap, then on my way.”

A few seconds later, a reply from his mom. “I would call but I’m in the waiting room. Reese isn’t coming with you, is she?”

Heat rose up her neck.

Another text. “Because she really doesn’t need to be here right now. I need you, Elliot. Here and focused.”

Reese didn’t respond.

Elliot pulled into his driveway and threw the Jeep into park.

Reese helped him unload all their camping gear and set it on the porch.

He unlocked his door and flew in.

Reese eyed the neglected crutches in the corner. He’d insisted on leaving them when they left for their trip.

Elliot zoomed past her to his bedroom, but coming back through, he caught her staring at the crutches. “I’m leaving them. They slow me down.”

“How’s your leg?”

“Sore but fine.”

He carried a bag out to the Jeep, and Reese watched from the doorway as he shoved it on the floor behind his seat. He flew back in.

"Do you mind getting my mail and—just take care of things for me for a few days?"

She shook her head. "Need help with anything right now?"

"My phone, my phone—"

"I left it in the cup holder for you…"

"Right."

"Elliot—"

"What?"

"Elliot—" She grabbed his arm as he walked by.

"Reese, I don't have time—" He stopped short and put his hands in his face.

She grasped his trembling hand against her chest.

He clutched her in a tight hug and kissed the side of her head.

"Just breathe. You have my number—I have yours."

"I'll call you as soon as I land."

Reese helped him carry a couple smaller bags out to the Jeep.

After they tossed them inside and made sure all the camping gear was out on the porch, which Reese said she'd put away, they said their goodbyes.

She rubbed the prickles on his face.

"God, I'm going to miss you," he said.

"You need to go."

"I love you."

Reese dropped her head, breathing in the scent of his cologne.

He leaned in and kissed her lips. "Maybe you should come. Maybe I'm rushing."

"No, Elliot. You're right. There's no time—go, and I'll take care of things here. Just keep me updated. Love you."

He drew in a deep breath and released her from his grip.

"Um—and your mom sent a text. I replied in your place. Hope you don't mind."

He opened the door and grabbed his phone. He scanned the screen and looked at Reese. "Sorry you had to read that." Elliot hopped in the seat and started the engine. "Mom's the jealous type—but she's going through a lot right now. Apparently, I don't know the half of it."

"Maybe you can get caught up now…"

"Yeah."

Reese waved as he backed out. She hoped Amelia would be all right and prayed Elliot would be too. *He's rescued Amelia before—but what if this is beyond him?*

CHAPTER 38

One week until Thanksgiving.

The shower water smacked Reese in the face while she dug for ideas of how to stay busy the next few days. The temptation to speed to the airport and get on a plane behind Elliot was growing. He'd left a little over three hours ago.

No, Reese. It'll be fine.

She rinsed the soap and let the hot water hit the back of her neck long past the last of the suds were gone.

Her phone rang from the bathroom sink.

Reese shut the water off and ripped the curtain back. She reached for it on the last ring. "Hello?" she answered, wrapping in a towel.

It was Elliot. He wanted to call to let her know he'd made it safely, but that he was nervous as heck.

"She just needs you there, Elliot. You don't have to do or be anything else."

He let her go, but not before Reese told him to keep her updated—and to try to call back before bed.

She rubbed the towel across her face and imagined Elliot

hearing good news soon. *May as well picture the best until we know more.*

Baby step. Check.

Miss Rosa's face turned red. "No, no, no. Further that way—" she pointed.

Reese laughed at the spectacle happening between her and Ron. He was trying to help get the rest of the decorations mounted and propped.

Reese sat in the gazebo testing another few boxes of lights someone had set in front of her. *My pleasure.*

Anything to get her mind off what she couldn't control.

Her phone lit up on the bench. Mom.

"Hello?—Yes, I need to talk to you, but I really wanted it to be in person."

Reese went through each strand while she spoke, but she couldn't bring herself to admit how close she and Elliot had become. *I want to tell you in person—not like this. Not spread across land and sea.*

Her mom confirmed what her sister Dana had tried to say on the phone weeks before, that they wouldn't make the main holidays but would be home soon after.

"I think I can stand to wait—if you come back for New Year's, at least." Though inwardly, she didn't understand. She caught herself biting the inside of her mouth and stopped. "By the way—are you ever coming home to stay?" She conjured up a laugh to cover up the wondering and dropped the lights before moving on to the next batch.

Miss Rosa smacked Ron's butt twenty feet away. He let out a yelp.

Reese looked around. *Oh, my—Miss Rosa, you're going*

to give our town a reputation. "No, I'm here, sorry. Decorating with Miss Rosa. You know how that goes." She threw a dud set of lights to the side.

Miss Rosa motioned toward her but didn't realize she was on the phone and made an *oops* face.

"I know. I love you too, Mom." She set the lights aside. "Yes, Dayl has helped. A lot. I'll fill you in when you get home."

Miss Rosa walked up to the gazebo, waiting patiently but making Reese feel bad about not having hung up yet.

"Okay, Mom. Love you. Bye."

"How is she?"

"Apparently their signal's still flaky. But they've accomplished much more than they hoped to, so that's good."

"And you are the fastest light tester in Kentucky."

"Yep. Here ya go."

Ron walked over with a poster board attached to a wooden stake. "Think you could turn this into a photo thing?"

She made a face. "Me? Non-crafty Reese Lockhart?"

He nodded and shoved it forward. "Yes, you. Thank ya, ma'am."

She pushed her glasses back in place and stared at the blank cardboard. "Sure."

Ron walked away, toothpick in mouth.

Miss Rosa sat down next to Reese and lowered her voice. "So, any word from Elliot?"

Reese shook her head. "He was supposed to call last night, but I never heard from him."

"Try not to worry. I'm sure today you will."

Reese stood, moving the boxes out of the way. "And there's something I need to tell you."

"Oh?"

I don't feel bad about this—telling her before Mom.

She's family. She's here.

I have to tell somebody.

"Elliot proposed while we were away."

Miss Rosa lurched off the bench and picked Reese up off the ground, spinning her in circles. "Oh, my sweet tangerines, Reesey!"

"That's pretty close to what I thought too."

"So…you said yes?"

Reese nodded and smiled.

"You two are like a movie, kid." She clapped her hands and turned toward the crowd of helpers.

"But if you could keep it between us, that'd be great. I haven't told my family."

"Oh."

"Yeah—I want to tell them in person."

Miss Rosa pursed her lips. "You torture me, Reesey—but okay. For you, I can keep quiet."

"Now, I need to get to work on this…thing," she said, holding up the poster board.

"Do you know how hard it's going to be trying to decorate for Thanksgiving while I have wedding bells playing in my head?"

"You can do it," she winked.

Miss Rosa walked away but spun around one last time. "You're both keepers."

CHAPTER 39

Burlap. Wreaths. Twine. Burlap. Wreaths. Twine.

Reese didn't want to forget what she was looking for in the shed.

She pulled the wagon across the lawn and swung the doors open.

Miss Rosa had called with an SOS just a few hours before. "Your mom has this hidden stash of holiday bling in the shed, Reesey. They were your grandmother's, so she takes good care of them—so do I. Every year they're the first ones I take down. So how 'bout it, honey? Want to dig for those real quick? The library needs some TLC before next week."

There was no way Reese could turn her down. She found the light and began sifting through the mounds of boxes. The smell of damp air left no room for anything with a holiday scent. Unless she came across Grandma's potpourri. That'd knock an army out.

Reese lifted a box labeled *Grandma's Holiday.* She set it aside, but something caught her eye. It was a large black container or bin of some kind. One she'd never seen before. It was sitting in plain view now that the other box was out of the way. She ran her fingers under the lip of the lid and pulled but the seal was strong. After a few minutes of messing with it, she gave up and decided to take it inside.

She lifted the two large items into the wagon and pulled them to the house.

Her phone buzzed from her back pocket. She dropped the wagon handle and yanked her phone out.

It was a text from Elliot.

“Sorry I didn’t call you last night. Amelia’s pretty banged up. She’s conscious. We stayed up and talked. Fell asleep on the couch in her room.”

At breakneck speed, Reese typed a reply.

“No worries. Glad she’s okay and you got to talk. How is everyone otherwise?”

Send.

She slipped the phone back into her pocket and carefully lugged each box inside.

Dust grabbed her throat as she flipped open the flaps on Grandma’s box. Burlap, wreaths, and twine were there all right. They needed a good shaking out.

She closed the flaps back and lugged it through the house and out her front door.

Am I supposed to decorate the decorations or this good enough?

This was her mom’s cup of tea. As much as Reese wasn’t a fan of creating the festival’s raffle items, at least they were smaller and didn’t require a ladder. The library was tall, and if she remembered right, last year they were hung fairly high.

Library.

I wonder if Elliot’s book signing is still on.

She loaded the box into the car.

Before walking back inside, she stopped. The place didn’t seem right without his Jeep.

I never knew what I was missing.

Reese stared at the black tote. She jabbed the butter knife into the crack and pressed the bottom down, hoping to lift the lid just enough to slip her fingers under. It took a few tries, but the lid finally gave way.

It flung off and landed a few feet away.

"That works."

She dropped to her knees, eyeing the contents.

Her jaw tightened.

"This was from Grand's house. This is Jett's stuff."

She threw the lid on and snapped it shut.

Her heart pounded in her ears, and she shook her head to try to make it stop.

Hot tears spilled down her cheeks. She shoved the tote across the wooden floor until she got to the mudroom.

Her eyes darted around.

She grabbed a sheet from the shelf above the dryer and spread it over the box. Her eyes stung. She tried to see as she looked around for something else to add. "There."

She set a few recipe books from the shelf on top of the sheet, as if the contents would try to escape. She closed the mudroom door and ran upstairs to grab her jacket off the end of the bed but opted for Elliot's cardigan instead.

Her hands trembled as she locked the door. This time, she wanted to talk to someone before she let her brain take her down a dark road. "It's going to be okay. It's going to be fine."

But as she drove out of town, she fought to believe her own words.

CHAPTER 40

Double yellow lines meant she was getting close. Close to Dayl's office.

Reese practiced her deep breathing technique and found the closest parking spot she could find. She wasn't even sure she'd be able to get in today, but she had to try.

After a look in the mirror and a few wipes with a tissue, Reese grabbed her purse and tried to calmly walk inside. It was ridiculous the shame that always seemed to accompany a panic attack. She felt like some alien from another planet and did her best to dial back the emotions, but the shaky hands weren't something she could control.

The lady at the front desk greeted her.

"Hello, can you please leave a message for Dayl?"

"Sure? What is it?"

She grabbed a pen from the mug.

"Actually, can I just write it down and let you give it to her?"

The woman smiled. "I'd be glad to. She's about to go on lunch so I can hand it to her on the way out."

Reese nodded and scribbled her thoughts down, signing

below and adding her cell phone number in case Dayl forgot or didn't have it.

She slipped the paper to the woman and took a seat, but it was a challenge to sit still. After a few minutes, she walked outside into the cool. The sun was out, but the air was crisp. She paced the sidewalk.

Why am I back here in this place again?

"I should have never looked in that tote."

Her phone buzzed. A message from Elliot.

"Mom's stressed but she's only been here once. I wish you were here. How are you? I miss you."

She spotted a bench near a different set of doors and sat.

She replied, "I'm okay. Wish I was too. Love you so much."

Send.

He replied almost right away.

"Can I video call?"

Reese swallowed.

"Sure."

It rang, and she connected the call with the video option.

"Hey—there you are. Much better."

Reese struggled to laugh and hoped he didn't notice her reddish face.

"Where are you? I see brick."

Reese smiled and shrugged. "Well…I'm at my therapist's office."

"Oh, okay, that's cool. You okay?"

The truth was, calm settled over her when she saw his face. And sitting outside was helping.

"Yeah—I am. Just need to talk, but I knew you were busy…"

"Don't feel bad about talking with her, Reese. She's an asset in your life."

"Where are you?"

"I came down to the lobby a few minutes ago. Didn't want to wake Amelia."

Reese nodded.

"Listen, Reese…her condition isn't so good. I may need to stay here longer than a few days—" He stopped before continuing. "Mom's going to need help—I don't know how she's going to do it, with her in recovery and all, at home. Therapy—all that. It may be a few weeks." He just shook his head, looking like he was trying to figure it all out.

"Of course."

"Thing is—I still need to come back in a week for my follow up. I thought maybe that'd give me a chance to get more stuff packed up and take care of my book signing."

"I was going to ask about that."

"Yeah—if I juggle it right, I think it'll work out."

Her screen said Dayl was trying to call.

She ignored it and went to sit in the car.

"Sounds like you have everything under control."

Elliot grinned. "I don't know about that. Just trying to stay positive."

Sounds familiar.

"I have an idea but wanted to run it by you first."

"Oh?"

"Since it looks like Thanksgiving's going to be a bit chaotic—and Christmas is up in the air with your family—what do you think about getting our families together during New Year's?"

"Sounds good."

Elliot's eyes narrowed. "Are you sure?"

"Yes, it's a great idea."

"Is that my long-lost cardigan?" he laughed.

She pursed her lips. "Maybe." And then she broke into a laugh.

"You do miss me."

"Uh huh—and it's soft."

"I want to hold you so bad."

"It's all I can do right now to not buy a ticket and hunt you down."

Elliot looked away for a moment.

"What?"

He shook his head. "Nothing. I was just thinking."

"About?"

"Mmmm—if there was a way you could."

"Hunt you down?" Reese fidgeted with the hem of the cardigan. "I mean, I have the money—it's just—I need to be here for Thanksgiving. I already told Miss Rosa."

"Like I said—I need to reload my bag and either cancel or reschedule my book signing, so if I time it right I can get there the day before—get all that done, spend Thanksgiving with you, and then we could both head out the next day."

Reese straightened. "And I have off through New Year's, so I don't have to worry about work."

"Let me talk to Mom. There's a spare room plus my old one. This would give you all a chance to meet, since she won't be coming up now. You be okay with staying there? A hotel could rack up a big bill."

Though the idea of meeting Elliot's mom made Reese nervous, she knew it was inevitable and necessary. Plus, she could probably use some support right now. His mom, that was. Or maybe they both could. Woman to woman.

Reese smiled. "No sense in racking up a bill when there's room at your house. Her house—"

Elliot grinned. "Great." He looked up from the phone. His expression changed, and he nodded to someone.

His eyes dropped back to Reese. "I love you, and I will call you tonight. This time, I will. Even if I must drink—coffee," he said, eyes widening.

"Wow."

"Yeah. I would do that for you."

Reese laid her hand on her chest. "I'm touched."

"Well don't get used to it. But desperate times call for—coffee, apparently."

"Love you. So much. Take care."

After they hung up, Reese could feel the heaviness float away.

She took a breath and called Dayl back and put it on speaker.

She answered right away.

"Hello, Dayl. Sorry I missed your call."

Her therapist let her know a cancellation opened a slot in thirty minutes.

Reese looked at the clock on her car stereo. "Sure, I'm free."

Click.

Reese reclined her seat and set her phone alarm for twenty minutes. She let her mind drift back to Elliot.

"Reese Jacobson." It sounded good aloud.

She shut her eyes.

"Has a ring to it."

Her eyes popped open.

Ring.

CHAPTER 41

The aisles of the library were narrow, and the purple carpet reminded Reese of one of the many galactic movies she'd watched as a kid. She devoured them. Her parents thought for sure she'd be an astronaut when she grew up. After her parents ditched the television, Reese engrossed herself in books, and that was how she discovered her true love. It wasn't that she didn't appreciate movies—she did—but sometimes the movies didn't get the scenes right. She wanted to picture them herself.

Reese moved her finger across the spines of the books. A habit when getting near them. Each texture made her wonder where the story was headed: Bumpy, smooth, paperback, hardcover. Each look gave the reader a hint: Bright, dark, bold, inviting, imaginative, flowery, piercing, clean, artsy.

Right now, she was searching for an entirely different section altogether. One she'd never been interested in until now.

She walked the aisle and scanned the rows.

"Complicated grief," Dayl had said.

When describing it, she said it looked a lot like depression, because unlike the normal experience of grief, this didn't dissipate over time. She said symptoms would come in waves depending on the triggers.

"For instance, Jett's birthday, finding the black bin—even living near his house—can cause an episode. That's not to say you can't learn how to cope well. This is possible."

It explained a lot.

Her uncle, who'd suffered from post-traumatic stress disorder, passed away when Reese's mom was only twenty years old. Her mom didn't talk about it. It seemed stuffing things down ran in the family. Or maybe she'd worked through her grief already, and that just wasn't on the table for discussion.

Either way, Reese knew it must be possible to live well while dealing with the beast. She had, after all, been in and out of Grand and Jett's a lot the past year—and her mom had plenty of happy days she could recount.

Reese wondered if the panic that swept her off her feet when experiencing triggers was extreme because she wasn't expecting them. But now—knowing it was normal to sense some type of grief depending on the object attached to the memory—maybe she could calm down quicker than before.

And not making yourself feel bad about it will help for sure.

She decided on a book and tucked it under her arm.

The lady at the front checked her out.

Reese worked up some courage. "Ma'am, are you the one a person needs to contact if an author wants to set up a table? For a book signing?"

She handed the book to Reese. "No, but I can get her."

"Oh, no—it's okay."

"You an author?"

Reese shook her head. "I wish. No—it's my fri-friend.

He's an author and something's come up—didn't know if you could help."

Friend?

Fiancé.

Fiancé?

Yes—fiancé.

But do you wait until you have a ring to say so?

"Oh, neat. And perfect. She's right behind you."

Reese spun around to see a cheery older lady wearing a dress. She wasn't the woman Reese had known growing up. It had been a while since she'd come into the library. She and Jett used to sit in here and study.

After his passing, she began getting books from the bookshop. Cash for sanity. But now, here in the beloved space she'd spent so many hours in, she was ready to admit it wasn't very economical to pay for every single book she needed.

"Can I help you?"

"Yes," Reese held out her hand. "I—I was wondering if you would consider rescheduling an author's book signing. It's coming up soon, but his sister was in accident of some sort."

The lady walked behind the counter and pulled out a giant planner. "Let me find our events section—just a sec."

Reese set the book down and lay her arms across.

"We have a few holiday events and—" She moved her finger over the paper. "Is the author a he or a she?"

"He."

"E. L. Jacobson."

Reese grinned. "Yes."

"We only have one other slot open, and that's for after the holidays are over."

Reese bit her lip. "Ehhh—hang on. Keep him on there. I need to ask first."

"He has my number. We spoke a few months back when he set it up. Just have him call me if things need to change."

"Sure thing." Reese grabbed the book and walked to her car.

She opened the back door and saw her grandma's box. "Oh no, I forgot!"

Reese hung a right and went a few blocks over.

Miss Rosa wasn't outside, which was odd for her. Usually after harvest season was over and right up until the festivities, she was delegating to everyone right down to the farm animals.

She pulled over and whipped out a text. "You want the decorations in the gazebo?"

Reese waited. A few minutes later her phone buzzed.

"No. Set them in the library, please."

Reese scrunched her nose. "Okay."

She pulled out and went back to the library. As she walked to the door with the box in hand—someone opened the door for her.

"Thank you," she said.

The lady she'd just talked to walked forward. "What's this?"

"Miss Rosa said to set the holiday decor in here. You know her, right? Is that okay?"

"Oh—yes. I spoke with her last week. Thanks—I'll take them."

"Great," Reese handed it over.

"And I didn't get your name earlier, I apologize."

"Oh—Reese."

"And you said you were E. L. Jacobson's assistant?"

"Uh—no. Fiancé."

The woman's lip perked up. "Well, congratulations. Would you mind taking these papers I found after you left? They may interest him."

"No problem." Reese rolled the papers into a cylinder and left, feeling peppier than usual.

CHAPTER 42

The glass casing held dozens of ring designs, but Reese just folded her arms. "Thanks so much for letting me look. This gives me a better idea of what I'm looking for."

The jewelry store employee nodded and locked it back up. "Anytime."

She hopped in the car and drove home.

Which house was home?

She'd grown up in both—and practically lived in both. She'd spent at least a couple hours at Elliot's tidying up, getting mail, killing time. The killing time part just made her feel close to him. It was a relief that the house was no longer a trigger itself like Dayl had said. Then again, Reese hadn't gone upstairs. She couldn't bear to see Jett's room.

But how long will this last? Do I avoid it forever?

Her phone rang in the cup holder, and she instantly thought of her and Elliot's trip.

She answered Elliot's call with the video option. "Hey."

"How are you?"

"Trying to stay busy."

"That's a good idea."

"Any news?"

"I talked to Mom. She's not easy to talk to, ya know."

Reese rubbed her forehead. "So you've said."

"You can come. You should come."

"She's okay with it?"

Elliot had a slight hesitation. "You can come. It's going to be good. We need this."

She pushed her glasses back into place. "Okay. I'll make sure all the laundry's good to go, and—"

"Reese?"

"Yeah?"

Elliot's face started turning a slight shade of pink.

"Are you okay?"

He shook his head. "I don't even want to say this, because when I do…it's going to make it more real."

Reese waited.

"They're saying Amelia's not going to be able to walk."

She closed her eyes. "Oh, Elliot. I'm so sorry."

A few tears slid down his cheeks. "Yeah—it sucks. One of the doctors said it would take a miracle with her injury—the way it happened." He shook his head. "It all feels like a dream. A bad one."

"I wish I was there with you. Are you going to be able to leave her for a couple days? I can just come down there—bring all your stuff—"

Elliot wiped his face with a tissue. "No—it's okay. By then it'll be good to get some fresh air. Plus, I'm picky about my clothes—" He laughed.

Reese smiled.

"And speaking of that—I really want to tell Mom about

us when you get here, but I'm thinking it may be a good idea to hold off until Amelia's discharged and settled in. You okay with that?"

"Oh, yes. Completely. I can't imagine what she's going through right now."

Elliot tensed. "It's only been me and Dad here mostly."

Reese dropped her head.

"Yeah—Mom's somewhat in denial. Things were rough before Amelia stormed out and got into this accident."

"Awful."

They both sat quietly for a moment.

"It isn't the same without you here." Reese finally spoke up.

He gave her his Elliot look. The one she'd fallen in love with right away. Where his eyes did all the talking. "I'm not the same without you around."

She tilted her head. "Aw—you seem good. Strong."

His eyes dropped. "I don't feel like it. Amelia wants to meet you, by the way—and no, I haven't told her either—"

She threw her head backward. "Oh, no."

"What?"

"How could I forget? I have my final the first week of December."

"Oh, crap. Could they let you take it early?"

Reese shook her head. "I don't know. Let me get a hold of them—see what they can do."

"Your list just got longer."

"Yep. It's okay though. I just want to be with you."

"It's about Amelia's dinner time—I'm going to help her."

"Sure. Talk to you later."

"Probably tomorrow?"

She nodded.

"Love you."

"Love you, too." He winked.

Click.

Reese felt a surge of energy course through her.

So much to do.

CHAPTER 43

Anette pinched her lips together. She brushed a single curl out of her face and turned away, skirt twirling.

"I'm sure it'll look just fine," Reese reassured, touching the turkey-infested garland Miss Rosa insisted on hanging across the main windows of the book store.

Anette poked her head out from behind an aisle. "Turkey heads." She rolled her eyes.

"What did you expect?"

She came around the corner, arms full of misplaced books. "I don't know. But turkey heads? Who ever heard of decorating a bookstore with turkey heads? At least give me the entire body!"

Reese tried not to laugh and took the books from Anette. She wanted to help as much as she could before the big day, but she happened to walk right into one of Anette's fits. They were rare, but when they happened they lasted a while.

Miss Rosa entered. Her glance caught Anette's.

Reese looked away. *No way. I'm not getting in the middle of this.*

Anette walked into a different aisle, probably to avoid saying something her mama taught her not to.

Reese set the books down so she could flip through them one by one. "Is that what I think it is?"

Miss Rosa gave a side smirk. "It is. Push it."

Reese pressed a button on Miss Rosa's colorful shawl. It lit up and played a song. "Oh my."

"Don't be jealous, Reesey. But if you want one of these, I still have the catalog."

"Oh, wow—thank you, but I'm okay. I like my clothes low key."

Miss Rosa patted Reese on the head. "Apparently Anette likes her decorations that way too."

Picking up a book, Reese headed to place it in the right spot. "We all have different taste, I guess." She clutched her chest. "You almost gave me a heart attack!"

Anette ducked and slapped her back against the row of books next to Reese. "Don't tell her I'm free. I refuse to hang another turkey head in this place. I refuse!"

Reese snorted a laugh and slid the book into position. "I think you need a vacation, Anette."

She squinted and rubber her chin. "You're probably right."

Reese stopped in her tracks.

"What?"

"I have an idea."

"You always have ideas."

Reese ignored her.

Footsteps came closer. Anette darted toward the back of the store.

Miss Rosa's voice rose. "Where are you, Anette? I found these—"

Reese swung around the end and almost bumped into her.

"Oh—sorry. Do you want to take over running the bookshop during the holidays?"

Miss Rosa flared her nose. "What are you up to, Reesey?"

She swallowed. "Anette seems a little frazzled. Burnt out. Something. Just a thought."

Miss Rosa's brow arched, and she scanned the walls of the place. "It would be fun. But I'm so busy during this time of the time, honey. Maybe she can put up a help wanted sign?"

"That's a great idea."

Miss Rosa put her hand on the door before walking out. "It is. And when Anette comes out of hiding, tell her I have another box I need hung up. It's slow today—she should have time."

Reese twisted her lip. "What kind of decor?"

Miss Rosa stretched a grin. "Little pilgrim hats." She walked out.

Anette flew to the front. "Great. First, turkey heads. Now, pilgrim hats with no heads at all."

Reese threw her hands up. "It's Miss Rosa. Just roll with it."

And right then, as if she could hear through walls, Miss Rosa bounded through the shop.

"Reesey, it's your mom. Said your phone's dead or something. Here—" She handed hers to Reese.

"Oh—thanks." She took the phone to the stock room. "Hello?"

Reese set the clean, folded laundry in her large rolling suitcase and moved the wireless mouse to see if her professor had emailed back yet.

Nothing.

She mentally rehashed the earlier conversation with her mom. They were wrapping up the mission and had bought their plane tickets back to the States to be here in time for New Year's. Reese's stomach flipped in knots. She had gotten so used to not seeing them. Not hearing from them.

She'd been able to say hello to her dad for a few minutes but not her sister. Apparently, Dana had taken to a young man, and he'd invited her over for his mother's famous palm nut soup.

Reese smiled at the thought of her sister actually having fun. She was a workaholic too. They all were really.

She zipped the suitcase up and stood it on end. Was she forgetting something? Oh well, they'd go through the check-list one last time when Elliot arrived. "Two more days."

CHAPTER 44

Reese wrapped the cardigan tight and rocked in her chair, coffee next to her, final exam notes in hand. She looked across the lawn. Something in her felt detached from this space. Maybe it was because Elliot was gone. Maybe this trip would help reset her. She'd been here so long—*I need a new scene, just wish it were under better circumstances.*

It would be her first time flying. Dayl seemed excited for Reese when she shared the news. She confirmed it would be a healthy experience all around, no matter the circumstance.

Elliot had already purchased a ticket back for the both of them—there was no going back now.

Reese took a sip of her coffee. She hadn't gone into the details of the engagement with her parents on Miss Rosa's phone. It would have to wait until New Year's for sure. Maybe by then Amelia would be settled and Elliot's mom would be more open minded. Maybe.

REESE PERCHED ON THE EDGE OF THE BATH. SHE SLID THE razor up and rinsed. Repeat. Her Bluetooth speaker blasted the artist Hilary Hahn. She bobbed her head to the rhythm of the violin.

A glow caught her eyes.

Her phone was a few feet away on the bathroom floor. She reached for it but fell backward, tailbone hitting the hard floor.

It was Elliot video calling.

She almost bit her tongue gripping the nearest towel, tossing it over herself.

She raised the phone up to head level. "Hello."

"Hey there," a confused look on his face.

Reese rubbed her back with one hand. "Uh—yeah. I fell."

"Out of the bath?"

"Never mind," she laughed. "Any updates?"

He shook his head. "Not for Amelia. She's been eating but seems really weak. Sleeps a lot."

"Probably needs it."

"Mom's still MIA for the most part. Dad and I been able to catch up. Hey—think I'm going to cancel my book signing."

Reese nodded. "Understandable."

"So…you'd do it too?"

"Under these circumstances…"

"My head's just not in it right now."

"That's a lot to juggle if you don't have to."

"Thanks. For everything, Reese."

"Of course. Mail's forwarded, my stuff's mostly packed. Your laundry was already good."

"I don't have too much to get, but what I do, is important."

"So…"

"Tomorrow."

"What time you be here?"

"My flight's at one thirty. Should be back by four."

"You going to feel up for the festival or just want to sleep?"

"I don't know yet. I may play it by ear."

Reese sat up, holding the towel tight against her chest.

"I better let you go so you can—uh—finish," he laughed.

"Yeah. Well, I'll see you soon."

"See you soon, Reese."

She hung up and finished getting ready but laughed as she jammed her leg into her right pant leg. She forgot to finish shaving.

CHAPTER 45

Reese pressed her knuckles into the ivory dough. She smoothed it. Flattened it. Sniffed it. Rubbed it. *Soon, we'll eat it. Don't know how it's going to taste. That's beside the point.*

She eyed the chicken, cooling nearby. "I should save some of you for a salad later." She slid a knife into the dough. "Look at me making dumplings. Miss Lila's recipe just may be fail-proof. Elliot, you need to come back. I'm talking to my food. I need a cat."

A knock at the door made Reese jump. She hadn't had anyone over since—well, since Elliot was here, and even then, it had been a few days.

"Hey."

Miss Rosa stood at the door holding a bag open. "Here for your apple contribution, honey."

"Of course, just a sec—" She slid to the kitchen to grab her bag out of the fridge.

"Here ya go."

"Thanks, Reesey." She poked her head forward, eyes

darting both ways. “So it is quiet without them here, eh? And Elliot? How’s he?”

Reese shrugged. “His sister isn’t so well.”

“I’ll keep her in my prayers.”

“Thanks. I’m sure she needs them.”

“Don’t we all?”

Reese gave a short smile and wiped her hands on her apron.

“I’m bothering you, so sorry.”

“No, no—you aren’t. I’m just hoping I can get this right. Nervous. Haven’t made anything like this since…well—been a few years. Even then, mom was here to monitor me,” Reese snickered.

“You’ll do great. And worst-case scenario, drive over to my house and I’ll load you up.”

Reese shook her head. “You’re great.”

“I wish Anette thought so.”

“She isn’t really mad. I think she’s just used to having control there.”

Miss Rosa tilted her head, twinkle in her eye. “You’re right. Maybe I should throw her off. Take all the decor down and let her do it?”

Reese leaned into the door frame. “Not sure. You could try.”

A beep sounded from the kitchen.

“Oh, I better get that. You want to come in?”

Miss Rosa did a hand toss. “Oh, no, Reesey. I gotta head over to Miss Lila’s and snag their apples.”

“Will we have enough, or you need me to pick some more up?”

“We have enough. You and Elliot better do it this year.”

Reese’s eyes got big. “You know I always hide out.”

She wagged a finger. "Not this time. You two were made for this moment."

"Oh really?" Reese laughed.

"Go get your dumplings, Reesey. See you tomorrow. Bring extra clothes!"

Reese waved. "Yeah—right!"

She ran to shut the timer off. "Time to get you puppies into the water."

Elliot would be here soon. She breathed in the smell of freshly simmered chicken and hoped it tasted as good as it looked.

NOT CHEWY. NOT SOGGY. *PERRRRFECT.*

"It's how a dumpling should be right?"

"They're just fine, Reese. You did it!" Miss Lila swallowed her bite. "See? I told you if you followed the directions you couldn't go wrong."

"You're telling this to the kid who lit the ends of her hair on fire when making crème brûlée with her mom."

"Now you know—always pull your hair back when using a torch." She winked.

"Still. Pathetic right?"

"A haircut solved your woes, my dear. Now, get on back over to the house before Elliot beats you there."

"Right. Thanks again." She gave a side hug and kissed Miss Lila on the cheek. "When Stan wakes, tell him I love him."

FLUTTERS.

Reese grabbed at her stomach.

She opened her email, trying to ignore the clock on the laptop screen.

The countdown was making her queasy.

An unread email. Finally.

She clicked it open.

Her professor kept it short and sweet.

> Reese, sorry to hear about your fiancé's sister. You don't have to do it early. I can just extend the test due date. You'll see it there in your blackboard when you log in. Don't worry about coming to the last class. Hope you have a good Thanksgiving. See you in May.

A sigh of relief escaped her mouth. She was also glad to have finished up her edits a week early. "I can tell Mom I'm officially on vacation."

The family photo near her desk made her miss sharing good news face to face. "You'd be proud of me, Mom."

New Year's can't come fast enough.

I've come such a long way.

Such a long way.

She glanced at the clock, unwilling to dodge it any longer. 3:05. "This is driving me crazy."

Her phone buzzed from the chaise behind her, and she spun in the chair.

"Hello, Anette. Are you okay?"

She sounded even more frazzled.

"What?—Uh…"

After listening to Anette stress out about Miss Rosa wanting some kind of information on a plant, Reese agreed to find out in order to save Anette's sanity.

She threw her purse over her shoulder and hopped in the car. Hopefully she could it done quick and get back here to go through the five outfits strewn across the bed.

She gripped the steering wheel. “These people drive me nuts.” But she loved them.

CHAPTER 46

The tire brushed the curb and Reese's head jerked. "Oops."

She pushed out of the car, crossed the sidewalk to the bookstore, and flung the door open. Apparently, Miss Rosa was having a meltdown. Or Anette. Or both.

She stood there, unsure what to say.

Anette was fanning herself. Miss Rosa dug her fingers into her hips.

Reese looked back and forth. *So dramatic.*

She plopped in the leather chair and put her chin in her hands, eyeing them both. "So, what exactly do you need help with?"

Miss Rosa glanced at Anette, then back to Reese. "Don't laugh."

"Okay—I won't."

She tightened her neck and unfolded her arms. "Look at this." She held a book open.

Reese narrowed her eyes. "Yeah—it looks like a watercress."

Miss Rosa crossed her arms again. "See? I knew it."

"What? Knew what?"

"Anette didn't believe me. I told her to go pick some for Ron. He's making this new soup and needs them. She argued that it wasn't watercress. I made her call you."

Anette's jaw set. "I have to be at my brother's in a half an hour for dinner. They eat early. I can't go traipsing through the woods looking for a wild plant."

"Edible wild plant," Miss Rosa corrected.

"Can't he just use something else in its place?"

Miss Rosa had the look of someone who was very annoyed to be asked such a question. "No. It's a unique flavor. Look it up."

Reese glanced at her watch. "If I go for you, I don't have to bob for apples. Deal?"

Miss Rosa's jaw dropped. "Now—"

Reese crossed her arms.

"Oh, fine. You don't know what you're missing."

Reese thought she saw a gleam in Anette's eye but shrugged it off. "You all better know how much I adore you." She pinched Anette's cheeks, being funny.

"Oh, we do."

She shook her head in disbelief. "So where are these things? When does he need them by?"

Miss Rosa pushed her lips out. "They grow near ponds and lakes. Can you get it to him in forty minutes?"

Reese jutted her chin out. "What?"

"Just try. If not, he'll get over it."

"Then how come it's such a big deal?"

Miss Rosa glanced around. "Forget it. Just go. The soup is a special treat he makes his old mom every year. Don't let her down."

"How come he waited until now to get what he needed?"

Miss Rosa nudged her toward the door. "Too many questions."

She sighed. "All right. Here—let me snap a photo of it."

Miss Rosa held the book out. "Okay, now off you go."

She waved from the shop as Reese pulled away.

"Why do I agree to these types of things again?"

Reese put the car in park and ran into the house to throw on Elliot's cardigan. She hated coats, but this would do. *Hopefully I won't tear it.*

She fast walked to the woods behind her ugly, dead garden. It was funny now. At least, she told herself that.

The breeze was sharp.

She pulled the cardigan closed.

Reese tried to avoid the muddy areas, hopping over those, steering for the spots covered with fallen leaves. She shoved the branches out of her face. "I'm going to be late. I already know it."

A crunch and a snap.

She held her breath. A bird flew away. She rolled her eyes. "Hello, woodland creatures, don't mind me—just picking ingredients for my car dealer who doesn't shop at the grocery store anymore. He's boycotting big brands, you know. Soon, everyone will follow his trend, and we'll be out here by the dozens, buckets in hand. So be on the lookout for my face again."

She was getting closer to the water. Was that something behind her? She could have sworn she heard a noise.

Reese rounded the corner, trail dumping her out into the clearing she knew so well. Everything looked the same except—it wasn't. She stopped. "I almost didn't come here this fall." How tragic would that have been? She would have missed out on the beauty of the colorful arrangement, soon to be lost to the ground.

And fall was her favorite season. Here today, gone tomorrow.

"Okay, get to work, Reese." She high-stepped to the edge of the lake—head down, eyes skimming the bushes and weeds. After a few minutes, she looked up to the sky to give her neck a break. She tugged at her phone to recheck the picture of the plant. "Oh geez. I'm not seeing this thing."

She walked further down, mumbling under her breath, glancing at the time on her phone. 4:12. "I'm late. Might as well keep looking. Elliot's going to be really confused. Car's sitting there. Reese is nowhere to be found. Ugh."

She saw one that looked similar but when she bent down to get a closer look, it wasn't watercress at all.

"Watercress, where are you?"

"I'm not watercress, but will I do?" She heard Elliot's voice yell.

Reese spun around.

Elliot was standing in the gazebo a ways off.

Her eyes about popped out of her head. "Elliot!"

She sprinted toward him, completely forgetting the reason she'd come.

He held his arms open, and she lunged forward, burying her face in his neck.

"I missed you, beautiful." He looked into her eyes.

"Wait--you tricked me?"

"I wouldn't call it that."

"How—?"

He leaned in, pressing his lips into hers, and she didn't even care how he pulled it off.

He was here. *All is right with the world.*

CHAPTER 47

Elliot clutched the rope and looked back at Reese. It was the final game at the festival before fighting for pies and bobbing for apples.

"If I fall on you, don't say I didn't warn ya."

"I don't care, just pull!"

Ron blew the whistle.

"Go, go, go!"

Elliot was at the front of a long line. Two minutes into their first game of tug-o-war, the red ribbon crept closer to their side.

"No, he's too strong!" An older gentleman hollered.

"I'll get him next time!" A small kid from the sidelines shouted and spit.

"Come on everyone, one last hard pull!" The red ribbon pulled over to their side, and they all whooped and cheered.

One of the big guys from the motorcycle crew nodded. "I got you next time."

Elliot put his hands up. "Think I'll pass."

Reese laughed.

"Okay, everyone who wants to, head over to the pie contest. Miss Rosa, cue the music when they're ready!"

"We can sit this one out," Reese said.

"Because you don't want to lose to the older ladies, right?"

She threw him a look. "I eat enough pie as it is. Wish my family was here."

He kissed her cheek.

"Oh, there'll be none of that," Stan joked, slapping his knee from his wheelchair.

"Okay, go!" Ron hollered over to Miss Rosa.

She hit *play* on the radio, and the ten older ladies walked in a circle, acting paranoid—holding their arms out ready to shove someone out of the way.

"They do get wild, don't they?"

"I wasn't kidding."

They walked over to a booth selling goods.

Elliot picked up a basket and turned it around in his hands. "This is one you made."

"Blingy, huh?"

"In a *Better Homes and Gardens* sort of way—yeah," he laughed.

"Wanna eat?"

They walked up the sidewalk and around the corner to the clerk's office.

He pointed. "In there?"

"Yep."

He pulled the door open for her and let her walk under his arm.

The smell of home cooked everything took over the building.

Anette oversaw the area, greeting them cheerily, winking

at Reese. "Nice to see you two. Your dumplings are over there, Reese."

Reese wagged her finger at Anette. "You're smart. We'll talk later," she winked back.

Elliot made a face. "Food. Show me your favorite."

Anette shook her head and turned back to the other people walking in.

They sat at a table with plates full and chowed down until Miss Rosa walked up to the glass door.

"Oh no."

"What?" Elliot said, tossing their plates in the trash.

"Apple bobbing. The master has found me."

"Oh, come on—it'll be fun."

"That's what she says. Has she conformed you?"

"If I do it, will you?"

"No way. I didn't bring extra clothes, anyway."

Miss Rosa walked toward them, appearing overly energetic.

Elliot looked apologetic. "Actually—I brought you some."

"You didn't."

Then a grin replaced it. "No excuses now."

She threw her head back. "You owe me."

Miss Rosa lifted her brow and crossed her arms, bangles clashing against one another. "Reesey—we don't owe you. You never did find the watercress. Game on."

THE COLD TIN UNDER HER FINGERS FORESHADOWED THE regret Reese was about to feel when her head would be submerged into the cold water.

"Everyone's watching."

"That's the point," Elliot chuckled.

She rolled her eyes.

Miss Rosa had a wireless mic and stood ready to launch into a speech. Instead she looked down and then back to Reese. "Reesey, we love you. We've all been waiting for this day."

"It's just apples," she laughed. "But if it makes you that happy—here goes."

Miss Rosa rang a buzzer. "Go!"

She and Elliot had separate bins full of water. They both stuck their head down at the same time—competing against one another.

Reese shot water out of her nose, remembering why she hated this game. Kids and adults alike cracked up at the couple.

A few minutes later, she heard Elliot yell but couldn't quite hear—her head was coming up.

"He won! He won!"

Reese had one more to go. She dove back in, not caring that her clothes were soaked. She pulled it out and left it in her teeth.

"You're funny." Miss Rosa rubbed her head and threw them towels, walking back around the bin.

Everyone cheered.

"Oh, hold up!" She interrupted. "Looks like Reese forgot one!"

"That's impossible," she refuted. She looked back in and sure enough, there was one more left.

"I know I got them all!"

Elliot held up his hands. "Gotta do it, Reese."

She scowled and laughed. "Whatever."

She took a breath, stuck her head into the cold water and fought to get it in her mouth. She came back up for another gasp of air. *Of course the last one would give me trouble.*

She finally got a good hold on it and yanked her head up.

Why was everyone so quiet?

"There. You happy?" Water droplets slid down her cheeks.

Elliot looked calm but had a curious look in his eye.

She pulled the apple from her mouth and felt something. She turned it over in her hand to discover the lump was a diamond ring, jammed into the flesh, stone sticking out.

Am I alive?

Elliot, shirt soaking, water running down his face—took her hand, slipped the ring out and fixed his position to a kneel.

"Reese Lockhart, will you be mine forever? Will you marry me and be my Mrs. Jacobson?"

She knew he'd already asked, just the two of them. But this was a different kind of magical. Both were amazing. This made it all the more real.

CHAPTER 48

A cloud settled over Reese. The dizziness was no match for his face. His care. His compassion.

Elliot searched her eyes.

All the things she ever thought she'd say or ways she'd assumed she'd react slipped away—off the edge of Earth's outer corners.

Flashes of the first time she saw Elliot standing on her porch, images of him running down the road, were reeling in her mind, all in a matter of seconds.

She closed her eyes and felt his hands move onto hers. Every reason to marry Elliot was summoned in the short moment that felt so long. The image of his face the night he found out she was sick, the moment his eyes met hers in his kitchen—the morning after she pecked his cheek. The hilarious memories they'd made and his text on the beach when she wasn't sure he'd forgive her for freaking out. In such a short time, they'd accumulated quite the collection. They'd truly grown close. Maybe this was the first time she could trust her own gut without having to get it confirmed. *Life has done something here—and I know what I want—now, I'm going after it.*

Reese opened her eyes and nodded. "Yes. Yes!"

Elliot lunged forward knocking her backward on the wet grass while everyone cheered. He dipped the ring in the water and slipped it on her finger. Their surroundings faded. Elliot Jacobson was over her, running his fingers through her hair—staring into her eyes. "I love you."

She death-gripped his unbuttoned overshirt, pulling him down into a kiss. The faint sound of people somewhere far away echoed as the world around them spun.

THE EVENING CREPT CLOSE. THE STRUNG LIGHTS CAST shadows across faces of festival goers walking by. Miss Rosa, Ron, Anette, and a few others had gathered near the gazebo after wrapping up the fun and games and passing out prizes.

A woman standing near a wooden bar table poured wine into glasses, while another passed them out.

Miss Rosa spoke into her mic. "I've known Reesey for seven years, but it feels like I've known her all her life. She is like a niece to me—wouldn't have it any other way." She turned to Reese, wiping a tear. "Honey—you are special. Never forget that. Elliot—you are the one for her. No matter where life takes you, I know you'll be there for her. And now I'm shuttin' up or I'll break down, so here—"

She passed off the mic to Anette and one by one, they gave a short message. Many people had gone home by now, except for those closest to Reese. After they finished passing the mic, Miss Rosa handed it to Elliot.

He turned to face Reese. "Kentucky wasn't so random."

He looked around. "I don't believe in coincidences anymore. You're the best person that's ever happened to me, Reese." He set the mic down and held up his glass.

Miss Rosa raised her voice. "Let's toast!"

"Anette, can I have the shop key for a sec?"

"Sure. You okay?"

Reese nodded. "Yes."

She pulled the key from her pocket and handed it to Reese.

Reese unlocked the bookshop and let herself in, shutting the door and locking it behind her. She just needed a minute to gather herself.

The street was lit up like Christmas. People hustled to clean up the Thanksgiving mess, and she could see Miss Rosa directing the younger ones in an attempt to finish faster.

Reese held her left hand out, admiring the ring.

She looked up. The window provided a perfect view. Someone was dumping the water out of the apple bins. She saw Elliot looking inquisitive.

He was asking something or talking—Reese wasn't sure. He helped a gentleman with a table and walked across looking inquisitive still. *He's probably looking for me. Duh.*

Reese stood by the window. His eyes moved about, scanning the area and stopped on her. She gave a sheepish wave, and he walked to the door. Reese had it unlocked by the time he reached for the knob.

"Hey—everything okay?" He closed the door and locked it again.

She nodded, and he pulled her into a hug. "Just tired."

"And we have a big day tomorrow. Miss Rosa said she's good now—we can head out."

"Elliot?"

"Yeah?"

"I am so happy; I just wish our families could have been here."

He nodded. "I know. But can I tell you something?" He pulled a paper from his back pocket and handed it to Reese.

She unfolded the paper.

Elliot,

Thank you for contacting us. We are honored you would reach out—to share your heart and how you feel about Reese. Over the last couple months during our correspondence, we've been inclined to tell Reese you have been writing us, but it's not our place. At this point, if she feels the same way about you—and you want to move forward in asking for her hand—we say, go for it. Though we have not met in person, we trust that Reese has good judgment and will use it. If she loves you, we love you too.

See you both soon.

Reese folded the paper. "They know."

He nodded. "Yeah, I hope it's okay. Felt better about it this way. Since they weren't around."

Miss Rosa's voice boomed from nearby.

"You said you were a city boy, but you have country blood." She chuckled.

"City compared to here—and old fashioned. What can I say? I asked Miss Rosa for their mailing address in September."

"It's sweet. I should have been writing them, too.

Assumed it was all on them to contact me—but that's the old way of thinking."

He moved a hair behind her ear. "So—we're good?"

She nodded and smiled. "You gonna kiss me before you take me away?"

"I can arrange that." And he pressed his lips into hers.

CHAPTER 49

Reese climbed into the car and put the window down.

Miss Rosa lifted a small basket through and laid it on her lap. Stacks of envelopes filled the inside. "These are from the community. Save them for a rainy day, or when you need money."

"What? Oh—Miss Rosa, you didn't have to—"

"Shhh. We did. We love you, Reesey."

Elliot touched her left arm and looked at Miss Rosa. "Thank you."

"You take care. Call me when your plane lands."

"And we'll be back by New Year's."

Miss Rosa put her hand to her chest. "Christmas won't be the same without you—but you need this, Reese. It's good to explore and live a little—and, Elliot, give Amelia and your parents my best."

He nodded. "Will do."

She slapped the side of the Jeep and backed away.

"How's your leg doing?" Reese asked on their way home, whichever house—she still wasn't sure.

"Really well. I called my doctor and told them I'd be out of town during my appointment, so they said I can get seen down there and have them fax the papers over. Think it's pretty much healed though."

"Good."

A few minutes later, he pulled into his drive.

They sat for a moment. Finally, Elliot spoke up. "So, where are you sleeping tonight?"

"How old fashioned are you?"

"You've already slept on my couch, taken a nap on my bed, and slept in my tent—so apparently not enough. Why?"

Reese pressed her lips together, holding back her smirk. "All my stuff's at my house. I'll just stay there and see you in the morning."

He hopped out and opened her door.

"Thanks."

He wrapped his arms around her shoulders and kissed her head. "Flight's at ten a.m., so try and get some sleep."

"Are you going to bed right away?"

"After I pack my work bag, yeah."

She bit her lip.

"What?"

"Nothing."

Elliot narrowed his eyes and rubbed her jaw with his thumb. "I guess we need to talk about—"

Reese swallowed. "The date."

"Oh—"

"Wedding date."

"Right…"

Reese kissed his cheek. "Because I've never been a very patient person."

"Oh really?" His eyes twinkled in the moonlight. "Let me walk you to the door."

Reese gave him a soft elbow to the side.

He walked back home, but she had to force her body to stay.

Sleep. Just go to sleep, Reese.

JUST THE THOUGHT OF FLYING GAVE HER CHILLS. SHE GRIPPED Elliot's hand when they took off.

He leaned over and kissed her. "You're doing great."

Her eyes pinched shut. It felt like an hour before they were up and leveled out, but she knew it didn't take that long.

"You bring a book?"

She opened her eyes and dug into her carry-on. "Good idea."

Elliot set up his laptop and pulled something out of his bag. "Here—this is for you."

He placed green earbuds in her hand, attached to a small device. "I made you a playlist. Thought you might like one."

"Wow, thanks. Perfect." She felt the rush of anxiety slink away in defeat.

They both popped their earbuds in at the same time.

He gave her a wink and started typing.

I love this man.

REESE FELT A NUDGE, AND SHE FELT FOR HER BOOK. HAD SHE fallen asleep?

She tugged an earbud out.

"We're here." Elliot had all his stuff put away.

Thirty minutes later they were filing out of the plane, walking into the terminal.

They found their bags, and Reese stopped.

"What?"

"If we flew, what will we drive?"

Elliot laughed, dimples showing. "Forgot to tell you—my dad's picking us up. Called him last week. Said he'd make sure he was in town and not out on a flight. Mom has three cars. We're just going to use one of those while here."

"Three. Wow." Reese shook her head and followed Elliot out the door.

"Traffic's crazier down here—you want him to stop for food before heading to the house?"

She shook her head. "No, I'll be okay."

A black sedan pulled up, and Elliot recognized it was their ride. The passenger window rolled down and he stuck his head in. "Hey."

His dad did a two-finger wave. "Good to see you, son. And you, Reese."

They look so much alike. So…is this what Elliot will look like in thirty years?

Elliot put their bags in the trunk and opened the door for Reese.

His dad pulled into the busy traffic. "Lunchtime. You warned her right?"

"Thanks for picking us up," Reese said.

"I wish it were under better circumstances—well, Amelia, I mean. But yes, my pleasure. And congratulations. Elliot, she's as gorgeous as you said."

Reese looked at Elliot.

He met her glance out the corner of his eye. His mouth curved into a curious grin. "Yes, she is."

Elliot, you are making it hard to hold back. "So, you live in Georgia too, sir?"

"Don't call me sir. Just Rob. Yes, but his mom and I are

separated right now. Not because I want to be—"

"Dad, it's okay. I'm sure she doesn't want all the details—"

"No, it's okay. Sorry, I shouldn't have asked." Reese blushed.

"It's fine. You should know, or you may be confused when I drop you off and leave."

Reese squeezed Elliot's hand.

"Did you get to see her yesterday? Amelia?"

Rob's eyes met Elliot's in the rear-view mirror. "Yes. We talked." He got quiet for a second. "It hurts my heart to see her like this. Do what you can for her—but, Elliot, take care of yourself too."

"I know. I do."

"And if you need to get away for a few days between now and New Year's, call me. I have an extra room in the condo."

"Thanks. Have you spoken to Mom today? I told her we'd be arriving after lunch."

He cleared his throat. "Yeah—but she didn't talk for long. Seemed preoccupied. Trying not to push her."

Elliot nodded.

"Reese, I apologize. So—how are you?"

She smiled at Rob in the mirror. "Good. Just feel wiped out from the past few days."

"She helps everyone back home. The festivals are nuts. Did all that and got sidelined by me asking her to become a Jacobson." He laughed, and she threw him a snarky look.

"I see you two are perfect for each other," Rob chuckled then became serious. "Thanks for calling me and making me feel included, son. Reese, I want to say—our lives may be messy, but this one, he's a gentleman. We raised him right."

Reese felt her face grow hot. She smiled and squeezed his hand again. "I think so, too."

CHAPTER 50

Elliot took the bags out of the trunk and set them onto the paved drive leading up to a spectacular house.

"Is this a mansion?"

Elliot laughed.

"It's huge."

Rob got out and shook Elliot's hand. "I'm taking a vacation through the holidays. Call if you need anything at all or want to go out on the track."

Reese looked at Rob. He hugged her and put his hands on her shoulders. "You, my dear lady, are wonderful. So glad to be able to welcome you to the family." He looked back at Elliot and continued. "Set a date?"

"We'll probably talk about that soon. Mom doesn't know yet."

Rob's eyes got big. "Oh, don't wait too long."

"I know." Elliot cleared his throat, sounding a lot like his dad. "I just didn't want to freak her out last week. Wanted to share in person."

"Wise." Rob slapped his back.

"Bye, Dad, and thanks again."

Reese nodded and waved as he got in and drove away. “He’s nice.”

Elliot smiled. “He’s a great man.” He slung two big bags over each shoulder and gripped the handles of the wheeled bags.

“I can help,” Reese said.

“If you can get the carry-ons, I’m good.”

“This house.”

“What?”

“It’s just huge.”

Elliot laughed. “This is going to be fun.”

At the door, Elliot pushed a buzzer.

A woman greeted them. “Hello, Elliot! So good to see you! She turned and snapped. A butler-looking man walked forward.

“No, it’s okay—I got it, but thanks.”

The woman made a face. “Same stubborn Elliot.”

He threw her a smirk and kept walking. “Good to see you too, Joanne. Catch up soon!”

Reese followed him down a hall.

“An elevator?”

Elliot grinned, dimples showing.

“What else have you not told me?”

“You know all the important parts.”

The door opened, and she followed him down another hall. “There’s this room or that one, or the one at the end—take your pick.”

She looked around. “Where’s your room?”

“Downstairs.”

“Oh, okay.”

“You sound disappointed.”

Her eyes squinted, and she smiled. “Surprised?”

“This is my other favorite room.”

"Works for me." He pulled her bag into the giant bedroom and set her duffel on the bed. The ceilings were cathedral-style, the room immersed in an oceanic colors. It was relaxing. Made sense this was his favorite.

"This could be a house all by itself."

"I couldn't agree more." He wrapped his arms around her.

She pressed her face into his chest and breathed in the scent of his hunky cologne. His fingers intertwined with hers, and he pressed his lips into hers.

"What about that date?"

"We're going to decide that right now?"

She chuckled. "Okay—guess not."

"Let's go find Mom."

"Elliot? Aren't you forgetting something?"

"What?" He ran his fingers through his hair.

She held up her left hand.

His eyes widened. "Cra—" His phone rang. "It's Mom."

Reese laughed and plopped on the bed.

"Hello?"

She rolled over and pulled the diamond off, tucking it into a drawer by the bed.

Elliot gave a thumbs up to Reese. "Yeah—we're here. Okay, will do. Love you, too."

He hung up and opened the drawer. "Here." He took the ring back out and walked over to a wooden trunk. He moved it, revealing a black square with buttons. He punched a few and opened it, placed the ring inside, and closed it again.

"A safe. Sweet."

"Mom's heading home from the office. Ready to meet her?"

Reese swallowed. "Yes."

"THIS IS IT." ELLIOT SHOWED HER HIS BEDROOM. THE WALLS were lined with quotes, and a guitar sat in the corner. One of the walls was accented with dark gray, while the far wall looked like giant canvas covered in art of various types.

Reese ran her fingers across the wall, feeling the textures against her skin. Maybe his mom was on the grouchy side—or so she'd gotten the vibe—but at least she let Elliot own his room.

"These four walls caught all my emotion, can you tell?"

"You bet."

Elliot walked to the doorway and Reese followed.

His mom was just topping the stairs. She could really pull of the pant suit thing. Her hair was pulled back into a fancy up-do. She rubbed the carpet in a certain direction with the tip of her shoe, looking less than amused.

Reese could feel her nerves crashing into her chest. *I hope she likes me.*

Elliot spoke first. "Hey." He hugged her, and she awkwardly returned it with one arm.

His mom looked over. "Hello, Reese." She nodded.

"Hello."

"Tracy."

"Nice to meet you, Tracy."

His mom clapped her hands together. "Elliot, you get her set up in a different room?"

Elliot glanced at Reese, a side grin showing. "Of course."

"You both hungry? I can have Jo make you something."

"Yes," they both said at the same time.

Tracy made a face. "Well, all right then. Let's get to it."

She led the way, and Elliot looked to Reese, crossing his eyes.

Reese tried not to laugh. *Oh, this is going to fun. He wasn't kidding.*

Elliot stoked the fire in the fireplace but was quiet.

Reese tried to read his face but wasn't having any luck.

"What are you thinking?"

He poked another log and set the metal rod on the hearth. "Just a lot of memories flooding back, being here."

She nodded and rubbed his back. They were in a grand sitting room, as Tracy had called it earlier when she was taking Reese through the house.

"You want to talk about it?"

He shook his head. "Nothing to talk about, really. I grew up alone. Mom and Dad were always working—or having dinner parties. The house was always full of their guests on their days off, though I don't think Dad was really into it. He went along with it for Mom, but I think he got burnt out on playing the game. Mom's always had a hard time hearing the opinions of others."

"What about Amelia?"

"She was around somewhat. Always had a ton of friends over or was with her latest boyfriend. I stayed in my room painting or strumming guitar most days—until I started writing. That's when my imagination got the best of me and I started inching for change."

Reese took his hand.

The fire flickered and snapped.

"Being here just makes me sense that loneliness again."

"You're not alone."

"I know—but then, as a kid and a teen, I felt it."

"Why did you stay so long?"

Elliot dropped his head. "I think I thought mom would eventually grow tired of working so much. That she and Dad would finally get along. And there's so much room here. It felt foolish to move out. Once I started writing full time and seeing I could make a living from it—I just knew I needed to get out and experience life for myself."

Reese rubbed his arm.

"What kind of twenty-nine-year-old guy works from his parents' home?"

Reese chuckled. "I don't know."

"The money for sure wasn't bringing me joy—and I was tired of waiting around for someone else to dish it out to me. Moving was the best thing I ever did."

She ran her finger down his cheek, following the lining of his facial hair—where his sideburn met with the rest of his five o' clock shadow.

"Money does a lot of things, but not all."

He put his hand on hers. "Anyway."

"I'm listening."

"Yeah—but you need sleep. Been a long day. Plus, we should go see Amelia tomorrow."

"Of course."

He took her hand and walked her to the bedroom she was staying in.

They stopped at the door, both probably thinking the same thing, but unwilling to say it. Now that they were engaged, Reese wanted more than anything to fast forward and say, "I do," but it just wasn't possible. They had other things to tend to here—and she was just going to have to get over it.

If Elliot wasn't such a jaw-dropping stud. An irresistible gentleman from another planet.

He pulled her into one last embrace, hands clasped on the small of her back. He kissed her forehead and went downstairs.

Reese watched him until he was out of sight. She looked around the edges of the walls and wondered if there was surveillance installed. The thought made her laugh—but she gulped at the image of his mom viewing footage of Reese sneaking downstairs to poke Elliot awake.

She tucked herself in feeling lighthearted and free. *I just may try to pull it off before it's all said and done.* She reached over and tugged the chain on the ceramic lamp.

I just may try.

CHAPTER 51

Reese tiptoed down the carpeted staircase, unsure of who was already awake.

A bright blue blur in high heels flew across the floor.

Elliot was sitting at the breakfast bar with a plate of fruit, scrambled eggs, and what appeared to be turkey bacon. When he saw Reese, he immediately slid his chair back and pulled one out for her. “Good morning. Hungry?”

She stretched and sniffed the air. “Is that coffee I smell in the background?”

“You’re good. I thought bacon was the perfect cover-up.”

Her chin rested in her hands. “Nothing hides coffee. Fuel me up.”

“Yes, ma’am,” he joked. He poured a cup and set it front of her, along with a spoon, a few packets of sugar, and a creamer.

She mixed it while he fixed a plate and slid it in front of her.

Tracy rushed in and pulled something square from the microwave.

“Mom, I told you I made breakfast. Can you eat with us?”

"No, Elliot, I don't have time for fancy. I gotta run. We're crunching numbers this morning with a new client, and I don't want to be late."

"What about Amelia?"

"I told her I'd stop by on my lunch." She bit into the poor excuse for a piece a toast.

Elliot pushed his food with the fork. "Oh, I see."

"Don't get anything dirty, tell Jo what you want for dinner, and I'll be home by…"

Elliot looked up, waiting for her to finish.

"I'll be home—tonight." And she hurried out the garage door.

Reese ripped a slab of bacon in half, popping one side into her mouth.

"Some people never change," Elliot groaned.

"You never know. Miracles happen."

"I know…"

Reese wanted to change the subject. Get his mind off what he couldn't control. "I—I've been thinking. May is a really good month."

He swallowed his bite. "You have my attention."

"But—I'm not against upping this gig. We can shoot for March, February, January…"

"This gig?" He laughed and put his plate in the sink. "I never saw you as winter bride. Am I wrong?"

Reese didn't respond but scooped the remains of her bacon and eggs into one heap and downed it together. *No, you're spot on.*

He kissed her on the cheek. "April's nice too. I'm headed for the shower. Be ready in an hour?"

She nodded, and he turned down the hall, but she was tempted to get a running start, catapult herself into the air, and latch herself to Elliot's back. She loved seeing him laugh.

It would be fun. But, no. Another day. What—what did he say? April?

April. That's when they met.

She set her dish in the sink, looking around for Jo. She picked the plate back up and rinsed it. She didn't want to be rude.

Reese organized the condiments then wiped the counter down. Finally, she started hand washing their breakfast dishes. She couldn't take it anymore. The house was too pristine to leave gooey egg running down the side of a plate, for all to see. Besides, she could clean up after herself—and they already knew Elliot could, right? His house was always in shipshape condition. *Must run in the family.*

Joanne walked in and gave her a funny look. "No, ma'am. We don't let guests to the dishes here."

It was the first time Reese ever had someone grab a plate from her hands so they could take over. "I was just trying to hel—"

But Jo smiled and stood in the way. "You're here for Amelia, right?"

Reese lifted her brow. "Yes."

"All right then, have a good day."

Joanne and Tracy were eerily alike—but it made sense.

Reese went to the bedroom feeling like a five-year-old and wondering if everyone under the roof was told what to do at all times. "Yes—let's get ready and get out of here."

Mint green and cold, white walls. Hospital colors always seemed to scream, "Puke," or, "Hey, let's watch MASH reruns." Never, "Aw, you're in an awful state right now—let's see if we can't help you feel a little better by at least hiring an interior designer to make this room a little more comfy."

Reese felt a chill run down her spine. Maybe she was a little edgy right now. Maybe that's why her mind was running a hundred miles an hour. She looked down the hospital corridor. A woman with her son sat in a nearby waiting room, walls made of glass. The boy was holding a phone, eyes glued to the screen. The mom looked like she was having her fingernails for brunch.

Elliot came out from Amelia's room.

"Well?"

He rubbed his hands together. "She's tired—not up for talking just yet. The pain meds are strong too."

Reese released her grip on the window ledge outside Amelia's room. "Understandable."

"I held her hand, told her we loved her and would be back around lunch when Mom gets here. Give her time to nap—if she's still out at noon, we can try again after dinner." Elliot took Reese's hand and headed for the elevator.

"Where to?"

"I thought I might take you to my favorite coffee shop."

"But you don't like coffee."

He gave her the Elliot look. "They serve the best sage tea."

"That's why you're so alert without coffee involved," she snickered.

"You never asked."

She thought for a moment. "You're right. I think I now know what a coffee snob is."

"SHARP SUV."

Elliot shrugged. "If you've seen one, you've seen them all."

"It's nice of your mom to let us use it." Reese was trying to keep a positive attitude. His mom seemed annoyed at her presence. If Reese was going to be a Jacobson, it would benefit everyone if she could get a head start by finding admirable traits in Tracy. Dayl had taught her that this was one way to replace negative thinking.

The lady at the counter took their orders and they found a corner table.

"You mind if I write for a bit?"

"No, go ahead." She really didn't mind. He'd been so busy thinking of everyone else lately, writing would probably be good for him.

Reese twirled their place number across the wooden surface.

"Oh my—is that you, Elliot?"

Reese shifted in her seat to see a young woman walking toward them as she adjusted her scarf.

Elliot's eyes shot up. "Well, hello." He looked around. "How are you? Been a while."

"Right? Where'd you run off too? Miss seeing your face in this place."

Elliot clenched his jaw.

Reese could tell he was uneasy.

"This city boy needed some fresh air."

A woman walked up with their drinks and traded them for the number.

Elliot nodded. "Thanks, ma'am."

"Still polite as always," the woman said, pulling her jacket closed.

"Reese, this is Piper. Piper, Reese."

Reese smiled, stretching out her hand.

Piper shook her hand and added, "If he said anything about me—I promise, it's probably all true."

Elliot sipped his tea. "What are you up to these days?"

She slipped her hands into her jacket pockets. "Still working at the downtown branch. Ed's talking about marriage, but I don't know—"

Elliot cleared his throat. "How is Ed? He finish his degree?"

"Not yet. This spring. You know, if Em knew you were here, she'd want to see you."

"Not necessary. I can't talk about this here, but I'm glad you and Ed are doing good."

Reese searched his body language.

Piper pulled her lips in. "Elliot—"

He stood and gave her a pat on the back. "Piper, Amelia's in the hospital. I really can't talk right now."

She relented. "I'm sorry to hear that. Well—" She dropped her head. "Maybe we'll see you around."

He nodded, and she got in line to order.

Elliot shut his laptop and adjusted his messenger bag. "Let's go."

Reese slid down from the stool, grabbed her drink, and tried to keep up with him.

She chewed on her lip before speaking up. "So…"

Elliot sighed. "You don't know everything. I'm sorry, Reese—I messed up."

Reese felt her heart burn inside her chest. "Okay—what is it?"

He turned onto the highway and continued. "I was engaged before. Emma. It was three years ago."

She rubbed her neck. "For how long?"

"Six months."

"What happened?"

"She chose someone else. While we were together."

"That's awful."

"I'm sorry I didn't tell you. I guess I thought it didn't matter—but you sitting there, Piper walking up. It hit me. I knew I should have told you."

"Well—I know now."

"Still. I'm an idiot."

"No. You aren't. But who is Piper to Emma, then? Just curious."

Elliot gripped the wheel. "She's her best friend. Ed and Piper have been together for as long as I can remember—but he was always into the parties and stuff. Anyway, one day I found a text from him on Em's phone. It rang, and I brought it to her. You know how some phones show the partial of a new message?"

Reese nodded. "Yeah."

"Well—Ed's showed up."

Reese swallowed.

Elliot turned into his mom's drive and pulled up to the house. "They had been seeing each other behind our backs. After that I stopped talking to him."

"What about Piper? Does she know?"

"I confronted Em about it. She got angry. I asked her why. I told her she needed to be honest with her friend."

Elliot opened his door and stuck one leg out. "I'm not sure if I made the right choice in how I handled it. But I felt it wasn't my place to tell her."

"I don't know," Reese said.

"There's more."

She looked over. Elliot put his head on the wheel. "Em and I didn't really know each other. I think going out with her—getting engaged—it was a way for me to try and take control of my life. I hadn't started writing full time yet. I was in limbo about a lot of things. I just wanted to make a concrete decision, ya know?"

"That's pretty concrete."

He nodded. "Too much so for being unsure."

"You know, you're not perfect."

"Trust me, I know."

"I didn't mean it in a bad way. Elliot—you told me before that I didn't know everything. I didn't pry. If this was it—it's out there. It's done."

"When I left Georgia, I was in search of peace. I really never intended on—"

Reese touched his arm. "I know."

He shook his head. "Please forgive me. If any of this makes you uncomfortable—I get it."

Reese tucked her lip inward. "I'm fine. Let's go inside so we can reset before seeing Amelia."

He hopped out but didn't get to the door before Reese climbed out.

She shut it and spun around to face him.

"This day."

"Let's reset."

He took her hand, and Jo opened the door.

Reese followed him to the kitchen. He started fishing through the freezer.

"What are you doing?"

Finally, he gave up. "Is this what women do when they feel crappy? How come there isn't any ice cream in here, Jo?"

She wasn't in the room. It was sarcastic.

Reese laughed. "Wow."

Elliot kept a straight face, though. "So sad."

She followed him to his room and leaned on the door

frame. "I feel like I need something to do while I'm here, or I'm just going to keep trailing you like a puppy."

"Go for it."

"Does your mom need help with—something?"

"You're supposed to be on vacation, remember?"

"From editing, not living," she laughed.

"True. I mean—there's plenty to do for fun—just not work. Unless you want to work for her at the company. I don't recommend it," he smirked.

Reese sat on the edge of his bed.

Elliot walked over to his closet and pulled it open. He slid his shirt off and replaced it with a fitted workout shirt. "I didn't move completely out."

Reese didn't drop her head this time. She studied his tan skin. Not tan from a tanning bed—but a naturally darker skin tone kind of tan.

He pulled shorts from his wheeled bag. "Can you—um, never mind, be right back." He jogged out of the room and came bag changed in under a minute.

"Maybe I'll go out back and walk around until we leave. I may even try to call Mom."

He stooped down to Reese's eye level, hands on her knees. "Sounds good. I'm going to try to run. I need it."

"Are you sure? Don't you want to wait until the doc here gives you the green light?"

He shook his head and slid his fingers into her hair. "No, it'll be fine." He pulled her face toward his, pressed his lips into hers.

Just then—a sound came from the hallway.

"Cut it out you two." It was Tracy's voice.

He looked up, and Reese turned. Apparently, Tracy had passed by the doorway.

"Guess Mom's home for lunch."

CHAPTER 52

After Elliot showered and Reese left her mom a message, she sat in the SUV. Tracy walked by and eyed her. Reese smiled anyway. Elliot came out, wearing a fresh change of clothes and with his hair fixed his favorite way. He shot her a grin, but Tracy walked up to him and started in about something. *Man, she can be grueling.*

Elliot was too far away for Reese to tell what he was saying. He looked annoyed but calm. He nodded and put his hand on Tracy's shoulder. She dropped her head, and then he pulled her into a hug. It was a few minutes before he got in the vehicle, but when he did, he was quiet.

"Everything okay?"

"I have a favor to ask."

"Sure, what is it?"

"Or—I'll pay you, I mean."

"Pay?"

He laughed. "I need my manuscript gone over one more time. Thought you might want to. I know you're off—but I wanted to ask you first, before passing it off to my usual editor."

"They say never hire anyone close to you. How do you know you can trust me?"

"More than anything, I just want to make sure there aren't any holes in the story. Relationship doesn't really hinder that kind of read through."

"True."

"And…"

"And?"

"Mom needs to talk about something with me. Tonight. After work. Are you okay with that?"

"Of course. You all need to spend time together, too. Elliot, I'm independent. I know it doesn't look like it lately—but I can be. I have been—"

"I know. Sorry. Being here is weirding me out."

"Have fun tonight. Do what you need to do."

"I don't think it's that kind of conversation."

"Oh?"

He shook his head and backed out of the drive, his mom proceeding them to the hospital. "No. She wanted to tell me something on the phone a while back, remember? Whatever it was, she wanted to wait."

Reese drew in a deep breath. "Well—I hope everything's okay. She's going through so much already."

Elliot flipped on the radio and took her left hand. "We need to get that ring back on your hand."

THE NURSE WAS ALL SUNSHINE. REESE SMILED, THANKFUL SHE was assigned to Amelia. "She's sitting up, ready to visit. Let me know if there's anything I can do."

Tracy nodded and looked to Elliot. "Are we going in together or separate?"

"You can go in first, have some time. Reese and I can wait across the hall here."

"Very well." She opened the door and shut it behind her.

Elliot led the way and slid a dollar through the vending machine slot. "You want anything?"

Reese shook her head. "No. Thanks."

"I hope whatever's bothering Mom won't, after she tells me." He bit into a pretzel stick. "It's eating her up. I can see it."

Reese turned the television volume down. "Yeah. I do too."

"She and Amelia need to bond. It just stinks if it took something extreme to make it happen."

Reese bent over and kissed his cheek. "You think a lot, don't you?"

He laughed. "Too much these days."

"When do you think she'll get to come home?"

He bit another stick. "Don't know bu—"

A knock on the entry way to the waiting room made them look up. A young woman and Piper stood in the doorway. Piper did a quick wave and turned to walk away. It was awkward behavior, really.

Elliot straightened.

Is this Emma?

The woman came closer and lowered her head, clutching her purse. "Elliot. Piper told me about Amelia."

"Um—hey."

"I asked your mom—she told me where she was."

Elliot tilted his head in clarity. "Ahhh, I see."

"I just wanted to say hi to her. Tell her she's in my prayers."

Elliot shifted. "This is Reese."

"Hello—nice to meet you," she held out her hand.

Reese awkwardly shook it with her free hand and smiled. “You too.”

Elliot gave Reese’s hand a squeeze—the one he’d been holding, and they looked at one another for a moment.

“I won’t stay long. Is anyone in there yet?”

“Actually, Mom is, yes.”

Just then Tracy walked into the waiting room. “Oh, good —you’re here.” She patted Emma on the arm.

Elliot led Reese out of the waiting room and into the hall by Amelia’s door. “We’re going to visit for a bit—I hope you don’t mind. She wasn’t up for talking this morning.”

Reese dropped her head. She didn’t want to look at Emma anymore. Really, she wanted to ask how in the world she could hurt a guy like Elliot. She wanted to flick her in the forehead. Looking away was helping.

“Oh, yes, right. I’ll wait…in here.”

Tracy shot Elliot a glare. “Let’s get you something to drink.” And she walked into the waiting room with Emma.

Elliot looked down, his neck veins bulging.

“Let’s go in.”

He nodded and opened the door.

It was dark and quiet, the only sound coming from the buzz of the vent. He shut the door behind them. “Let me pull the extra chair up next to the bed.”

Reese felt nervous but tried not show it. The last time she’d seen Amelia was when she was in Elliot’s Jeep, bright and chipper.

“Hey, sis,” he said taking Amelia’s hand.

She smiled. “Hey.”

“You remember Reese.”

She nodded. “Pretty as ever.”

“Oh, thank you. I—I’m really glad I was able to come.”

Amelia played with the edge of the sheet.

Elliot looked at the muted television. "Movie?"

"I don't know. It was on," she laughed lightly.

He rubbed her hand. "I'm hoping to talk to the doctors today. See if they have a better idea on when you're coming home."

She reached for her cup of water. "I heard my chair will be here in a few days."

His head dropped. A tear fell.

"Elliot…"

Reese wrapped her arm around him.

"Is there anything I can do for you?"

Amelia shook her head. "You are right now."

"What kind of stuff do you to read?" Reese asked.

Amelia tapped her finger on her cheek. "Fashion magazines, romance…"

Reese grinned. "Do you mind if I gather a few you may like?"

"That would be great."

Elliot smiled. "Amelia, I need to talk to you about something. It's a big deal. Would you rather talk about it now—or after you get settled in at home?"

Amelia looked back and forth from her brother to Reese. Her lip curved upward into a grin. "I think I already know. No—go ahead."

Elliot stood up and gave the 'one sec' finger. He opened the door, stepped out for a few seconds, and came back, Tracy close behind.

"Mom, have a seat please."

"Am I in trouble?"

He laughed and rubbed the back of his neck. "No, no."

Reese swallowed hard. *Is he doing what I think he's doing?*

"Mom, I need to tell you both something—Amelia said she's good with hearing the news now."

Reese crossed her leg and fidgeted with a loose thread on her jeans.

"As you know, Reese and I have become best friends over this last year…" He cleared his throat. "She means the world to me, and I wanted to tell you both in person—" He pulled something from his pocket.

The ring. He brought it.

"Reese and I want to make a commitment to each other—so we're getting married." He slipped the ring on her finger.

Amelia clapped. "I knew it."

Elliot stooped down in front of Reese, adjusting the ring. He looked into her eyes. "I love you."

"Love you, too."

He leaned in and kissed her forehead and looked over at his mom. "Mom, it would mean so much to me if you could support us in this."

Tracy looked down and nodded.

Reese tried to catch her breath, hoping no one had noticed.

"The day I saw Elliot's reaction to you—when he saw you walking down the road in the rain, and then you hopped in—I knew he felt deeply for you. I've never seen him act that way about anyone." Amelia's eyes twinkled.

"Not even Em?" Tracy stood and walked out, closing the door behind her.

Amelia grabbed for her brother's hand. "Don't go after her."

Elliot didn't listen. He was out the door in a flash.

"I'm sorry, Reese. Mom's—it's like she tries to find reasons to be mad at people. I don't know why. I think maybe —she's hurting inside, and it comes out."

If she can throw the fire at other people, she can keep running from her own burning heart. I get it.

Reese smiled. “It’s okay.”

“No—it’s not. Elliot and I—we’ve run from the sharp arrows all our lives. Dad never wanted to go—Mom kicked him out.”

“You don’t have to tell me, it’s okay—”

“You’re going to be part of the family. You need to know the truth.”

Reese fixed a wrinkle in her shirt. “Elliot told me some. Your dad is sweet.”

“He is, and mom was, before she took over as CEO. It took over life. I remember when it happened. It changed her. She knows it—and I think she regrets it.”

“So you think she’s living every day in regret?”

Amelia shook her head. “She feels bad inside but hasn’t forgiven herself.”

“So she keeps pushing through life…”

The door opened, and Elliot smiled, but Reese wasn’t sure how to read this one.

“Elliot—”

He put up a hand. “Mom’s all right. Em’s gone. Everything’s going to be okay.”

Amelia moaned.

“You okay?” Reese sat up.

Elliot poked his head out the door.

Amelia moaned again and grabbed her thigh. “Elliot, please don’t let Mom—”

She closed her eyes and grunted in pain.

“Can I get a nurse in here, please?”

Reese stood and backed away to give whoever was coming room.

Elliot nodded to someone and walked over to Amelia—taking her hand. "It's going to be okay, sis."

"I know—I'm due for another round of meds."

"We can go and come back tonight."

A tear slid down her cheek.

The nurse walked in and checked her vitals and the machines. "Let's get you fixed up here—and you need some rest. Small activities are going to wear you out easily for a while."

When the nurse finished, Elliot walked with her into the hall.

"You are doing great. He's so proud of you, I hope you know that."

Amelia leaned her head back. "I don't know what for. I've never done anything worth being proud of."

Reese hung her purse from her shoulder. "He thinks differently. And he loves you very much."

"What's the date?"

"Date? Oh—the wedding. We don't have one yet."

"I want to be there."

Reese smiled. "Of course."

He stepped back in. "You want us back here tonight?"

She shook her head and tucked a hair behind her ear. "No, I called Dad. He's spending the night here with me."

Reese smiled.

"I'm so glad." Elliot wiped the tears from his eyes. "Love you," he said as he hugged his sister.

"Hey, bub, my meds are kicking in—I'll be fine now. Dad and I have an ongoing game over there in the drawer. The nurse has specific instructions not to let housekeeping moving our pieces," she laughed.

"That's awesome," Reese said, peeking in the drawer.

"Look, but don't touch."

"Right."

"Hey guys, thanks for telling me in person. Today, instead of later. I'm happy for you, bub. Reese, he's the best man I know—next to Dad. Protector. Loyal as heck."

"And annoying big brother," he smirked.

"That too."

They said their goodbyes and left, Reese feeling torn inside. On the one hand, she felt relieved. On the other, she wondered if her marrying Elliot would do more damage to the already rocky relationship he had with his mom. She pushed her glasses back in place and got in the SUV but decided not to bring it up.

I just want them to be happy.

CHAPTER 53

Reese finished the test and hit *Submit*. That was it. Class was over. Gardening seemed like such a faraway thing right now. Almost as if she'd never done it. The funny thing was, through the process of seeing Dayl, living next to Elliot, planting those tiny seeds and watching them grow—she herself had been sifted, cultivated, and nurtured.

She shut her laptop and tucked it under the bed. *I just wish I could make their hurt go away.* On the drive back to the house hours before, she and Elliot talked about everything under the sun except pain. It didn't mean it wasn't there, but she knew Elliot had a burden for his sister like no other.

Reese was thankful for his dad. Hopefully, his mom would come around soon. She walked downstairs and peeked into Elliot's room, but he wasn't there. She looked for the downstairs bathroom and heard talking. A door was cracked.

"I left because I needed a fresh start, Mom. I needed to move on from my stupid mistake—and learn how to live on my own."

"It wasn't stupid, Elliot."

"Look—I was just going through the motions back then, okay? I was desperate to make you proud of me, to prove to myself I could man up and—"

"Elliot—"

"It was stupid because I knew we were rushing. I barely knew her. And the thing is, it didn't work. It didn't make me who I wanted to become. It didn't make you bat an eye—so don't act like that. Don't act like you care now."

Reese fast walked down the long hall searching for the bathroom. She knew she'd stood there too long. Her heart raced.

She opened a door, any door at this point. She took a breath and spun around.

The butler-looking man froze.

Reese dropped her jaw.

He was putting his shirt back on.

Reese grabbed the knob and ran out. *No, no, no.*

As she flew down the hall, Elliot and his mom came out from the room. "Reese?"

But she kept going and bounded out the back door through the hedged yard—and stood behind the nearest tree she could find. She slouched down to her ankles trying to catch her breath.

"Reese? You out here? You okay?" It was Elliot.

She didn't respond. *What is going on, Tracy? Why?*

Elliot called her name again, but she didn't want to respond. Not like this. She needed to calm down and get her head on straight. Spewing junk wasn't going to help anyone.

She leaned her head against the rough bark and shut her eyes. *Oh, Elliot.*

Reese pushed the door open. The house was quiet. She went to the room upstairs and pulled her phone from her purse.

Elliot had tried to call and text a few times. Then he left a text.

"Meeting dad at the track for an hour, be back soon. Hope you're okay. Call if you need anything. Love you."

She walked downstairs to poke through the kitchen. It wasn't dinner time yet—but she needed something.

Tracy walked in.

C'mon, Reese. Will yourself to turn this ship around.

"Oh, hey—you off early today?"

She poured a glass of something dark from a long neck bottle on the counter and took a drink. "Reese, it really was nice to meet you—but you don't know a thing about me, okay?"

Reese dropped her head. *Did she see me come out the room?*

"Elliot thinks he can just run off and make the pain go away—well, he's wrong."

Heat rose up in her throat. She buried her hands in her pockets. "No, I don't know you—but you don't me either—or Elliot for that matter. He loves you—can't you see that? Can't you see he's only ever wanted a healthy relationship with you?" She spun around and rushed out the front door, leaving Tracy no time to reply. And it was better that way. Maybe she'd think instead of opening her mouth and hurting someone again.

Calm down, Reese. Breathe.

She walked down the long driveway, unaware of where she was heading, but she didn't care. The vibe in that house made her understand why Elliot hadn't wanted to stick around.

"Elliot and Amelia deserve better than this..." She turned left out of the gated yard and fast walked. "I have an hour to kill, and I'm not spending it with Tracy."

CHAPTER 54

Reese had walked almost the entire hour—in the opposite direction of the house. She tried to keep straight so as not to get confused, but she hadn't factored in it would take an hour to walk back. "Crap. I should have turned around thirty minutes ago."

She walked another few minutes before her phone rang. It was Elliot. "Hello?"

She crossed over to the other side of the street. Maybe she could wait somewhere for Elliot to pick her up. "I'm okay—don't want to get into it right now. I took a walk and, uh…I'm not sure where I am." She looked around. "Can you pick me up at this place called The Poetree?" She sat down on a nearby bench. "I know. I just kept going," she chuckled. "Thanks."

A few minutes later, Elliot pulled up in his mom's SUV.

"That was fast."

"You're only a few miles away."

"It felt like I walked a hundred miles."

Elliot kept the vehicle in park. "Where did you run off to earlier?"

Reese looked ahead. "I don't want to talk about this right now."

He put it into drive. "Okay, then."

The drive back was a quiet one. Reese got out and went to her room.

Elliot folded his arms and leaned against the wall while she picked out her night clothes. "We haven't had dinner yet."

"I'm not hungry."

"What's going on, Reese? You can talk to me."

"I don't want to be here, okay? I don't think this is going to work out. I'm getting a shower." All the emotions she spent the last hour trying to pep talk away escaped in three seconds. She walked to the door.

Elliot reached for her hand. "Reese."

"Talk to your mom. It's not up to me to say. Now I know how you felt with Piper." *I need hot water, right now—running down my face. That is all.*

REESE CLIMBED OUT OF THE SHOWER FEELING REFRESHED. She dried and combed her tangled hair and threw it into a quick braid.

Sweatpants and a tee would have to do for now. When she grabbed her clothes she really wasn't paying attention. The whole situation had her brain in a fog.

After she finished cleaning the bathroom, Reese walked around to find Elliot. Maybe she was hungry after all. "Elliot?"

She knocked on his bedroom door. It was ajar.

"Come in."

"Hey—"

He was zipping up his suitcase.

"What's going on?"

"We're leaving."

He was laser focused, feeling inside the pouches, double checking everything. He set the bag down and rolled it toward her. "A cab's on the way now."

Reese bit her lip.

He rolled it past her and left it by the front door. "Can I help you get your things?"

She looked around, half hoping Tracy would run out and say how sorry she was for whatever she said—or the affair. She guessed Elliot knew. "No, I'll grab them."

He looked at his watch. "Okay. Should be here soon."

Reese nodded and flew up the stairs. What a day this was turning out to be.

THE SUN WAS GOING DOWN. REESE'S STOMACH GROWLED. She grabbed for it.

"We'll order something when we get to Dad's."

She nodded, fidgeting with her thumbs.

Elliot leaned his head on the window the entire ride across town.

When they arrived and got their luggage out, he finally spoke. "Here's the key."

Reese unlocked the door to the condo while he brought the bags up the stairs.

He left them in the entryway and walked through the house, sliding open the glass door that led to the view of the lake and pool. He gripped the steel railing and shut his eyes.

Reese's phone lit up, but she shut it off. *Not now.*

She wished she could make his hurt go away, but she didn't have that kind of power.

He sat in the patio chair. "Mom's digging her grave."

"What?"

"She's so angry, so lost."

Reese crossed her arms and looked at the ground.

"I'm sorry you had to see that."

Reese hoped they were talking about the same thing.

"The—"

"The guy in there. Mom's drinking." He pulled her close, and she sat on his leg.

"I'm not going back. I can't stay there, I mean."

Reese ran her fingers through his hair.

"She's a wreck. She needs counseling. I just wish she wanted it."

"We can't make people want to better their lives."

He brushed her cheek with his finger. "I know."

"It's one thing to do what you can and another to dwell on something you can't fix. Did you know I was contemplating going home earlier?"

"What?"

"Yeah. I was almost convinced what may help Tracy would be if I left and you two had time—just you and her, talking and making up."

"No. It's not like that with her."

"I see that now. I know there's always hope, but I realized this wasn't about me."

"You thought it was?"

Reese remembered the conversation she'd overheard between them. "I just knew her wounds seemed to be spread out."

"They are. And you're right—let's not talk about this anymore. I'll order Chinese, and we can get a good night's sleep."

He kissed her tenderly.

She wrapped her arms around his neck, and he picked her up and carried her into the house.

"Where do you want to go?"

She pulled back. "Huh?"

"Dad's room is that way—you can have the guest bed or the couch. Your choice."

"Oh—the couch."

He spun her around toward the guest room. "Just kidding. You aren't sleeping on the couch. Who do you think I am?" He laughed.

Finally. He laughed.

Reese felt a weight lift.

He playfully tossed her on the bed.

"This is nice," Reese commented, feeling the softness of the mattress.

"Just wait until I turn the light on and you can see." He clapped, and the light came on.

"No way. They still have those?"

He chuckled and bent over her body, kissing her neck.

"Elliot?"

He kissed her cheek. "What?"

"Are we going to—"

He kissed her other cheek.

"Order food?"

He pressed his lips into hers, and she went backwards on the bed. He slid his hands into hers, kissing her more.

"Elliot—"

"Food. Food. Right." He backed off and popped his neck. "What am I doing? Sorry, Reese." He shook his head. "I'll—I'll be right back—or, actually—meet me in the living room, or the kitchen. Somewhere else." He turned to walk out and shut the door behind him.

Reese sat up and touched her lips. *Whoa.*

CHAPTER 55

"Nice pad," Reese said looking around, sliding her chopsticks into the fried rice.

"It is."

"I hope Amelia is beating your dad at the game," she laughed.

"Me too."

"This is so good. Do you believe in fate?" She licked her lips and set the remains of the Chinese food on the coffee table next to Elliot's propped up feet.

"Fate? Yes and no." He swallowed his mouthful.

She lifted a brow. "Go on."

"I think life has a way of working things out—but I also think we have the ability to contribute to it along the way."

"Sure we do. Or—most of us do. But I was talking about the Chinese food," she snickered.

"What?" He shook his chopstick at her.

"Feel that?"

He took another bite. "Feel what?"

"The atmosphere. So calm."

"Ah. Yes."

This. Right here. This was what she wanted. But life was clearly not an ocean of calm waters every day. Her family was far away, serving. Amelia was possibly paralyzed. Tracy was battling—and from what she could tell, an innocent soul such as Elliot's dad was living alone. *Life is both beautiful and ugly.*

"Reese."

"Yeah?"

"You're right. We need to set a date sooner rather than later."

Butterflies. She straightened and pulled a blanket up over her body. "I'm all ears."

"Tonight made me realize—we're all human. Maybe I've been too hard on my mom."

Reese tried not to laugh.

"What?"

She couldn't hold it in. *Epic fail.*

"Did you just snort at me?"

"I'm sorry. You caught me off guard. You never told me you were human."

"Don't make me throw a noodle at you," he joked and set his box aside. He pulled his feet down and climbed next to her. "I'm being serious."

"Okay—we're all human. Now what?"

"This isn't as easy as I thought it would be, Reese."

"What isn't?"

"Being around you and—keeping to myself."

She nodded. "Oh."

He kissed her cheek and got up. "Let's get some sleep and mull it over soon. Sound good?"

"Of course, human."

"Wait—you're not supposed to sleep here." He scooped

her up in his arms, blanket and all.

"Elliot!"

"Have no fear—this is an innocent transport."

She gave the back of his head a love tap. "You're funny."

He plopped her down on the bed and zoomed out, returning with her bags. "Here you go, my love."

"You're a riot."

"Soon to be your husband." He winked and shut the door. "See you in the morning, my love," he said in a deep, formal voice through the door.

She laughed and rolled onto the bed. "I can't wait!"

The door flew open, and he poked his head back in. "Don't tell me that. Trust me. Don't tell me that." He closed the door again, and they both laughed.

April seems so far away, though.

REESE TIED HER ROBE TOGETHER AND POURED THE COFFEE Elliot had brewed. There was a note on the counter. He'd scribbled a sick emoji face with an arrow pointing to the coffee pot. He added little hearts too. *This is what it's going to look like isn't it? Life as Mrs. Jacobson.*

Joy permeated her body. She took a sip and peeked around the corner.

Elliot was out on the balcony, laptop in front of him, typing away.

All those years she wasn't sure where she wanted to spend her energy. She knew life wasn't all about her. Helping others had been the one thing that made sense. Months before, Dayl recognized Reese's dilemma in that her introverted nature grated against this personal conviction. But with Elliot in her life—she knew this where she wanted to spend her energy. The best of her energy, anyway. She'd still be imperfect, but Elliot already knew this. It was what made everything so golden. He was perfect for her—imperfectly perfect. She was perfect for him—imperfectly perfect.

REESE COULD FEEL THE SWEAT PUDDLING IN HER PALMS. SHE gave them a wipe just as Elliot reached for her hand.

He clasped tighter than he'd probably realized. They were waiting for the nurse to finish talking to Rob. It was nerve wracking waiting to find out when Amelia could go home to begin learning how to live a new normal.

"She gave me an estimate the other day when we were here—but I didn't want to tell anyone without knowing for sure," Elliot said.

Reese could feel the cold from the wall through her shirt. Why did places like this have the air blasting when it was almost winter?

Elliot pressed his head against the wall—eyes shut. "And where's Mom? Not here. She's barely ever here, from what Amelia's said. So frustrating."

Before Reese had a chance to reply, Rob and the nurse came out, shutting Amelia's door behind them.

"She's going to get some rest now—talk to you soon." The nurse pivoted, leaving Rob with a blank stare, rubbing his chin.

"Let's sit down, son."

They gathered in the waiting room.

Elliot didn't let go of Reese. "So?"

"She'll be able to go home. Very soon. At this point, there's no reason for her to remain here. As long as she has her medicine, her power chair, and I can get her physical therapy set up, we're good."

"Physical therapy?"

"They want to work with her, even if it's just basic motor skills and throwing a ball back and forth. Said it would also help her morale. There are groups across the state with others her age and everything. I think it's a good idea."

"Sounds helpful," Reese added.

"Yes," Rob said, "but here's the deal. The insurance is giving me a hard time with a few things. It's going to take a few days to get the kinks worked out. Also—and I hate to say this—but I don't think your mom's going to be able to give Amelia the attention she needs."

Elliot dropped his head and put his face in his hands.

Reese stood and poked a few coins into the nearby vending machine. She brought back an energy bar and put it in Elliot's hand.

"I'm giving up flying."

Elliot jerked up. "What?"

Rob nodded and rubbed his hands together. "I've already thought it over—it's the right thing to do. Amelia needs care, and even if there were a way she could fly with me…it's too soon."

Elliot bit into the snack.

"So where will you work?" Reese asked.

"I'm already working that out. I have a friend who owns his own company, and he said with my knowledge I can hop on board—no pun intended—and be working for him from home in no time. This'll ensure I'm available for Amelia."

"It's gotta be a pay cut," Elliot said.

"Sure it is. I don't care. I don't have any debt left. This is what I'm doing, but you need to brace yourself, Elliot."

"For what?"

"For what I'm about to tell you."

Elliot pulled Reese closer.

Rob continued. "Your mom has already given me the go-ahead. That's why I'm so sure about this."

"What do you mean?"

"She feels helpless in the matter. Said she can't deal right now."

Elliot stood, folding his hands behind his head. "Of course. It's always about her. What she can and can't do." He walked out.

Rob looked at Reese and took a deep breath. "Amelia's going to be just fine. Tracy—I'm not so sure—but she has my number. She knows I'm just a call away."

Reese bit her lip and shifted in the seat.

Elliot walked back in not looking much better than before. "So, you'll be taking care of Amelia—Mom's got a whole seven rooms to herself while you're in a condo not fit for a handicapped person." He shook his head. "It isn't right."

Rob held up his hand. "Now hold on, son. You haven't heard it all. Sit down. Breathe."

Elliot sat and leaned his head back.

"The condo's only a rental. I never figured I'd settle down there. I didn't know what would happen, truth be told. It was a temporary solution to a hopefully temporary problem. Since that didn't look to be as true as I'd once hoped, I have been making other arrangements."

"What do you mean?" Reese sat up.

"Well, that friend I told you about—soon to employ me? He has a few properties for sale out on Georgia's East Coast. St. Simons Island, actually."

"So you're moving?"

"He's selling all three at once—wants to be done with them."

"How are you going to take care of three properties with Amelia and working from home?"

"I can do it, but what I had in mind was renting the other two out—keep a stream of income flowing from those, plus what I'll make."

Reese thought about it. "It sounds like a creative way to go, but why so far?"

Rob shrugged. "Amelia needs a new view. All she's ever known is the city life. I talked with her about it. She thinks waking up next to the ocean will be a nice move."

Elliot was still thinking.

"Your mom knows, too. This is why I'm staying in Georgia. So she don't have to cross a state line to visit Amelia—and so Amelia's insurance won't have to change or hit any walls—except for the snags I'm working on right now."

"So other than that—everything's already worked out?"

"I keep busy," he laughed.

"Mom's house is so big. She could easily get a ramp installed and—"

Rob shook his head. "Elliot. We both know it's better this way. If your mom agrees—that tells you something."

"She knows her life's not compatible with taking care of her daughter because she won't try hard enough?"

"Elliot…" Reese took his hand.

"Sorry. I know. We're all human. I remember. I just need some fresh air. Be right back." He walked out of the waiting room and out of sight.

Rob was leaned over, but he looked into Reese's eyes. "I'm glad you two are together."

"Me too."

"I need to talk to Elliot—man to man. It's about some big decisions. Do you mind?"

Reese shook her head and smiled. “No, of course. Thanks for including me so far.”

He nodded. “And you’ll be included in this—but I need to speak to him first.” He stood and went to find his son.

Reese admired the man. Made her think of her own family.

CHAPTER 56

Reese pushed the door open.

"Come in," Amelia said.

"I thought you might be asleep."

"Nope. My brain won't shut off."

"Everything okay?"

She nodded. "I just want to get out of here."

"I bet. So, who won the game last night?"

Amelia laughed. "Oh—it's still going."

Reese rolled her eyes. "No kidding?"

"Dad's pretty awesome."

"So I've noticed."

"He told you and Elliot about the move?"

Reese crossed her legs. "Yep. Pretty exciting, huh?"

Amelia shrugged. "I need the kind of adventure that's good for you."

Reese smiled.

"The night I got in the accident, I was angry with Mom. Well, okay—it's been an ongoing thing for a while. But being in here's given me time to think."

"Oh, yeah?"

Amelia took a drink. "Yeah. I don't know how to word it—but I just know putting some healthy space between us for a while will be good. When I came to visit in Kentucky, it wasn't under good circumstances. When I left angry from our house a couple weeks ago and ended up in here—it wasn't either."

Reese searched Amelia's eyes. This young woman who had seemed so sure of herself before, now seemed a little more mature.

"If I go with Dad…maybe Mom can find her way. And maybe I can find mine."

Reese let out a breath. *Wow.*

The door opened.

Elliot came in. "You're supposed to be asleep." He flashed her a cheesy grin.

"I was talking with my future sister-in-law, thank you very much."

Now, there's the young woman I remember.

"Look what I got for you." He held out a bag of fast food.

Amelia's eyes widened. "Thank God. Real, unhealthy food."

He laughed and set it out on her table.

"Where's mine?" Reese joked.

"Dad has it, but he's on a call."

Reese grinned and helped organize the table.

"Guys, I can get it."

"Oh—"

She laughed. "It's okay—I was just letting you know."

Elliot stuck his hands up. "Overprotective me."

"Before you go. Elliot, I want you to know I've forgiven Mom. I hope she forgives me—but I'm not so sure she has. I've caused her a lot of grief."

"Amelia—"

"I am asking you to forgive her as well."

He dropped his head.

"Please. Don't let her mistakes trip you up. I hope mine haven't. I wasn't the easiest person to live with. You know this."

Rob stuck his head in. "Ready to go?"

"No cab this time?"

"No," Elliot said. "He's taking us back to the condo."

Amelia reached for her brother's hand. "I love you."

He hugged her and whispered something in her ear, and her eyes got big.

Reese tapped her foot pretending not to care.

They said their goodbyes, and Rob made sure to tell Amelia he'd be back. She was as bright and energetic as any of them remembered seeing her in the hospital so far. It made for a nice ride to the condo.

Rob dropped them off and went back to the hospital.

Reese nudged Elliot. "What was that all about? With Amelia. Or am I allowed to ask?"

He rubbed his unshaven face and smiled, dimples showing. "You've flown from Kentucky to Georgia. Have any adventurous itching left in you?"

REESE TUCKED HER FAVORITE SWEATER, TEE, AND JEANS INTO her bag. Simple was better.

Elliot rolled his into the entryway. "I feel like I'm having a major case of déjà vu."

"Tell me about it," Reese replied from the bedroom.

"Dad doesn't have to rent these places. He's just choosing to. He has enough saved up to live on for the rest of his life, probably."

"Sounds like a wise man not to assume."

He leaned in the doorway, hand in pocket. "Need help?"

"Nope. But thanks."

"The cardigan looks better on you than me anyway."

Reese looked down and touched the gray fabric. "You can borrow back it anytime," she winked.

"Sure. I think you've said that before."

"So the rental's ready to go?"

"Out front."

Reese threw her bag around her shoulder. "Here we go again."

THE FIVE-HOUR DRIVE TO THE GEORGIA COAST FELT LONGER in the torrential downpour that lasted for half of it.

She wrapped her hair in a messy bun, feet on the dash, and leaned against her door to watch Elliot drive. They'd already stopped once. She hoped if she dozed off, they'd magically arrive at their destination—the three properties Rob had asked them to survey.

Reese shut her eyes, picturing what a winter wedding would look like. *In the winter, it won't matter how pretty it is. What's a winter wedding going to feel like? Brrrr.*

"You asleep?" Elliot asked.

She kept her eyes closed. "No, what's up?"

"You okay with staying at one of the houses for the night, or do you want to drive straight back after? The owner said we could. Our choice."

"Sure. I'm excited to see it."

"Me too. I miss the coast."

"Did you visit a lot growing up?"

"We did. Before Mom got promoted. When life was

slower. There was this beach house we'd stay in for a week. Dad would take us fishing."

"Sounds amazing."

"It was. I kinda miss hanging out with him. Didn't realize it until recently."

"Maybe you all can get some time together soon."

"Yeah, maybe."

Reese's phone buzzed. She peeled her eyes open to check. "Mom says she'll be able to call later. Finally."

"They don't get much down time, do they?"

Reese sat up. "Hey—we're getting close."

The GPS led them a few more miles. Before they got to the property, the ocean was in sight.

"Oh, wow." Reese rolled down her window and poked her head out.

"Hey, that's cold."

"Hurry up."

"I can't drive fast on this road."

"It's a cul-de-sac from Heaven!"

Elliot laughed. "You're cute." He put the car in park, and Reese hopped out before he could say another word.

A big white beach house stood to their right, a light-blue French-style home in the middle—nearest the ocean—and a one-story house sat on the far left.

A man greeted them. "Hello, I'm Damian—Rob's friend."

"Hello," Reese said while Elliot shook his hand.

"So, I see that one already has handicapped accessibility—that's great." Reese pointed toward the one-story house with a ramp along the side, leading to the front door.

"Yes—these were all my vacation rentals, and it turned out to be a wise choice having one completely handicapped accessible. Would you like to start there?"

They followed Damian throughout the properties for the

next hour, and he gave them the freedom to roam without him, to discuss any question they may have had.

"They're pretty stellar."

"That they are. Pricey, too."

"You think your dad can talk him down?"

"He's going to have to. They'd be worth it—but man."

Damian walked up. "Don't forget to walk down to the dock. I'll be around if you need anything."

Reese walked down the steps of the middle house. They were so big—they hadn't even had a chance to really survey the yards and the ocean view from outside yet.

"We could dig this up and add a flat walkway—wouldn't that be neat?" She didn't stop to see Elliot's reaction. The steps wrapped around to the back of the house, which dumped into a large patio facing the water. More steps led to the dock. She followed them down.

"You're fast."

"Sorry. It's so beautiful." She turned to look at the view of the other houses from where they stood. "Look—that one has a ramp on this side too."

Elliot rubbed the back of his neck. "Sure does."

The wind picked up. Reese pulled the cardigan closed.

"Why did you leave your jacket?"

"I hate jackets."

"Then why do you own them at all?"

"Because it's the rule, right?"

He shook his head and took his off, wrapping it around her arms.

"I think I could live here."

"Whoa—you, Miss Homebody?"

She shrugged. "A fresh start sounds nice."

He was quiet and took her chin and kissed her lips there on the dock.

CHAPTER 57

Reese rolled the braid around and around, fastening a ponytail holder around the bun. "What do you think?"

Amelia held up a mirror and touched it. "Love."

"Now, if you two are done primping, take a look at these, sis." Elliot handed her his phone. They'd taken tons of pictures of the three houses, the ocean, and some random plants Reese had thought picturesque.

She swiped, jaw dropping, forming a wide grin. "Gorgeous. Has dad looked at these yet?"

"Yes. We showed him this morning."

"What does he think?"

"He's into them. Trying to negotiate a price—we'll see."

"This all seems so surreal," Reese said.

Amelia set the phone down and straightened. "I know." But the look on her face was serious. She eyed her legs.

Reese swallowed. *Idiot!*

Rob and the nurse came in.

"Big news," she said. "Your chair's here."

Reese got up and stood near the door to make room.

Amelia didn't say anything.

Everyone was quiet while the nurse did her stuff.

Amelia looked at Rob and then to Elliot. It looked like everything was hitting her. She broke down into a sob.

Reese got choked up.

Rob motioned for a moment with her, so everyone else left the room.

Reese walked toward the bathroom and jiggled the knob, but it was locked. Fat tears streaked down her face.

Elliot was behind her and pulled her into a tight hug.

"This sucks. So, so bad."

"I know. But we'll get through this—together. All of us—as a family."

"How? We're going back after Christmas."

She could hear Elliot's heart beating.

He took a deep breath and kissed her head. "We need to talk. Not here."

He led her into a quiet area and took her hands. "Reese, Dad jumped the gun."

She waited, confused.

"He's not going to be able to care for Amelia alone. It takes more than one adult to do this. The nurse was talking to us—and even with home health coming in to help on occasion—Dad's not going to be able to do this alone. I tried calling Mom, but she's prepared to hire a full-time caretaker before she'll do it herself."

Reese raked her fingers through her hair. "What does all this mean?"

"I'm going to have to help him, Reese. It's the only thing that makes sense. I'm her only sibling."

Reese could feel her heart twitch.

He rubbed her hand and kissed her forehead. "Take some

time to think about everything. But if this is too much for you —" He dropped his head. "I'll understand."

Tears formed in her eyes, and she lifted his face. "I'll go with you wherever you need to go, Elliot. Your family is my family too."

Amelia's face said she wasn't sure what to think.

Reese lay her clean blouse across the bed while the staff helped Elliot and Ron load up Amelia's equipment in their newly purchased van, compatible with her chair.

"Want me to pull the curtain?"

"Sure."

She cracked the blinds. Light flooded into the room.

"What's that playing on your phone?"

"Oh, just some music your brother introduced me to."

"He's always discovering the good stuff."

"He's not much into the mainstream, is he?" Reese laughed.

Amelia chuckled. "Oh, no. Not Elliot."

Reese set Amelia's toiletries in her small bag and zipped it up. "One down, two to go."

"Thanks for helping."

"No problem."

"Reese?"

"Yeah?"

"Can you help me with this?"

She adjusted Amelia's bra in the back.

"Thanks. Sorry to ask again. I didn't realize how nice it would be having a woman around. Mom's been so distant this whole time."

"I'm sorry you have to deal with this."

Amelia looked like she was chewing the inside of her cheek. "It is what it is."

"Are you excited about the beach?"

"I was."

"What do you mean?"

"Just not sure. I say it doesn't matter about Mom—I'm trying to be strong. But I need people in my life. Now more than ever."

Reese put the last of her packed bags on the sofa. She wanted to ask Amelia questions. Lots of them—but would it be right? Was it her place? What would she think? She wanted to tell Amelia about her and Elliot's conversation. But even then, they hadn't come to a full solution.

A knock came from the door. It opened a crack.

"We're ready. You need more time?" It was Elliot.

Amelia spoke up. "I'm good."

He came in while Reese pulled the curtain back. "You two have been busy."

"Well, Reese has."

They looked at each other.

"You're doing great." Reese said.

"We'll see about that," she fake-laughed.

"They said you did good learning all these gadgets on here."

Amelia didn't reply.

Reese put her hand on Elliot's back as they walked out, Rob in front, Amelia in the middle, them following behind, luggage in tow.

Elliot let the nurses, Rob, and Amelia go on ahead and pulled Reese to the side.

"Hey, you doing okay?"

"As good as I can be right now. Reese, when we get to the condo, I'm going to help Dad get her inside and settled—but

I'm taking you out tonight. We need to discuss our move from here—and I know Dad doesn't have a lot time to waste."

She nodded and smiled.

"I don't mean move—I mean, what we're going to do next."

"What if we need to move?"

He pressed his lips together, thinking about her words. "I've run through several scenarios—but I'm not sure how to make the best one work."

"Let's get her back and brainstorm. How does that sound?"

He kissed her cheek. "I love you."

CHAPTER 58

"Am I crazy? Tell me the truth." Elliot paced the floor of his house.

They'd flown back to Kentucky after getting Amelia settled into the condo, everyone knowing full well it was only temporary. Damian had agreed to go down on the price, and Rob was set to move into the one-story house on the coast just after New Year's.

It was one week away from Christmas.

"Elliot, you have to trust your gut. You said you felt like you needed to sell Grand's—your house and help your dad near the coast. I think you're right."

"I know, but I just moved here."

"Things change."

"Tell me about it."

Reese poured Elliot a cup of tea.

"Thanks. Have you thought of a date yet?"

"Actually, I wanted to share an idea with you."

He sipped his drink and sat at the kitchen table.

"What if we had a coastal wedding?"

His eyebrows shot up.

"It would be much easier for us to go to Amelia than for her to travel here."

"True."

"When Mom called the other day, while we were there, I asked her opinion about some things."

"Oh, yeah?"

"Elliot—I've changed. I don't feel like I belong here anymore."

He looked confused.

"I can't say what would have happened if nothing had ever happened with Amelia. Who knows? Maybe we would have gotten married nearby and lived happily ever…"

"We never discussed our long-term goals, did we?" He smirked.

"Nope."

"I have a feeling I would have itched to move again, down the road."

"Either way—" Reese looked around. The memories of Jett and Grand flooded back into her mind. "I'm ready for a new start, with you. And if Amelia's in the picture too, I'm okay with that."

"You're talking about more than a wedding. I knew you were serious at the hospital when you said that, but I wasn't so sure how you'd feel once you got back here."

"Yes. I know it seems extreme—but all of this has shown me family isn't about location. It's about connection."

"Profound."

She tossed a dry tea bag at him.

"Hey! I gotta lighten the mood somehow."

"My parents said they'd buy your house for now. They're thinking about selling, too, and moving closer to the nonprofit headquarters."

Reese walked down the hall into Elliot's room where her bags lay on his bed. She pulled a hoody over her T-shirt.

Elliot stood in the doorway. "I'm speechless."

She wrapped her hands around the back of his neck. "We hire packers and movers, fly back for Christmas, fly back here for New Year's—tell everyone goodbye—and voila."

"That's too much flying for my wallet."

"I can help."

"Do you trust me?"

She sat on the bed. "Yes."

"I think Amelia will be okay if we can't make it back in a week. Let's sleep on this and look up moving info tomorrow. Plus, your parents are coming in—"

She started to argue, but he leaned in to kiss her.

I'll argue later, then.

REESE STEPPED OUT OF HER PARENT'S HOUSE, ENERGIZED BY A fresh morning.

Elliot was running up the road and threw her a wave.

Just like old times.

He took his earbuds out and strung them around his neck.

"You're hot when you run," she commented as he came down the drive.

"Yes. I am hot. Gotta drink?"

She poked him and jogged back into the house, but he came in before she retrieved it from the fridge.

"Aren't you going to miss it here?"

"Yes and no. I've been feeling detached for a while."

He took a long drink.

She tucked a piece of paper in his pocket.

"Thanks?"

She smirked. "I got some moving numbers for you."

"Thanks." He set the glass down and moved closer to her.

"You are so sweaty."

"Thought you said I was hot?"

"Yes, you are—"

"Only from the road?" He laughed and kissed her cheek.

His phone rang. "Hello?"

It was early still. Reese wondered who it was this early in the day. *Is Amelia okay?*

"Hey—sure. Let me shower and call you back."

Reese stuck her head forward with a questioning look.

"Amelia. She wants to talk. It's about Christmas."

CHAPTER 59

Reese pulled a card from the mailbox. It was from Dayl.

Reese,

I hope you're doing well during these holidays. Please know I wish you all the best, and you are free to call me anytime—even if it's a phone appointment.

Sincerely,

Dayl

SHE TUCKED THE CARD BACK INTO THE ROSE-COLORED envelope and breathed in the winter country air. It was so different here than in the heart of Georgia. But the coastal air was marvelous too. She could see herself there—with Elliot, watching the tide roll in and out each day.

Elliot stepped outside and sat on his porch.

"What's the long look?"

"Amelia. I just got off the phone with her and then Dad. She's insisting on coming up here for Christmas."

"Oh, no. That wasn't supposed to happen."

"I almost didn't fly back." He kicked a rock.

Reese sat beside him, setting the card on the porch. "It'll be okay. You said you wanted to come back and think about everything—well, we did."

"I know, but she doesn't need to be traveling this soon."

Reese massaged his neck with one hand. "What did your dad say?"

Elliot sighed. "He was against it at first."

"Until?"

"Until Amelia told him why."

Miss Lila drove by and honked.

"She's out early."

"I thought she didn't drive?"

"Sometimes. Rarely." Reese waved. "I need to go visit them. Everyone."

"I talked to Amelia about me possibly moving in with her and Dad—before you and I finished talking about it."

Reese searched his face.

"I'm sorry. Maybe I shouldn't have. But it was like this: I knew I had to be there for her."

Reese bit her lip. "If I had been against moving—you're saying you would have broken our engagement off?"

He turned toward her and grabbed her hands. "No—not really. I didn't know what to do—I only knew the right thing to do was help them."

Reese wasn't quite sure what to think, but she knew she wasn't mad at Elliot.

"I'm—sorry. I need to learn how to communicate with you fully. Better. You first—if we're going to be married."

She laughed. "I do too. It's not just you."

"We're good?"

She nodded. "You've been under a lot of stress, Elliot. I think you're doing the best you can."

"So, Dad said he's driving her up in four days."

"Wow. Christmas here. Him too."

"Now that I think about it, I'm glad for Amelia's stubbornness. It'll be nice to have Dad here at least once."

"Of course."

Elliot stood and reached for Reese, pulling her to her feet. "What do you think about them staying through New Year's, and we can all head back around the same time?"

"Elliot. You're asking me a question about your own house."

He looked around. "You're right, I guess. It feels like we're married, but not."

They both laughed.

"This has been…interesting, to say the least."

She took his arm and they went inside his house. "Interesting is the best word you can come up with, Mr. Author?"

He gave her side a soft elbow and shut the door behind them.

REESE AND ELLIOT SPENT THE NEXT FEW DAYS MAKING THEIR rounds, visiting neighbors and updating them on Amelia. The town had even gathered for prayer after they flew to Georgia. Elliot was in awe of their thoughtfulness.

Butterflies in Reese's stomach arose as Christmas drew closer. She wanted to host Amelia well—but Christmas also meant New Year's and her parent's arrival the day before. Her nerves were knotted. She wrung her hands tight.

The timer went off.

"Thank you!" Elliot joked.

Reese pulled the cookie sheet from the oven.

"I was afraid you were going to rip your hands off. Come here—sit down."

"I can't. There's too much to do."

He grabbed her and pulled her down onto his lap as she walked by. "No—there's not. It's just Dad and sis. They know you, they love you."

"But—"

"They're not coming for the food and the decorations. They're coming for us."

She leaned back, head on his shoulder, spatula in hand.

"You know I'm right."

"Yeah, yeah."

He kissed her neck.

"You're trying to lure me into your dreamy dream boat, and I have stuff to do before they arrive. In only two hours!"

"Do we have to wait?"

She sat up. "What?"

He played with the ring on her finger. "Can't we just get married when your parents come in?"

"Where is this coming from?" She smiled, tilting her head.

"I—I just need you to be my wife already." He cracked a laugh that had Reese wondering, and he slid out from under her, stealing a cookie from the metal pan.

"I don't even have a dress yet," she protested and walked back into the kitchen.

"Just a formality," he said, biting down.

Redford barked from outside. "Oh, no—how'd he get out?"

Elliot peeked through the curtain. "They're already here."

Reese almost dropped the spatula and looked down at her messy apron, wishing she could press pause on the clock.

Get over yourself. Amelia's here now. And take her a cookie, for crying out loud.

CHAPTER 60

December 24 was cold and dry, but the sky was white, as if it snowed upside down.

Elliot had spent the previous day with his dad, showing him around town and introducing him to a few people while Reese and Amelia played checkers. Miss Lila and Stan and Miss Rosa dropped by to visit. It was a surprise.

Amelia had remembered Miss Rosa from before—even asked about Anette. A part of Reese wondered if she was making the right decision uprooting from Kentucky—but every time she imagined her life without Elliot or Amelia, she just couldn't.

Elliot had worked so hard with the car dealer, Rob—trying to get portable ramps in place for both houses before Amelia arrived. Seeing him kick into gear was one of the reminders that this was her man. Their hearts lined up, like two oddly shaped pieces of a colossal puzzle, snapping into place.

Those were the thoughts running through her mind when she dug through her mom's trunk the night before, after everyone had parted ways—leaving her alone, sleeping at her parents' house.

There it had been all this time. Her mom's ivory silk wedding gown.

Reese pulled it gently from the trunk, holding it against her body. It was long sleeved, with lace on the ends. She folded it back and shut the trunk.

Sometimes a gut feeling didn't bend the way logic did.

She let the memories of the night before fuel her. A moment of bravery took over.

She slipped into a different dress she had. She'd worn it during college for graduation. It was white.

She shot Elliot a text.

"If you are free for a sec, come here—please."

A few minutes later, Elliot was walking through the front door, gasping for breath. "Reese? You okay?"

She came around the corner.

He just looked at her for a minute, then understood. "Yes? Soon?"

She smiled and nodded.

He ran over and grabbed her up, spinning her around. He locked his fingers with hers. "Are you sure? I don't want to rush you."

"This is bigger than just you and me. And this *is* what I want." She touched his prickly face and pulled him down into a kiss.

"This works out perfectly."

"What do you mean?"

"You'll have to find out."

"You can't leave me hanging!"

"Oh, watch me. Now if you'll excuse me, Mrs. Almost-Jacobson, I have to go finish my casserole."

"I'm going to be learning about all your hidden talents for a long time, aren't I?"

He grinned ear to ear. "Probably so."

REESE FOLDED HER POEM. SHE HAD NEVER THOUGHT HERSELF a great producer of verse, but for Elliot, she wanted something real. Something she could read without tripping over her words.

Now, to just add twine.

"Let's write our vows and untie them in front of everyone," she'd suggested to Elliot. She stepped into the mudroom and looked for the box of decor Miss Rosa had given back to her.

Twine, twine, twine. Where are you?

Finally, she spotted it on the shelf past the dryer.

"Yes, that's where I put you." She opened the flaps and dug around until she felt the grainy fibers touch her hand. Closing her fist around a large ball of the stuff, she pulled it out.

"Ow!" She accidentally stubbed her toe on something. The black bin.

She clutched the twine and spun around but gave it one last look. "Goodbye, Jett. Rest in peace."

CHAPTER 61

"Miss Rosa's been trying to call you." Elliot waved the phone.

"Since when did she get your number?"

He gave her a funny look. "Did you forget?"

"Right," Reese remembered his sneaky arrival.

He tossed her the phone. "She wants in on the last-minute wedding plans."

"Oh—I'm in trouble now."

She'd been so busy trying to sort through her belongings at the house and then helping Elliot to prepare dinner, she hadn't paid attention to her phone. Plus, Rob and Amelia were too much fun for her to think about much else. She tried focusing on food and festivities, but it wasn't working too well. The ongoing game of charades was enticing. She and Elliot chimed in when they weren't busy, but he joked he'd fire her if she ignored the beep of the oven one more time.

It was turning out to be a wonderful Christmas Eve, despite the circumstances.

"I can't imagine Christmas without you two, now," Reese said.

"Still want to head into town," Amelia chimed in. "See all the lights."

"Of course," Elliot winked. "Just not yet."

Reese smiled; there was a gleam in his eye. *What are you up to now?*

The oven beeped just as a knock came from the door.

"You get the door—I'll get this," he said, with a hint of sarcasm in his voice.

"Who could that be?"

"Maybe it's Miss Rosa hunting you down!"

She turned the knob. Her family. Here? "Mom? Dad?" It was obvious. But what…?

Her sister Dana walked up behind them.

Reese's heart fell out onto the floor. "Oh my—"

"Don't just stand there, child, give us a hug!"

She lunged forward hugging them both at once.

"Don't forget me!"

She laughed through the tears that wet her dad's coat and grabbed for her sister. "Come in! What are you all doing here today?"

Her family exchanged glances.

"Who's fessing up?"

Her dad grinned. "It was planned all along. We couldn't not be home for Christmas."

Reese buried her face back into her dad's coat and squeezed him tight.

Elliot pulled the pot holders off his hands and walked over to greet them.

"So nice to meet you in person, Elliot," her dad said.

"He is quite the stud," Dana whispered under her breath, giving Reese a quick wink.

"It's nice to meet you, ma'am," Elliot said, shaking her mom's hand. "Let me take your coats."

Reese introduced them to Rob and Amelia and finished setting the table for their big Christmas Eve dinner. Everyone else was in the living room when she began pouring drinks. "You knew about them coming early, didn't you?"

Elliot took the rolls out of the oven and tapped them into a large wooden bowl. "You already know the answer to that."

She smacked him on the butt and took two glasses to the table. She set them down and called for everyone to come to the table.

Elliot grabbed her hands and twirled her in a circle. He leaned her back and planted a kiss firmly on her lips. "Merry Christmas Eve."

AMELIA PRESSED HER NOSE AGAINST COLD GLASS. "I WAS hoping it would snow today."

"White Christmases are the best, aren't they?" Dana smiled.

"Winter's just beginning." Reese handed Amelia a cup of hot cocoa.

"Thanks."

"There's plenty of time for the white stuff of Heaven to fall down."

Dana gave Reese's arm a squeeze. "I've missed you so much. I'm glad we get to spend the entire day just catching up and eating."

"Me too," Reese said.

Rob and Elliot were at the table working out moving plans, while Reese's dad went over to check on Miss Lila and Stan and see if they wanted to come over. He never did sit still. But now, Reese smiled about it. She could feel her heart healing, layer by layer.

Her mom was sitting cross-legged on Elliot's living room rug. They talked for hours about their trip overseas, plans for the future—including helping Elliot with the sale of his house. When Rob found out, he cried. Big, fat man tears. Elliot did too, as if it hit for the first time.

"You all don't know what this means to us," Rob said.

Reese had to get tissues for everyone.

Her mom looked straight into her eyes but was talking to everyone within ear shot. "We've always known Reese had a unique path—we just didn't know what that was."

Elliot stopped what he was doing and turned.

She kept going. "Now we see. You two are—"

"Mom, stop! I don't want to cry anymore today," Reese said, and they hugged, laughing and crying again.

Reese's glance caught Elliot's.

He blew her a kiss.

"But so mushy," Dana added for extra laughs.

"Speaking of mushy—you should have seen the garden after that storm."

Reese took Dana and her mom out in their back yard to fill in the gaps of her past year and the journey she'd taken with Dayl to help get to the bottom of the panic attacks.

Dana blew her nose into a tissue. "I didn't realize you were going through so much, Reese."

"All this shivering and crying calls for more hot chocolate," her mom said. She walked on ahead of them into Elliot's house.

"We need to stay connected this time," Dana said. She turned to face Reese. "I'm so sorry I wasn't there for you."

Reese just smiled and patted her head. "Let's go in."

"Sure thing."

They looked toward the back window of what used to be Grand's house, and Reese saw something entirely different now. The pains of yesterday were fading, and in their place, something new and beautiful was budding.

With the sun going down, the light in the dining room lit everything up. She could see Elliot stretch and lean back over his dad as they calculated and figured. "I get to marry my best friend." It didn't mean Jett never was—but she understood now that life wasn't one dimensional.

Rob hopped up and opened the door for the women.

Amelia was now at the table dealing cards out for everyone. "Get in here before you freeze, ladies."

Elliot motioned for Reese to follow him down the hall.

"Hey—what's up?"

He ran his fingers through her hair. "Dad and I pinpointed a move day. What do you think about January 7th? We couldn't really do it any sooner. The movers needed a certain amount of notice."

"That'll give us time to finish packing with the boxes you already have. And they'll bring more, right?"

"Yeah," he laughed. "It feels like I just did this."

"Well, you did."

"Something else—"

"Yeah?"

"You still want a coastal wedding? Because dad said he's willing to fly anyone and everyone out to the properties, pay for their hotel rooms, and fly them back here—so we can get married in front of the water, if that's what your heart is set on."

Reese grabbed his arms and laughed into his chest.

"I want this to be as special as it can possibly be for you, Reese. Just say the word."

CHAPTER 62

"Snow!" Amelia cheered from Elliot's room.

Reese opened her eyes. They'd all stayed up for New Year's Eve. When she realized what day it was, she squealed like a small child. "Happy New Year!" She rolled off Elliot's couch and ran to Amelia, who was sitting up on the bed.

Reese maneuvered around the lift and past her chair to peek out the window. "Woot!" She gave Amelia a hug. "Happy New Year."

Elliot came bounding downstairs and whirled into his room. He dug around and finally pulled his shoes from under the bed. He threw open his closet and pulled a hoodie over his head. "Be right back."

Amelia looked to Reese.

Reese shrugged. She loved that Elliot always kept her guessing.

The sound of a door slamming must have awoken Rob.

A few minutes later he poked his head into the room. "What's going on?"

"Don't know, Elliot's—"

He flew past his dad, snowball in hand, and set it in Amelia's hands. "It's sticking."

"It's cold! Elliot, what in the world?"

"Throw it at me."

"What?"

"Just do it."

Reese laughed, and Rob shook his head. "I need coffee for this."

They filed out and Elliot backed against the hallway where he could still see Amelia. "Go for it."

Without argument, she hurled the packed ball toward his chest. It exploded everywhere. "Feel better?" She asked.

"Do you?"

"What? I just made a mess!"

"But was it fun?"

"Yes," she laughed. "You're crazy."

Reese hurled a biscuit from the night before straight at Elliot. "I feel better now."

He scooped her up and kissed her lips. "See? Laughter's like medicine."

THEIR LAST FEW DAYS SPENT IN KENTUCKY BEFORE THE BIG move were a whirlwind.

Miss Rosa, Anette, and Miss Lila insisted on taking care of wedding decorations. They planned on boxing them up and either stuffing them in the van with Rob and Amelia or sending them on board their flight to Georgia when it was time.

A January wedding, which none of them had imagined Reese going for, was imminent. Miss Rosa promised her silk flowers were realistic looking, but Reese told her it wasn't a huge deal. Simple was preferred, a small gathering on the beach, but they could use their made-with-care decor on the tables for afterward during the meal.

It was the day before the move, and Reese was all jitters. Not from cold feet, but knowing she was about to say goodbye to her childhood hometown. Of course, they'd come to visit—but who knew when?

She pulled up a few websites on her laptop, searching for the perfect dress. Amelia was beside her. "We have to find one for you, Mom, and Dana too."

"Can I help?"

Reese handed her the laptop. "Please," she sighed. "My eyes need a break."

"More than happy to!"

Reese stepped out of Elliot's room where she and Amelia were chilling on the bed.

She went into the bathroom to splash her face. "Hey, Amelia, if Elliot asks where I am, tell him I went over to talk to Dad."

"Sure."

She slipped a coat on, along with Elliot's oversized slippers, and fumbled across the yard, trying not get snow inside the shoes.

"There's the bride-to-be," her mom said. "You just missed everyone. Look—" She held up more decor they finished putting together.

"I love it."

"What's wrong? You look heavy."

Reese bit her nail. "No, just want to talk to Dad."

"He's upstairs. Go on."

Reese slipped the wet shoes off and draped the coat

across the entryway table. She found her dad shaving with the door wide open.

She gave the wall outside the bathroom a knock, though it was obvious she was there.

"Hey, kid. How you doing?"

"Mind if we chat for a few?"

"Not at all. Pull up a chair."

She pulled the extra chair in the bathroom out the door into the hallway.

"What's on your mind?"

"I just wanted to say thanks."

He tapped the razor on the sink and rinsed it, then went back to shave the next section. "For?"

"For being there for me growing up. Some people don't have it so nice. I see that now."

"I know I slacked a lot when you got older—I'm sorry. But I do love you."

"I know you do. And thanks for the car. I mean who does that? And thanks for helping Elliot. I am beyond grateful, Dad."

"I know you are—that's why we have no regrets. We're doing the right thing. And the car—well, you deserve it, kid. You've never asked much all your life. You've always used what you were given or worked hard for what you didn't have. The car's a gift. The house thing—we felt a tug in our hearts to go the extra mile."

"You just got back from living this exact thing though."

He tapped the razor and rinsed it, then eyed her in the mirror. "Doing the right thing doesn't have an off button. You just live it, Reese. Your life is an example of this, too."

"Not me." She shook her head.

"You don't see it. We do. Elliot does, too. And he's a lucky, lucky man to have you." He finished and dried his face, throwing a shirt on before stepping out. "I am one proud dad."

Reese wiped a tear from her eye as he gave her a hug. "Love you always."

They went downstairs, and Reese tried to act normal.

"Whoa, whoa—do I see leakage?" Dana joked with her hands on her hips.

Reese laughed. "Yes—cut it out."

"Well, I hate to break up the fun, but, Reese, you—really we all—need to get to bed. You have a long drive ahead of you. It's going to be harder without having Elliot in the car to keep you awake."

They had to drive both vehicles down, so flying was out of the question for them. And Rob had to drive all the way back with Amelia.

"We're going to try to make it in a day, but if we get tired, we'll stop overnight."

"We used to make the drive to Florida in one trip, so you'll probably be okay—but you know your body better than anyone."

Dana gave her sister a hug goodnight.

"You okay sleeping over there? Sure you don't want your last night to be here?"

Reese shook her head. "Last night was good. I slept with Amelia in Elliot's bed. We stayed up talking about her favorite things until we were both too tired to say another word."

Her mom smiled and took her hand. "You are a true friend, Reese."

"I don't feel like someone special—just doing what I would want done to myself."

"That's why you are."

She kissed them goodnight and thought about her mom's

words. Elliot was on the front porch waiting for her. "Hey, what are you doing out here in the cold?"

"I didn't want to go to bed until I knew where you were sleeping. You still all right?"

"I'm great. Even better now."

CHAPTER 63

The wind blew hard the day Reese stuffed her car to the brim.

Everyone who wasn't leaving huddled together on the porch.

Reese tried to make them go in, but they refused to go inside until she was out of sight.

It was quite the sight. Miss Rosa, Anette, Ron the car dealer, Miss Lila and Stan, and her family were lined up across the porch.

Miss Rosa stepped forward, tissue in hand. "Reesey, don't forget to read the cards we gave you during your engagement. They'll be a comfort if you ever get homesick."

"That's a wonderful idea. Don't forget—I'll see you soon."

Miss Rosa nodded, teary eyed as ever. They hugged, and Reese went down the line.

Rob and Amelia had already said their goodbyes and were headed down the road.

"Now remember, no worrying about your stuff. The movers are coming later today. We'll make sure they get everything." Her mom kissed her cheek and gave Reese's hand a firm grip. *Mom. Always trying to be strong and hold everyone up. She'll probably cry her eyes out later.*

"Oh, sis. The next time I see you…we'll both be changing into dresses." Dana wiped her eyes. "Blah. I hate crying!" They both laughed and gave one last hug.

Her dad couldn't form words. He only pulled her into his arms.

"I love you, Dad."

"Love you, too." He turned to Elliot and held out his hand. "Take care of her, son."

Elliot nodded, but when he reached for his hand, her dad pulled him into a bear hug.

"Thank you, sir."

Reese and Elliot walked up the yard together.

"This drive is going to suck."

He laughed and slid his hands around her back. "It's only for today. Your GPS is set, just follow me so you have less to think about."

"You have snacks within easy reach?"

"Yes, ma'am." He grinned.

"Y'all already sound like an old married couple!" Dana said from the porch.

Reese gave an eye roll. It was true Elliot may have grown up a city boy, but his Southern charm was just a part of who he was.

They waved and gave each other one last kiss before getting into separate vehicles.

It felt like they were leaving too much for her family to do, but the couple discussed the possibility of an early spring visit to Kentucky to tie up any loose ends with Elliot's house. He had the next two or three months' worth of the mortgage covered, so there was no rush finalizing the sale.

Reese felt her sinuses burning as she backed out of the driveway. "Keep it together."

She smiled and waved to her family again before pulling onto the paved road behind Elliot.

This is it.

I'm going on a real adventure.

ELLIOT SPOKE TO REESE MIDWAY THROUGH THE TRIP. "I'D feel better if I could stop by Mom's. I'm going to hand deliver our wedding invitation—even if she's at work. At least she'll know we swung by."

Reese was glad for it. No one had heard from Tracy the entire time, though both men had tried reaching her throughout the past two weeks.

Elliot called Rob to let him know they'd be arriving later than planned.

Fidgeting with the radio scanner outside Tracy's house, Reese tried to ignore the pang in her gut. *What if Tracy doesn't show up at the wedding? What if she doesn't respond at all?*

Ten minutes later, Elliot came out.

Reese lowered the window. "Any word?"

He shook his head. "Jo said she's at work. I wrote her a note and put it under the invitation." He folded his hands behind his neck. "I've left her numerous voicemails. Hope I didn't push her away for good."

She squeezed his hand before he got back in the Jeep.

Almost five hours later, they made it to St. Simons Island.

Rob's movers were scheduled to have all his and Amelia's things at the new property around the same time Reese and Elliot's would arrive.

They'd packed enough in their luggage to last until the rest of their belongings finally caught up with them.

They parked the vehicles in the center of the cul-de-sac.

"Which house?"

"I figured we'd decide that later."

"Except—later's today," Reese laughed.

"I'm just glad they have the basic furniture, or we'd be sleeping on the floor."

Rob walked out of the far house. "Hey—look who loves the coast!"

He watched the door.

Elliot coupled his hand with Reese's.

Amelia came rolling down the ramp in her chair, blanket over her lap. "You're here!"

Reese knew this was a turning a point in her life. All the anxiety, all the butterflies, all the unknowns—were worth it.

She watched Elliot run to give his sister the biggest hug.

Three days until I'm all yours, Mr. Jacobson.

CHAPTER 64

The delight on Amelia's face spoke louder than words. Her lengthy new ramp was now in place, allowing her to travel to each house and down the rear side to the beach.

Rob worked nonstop with a hired crew the day after their arrival. Every fiber in Reese's body knew they'd made the right move in coming to live beside Rob and Amelia.

Elliot and Reese unpacked as much as they could in the two days that led up to the wedding, but when her mom showed up, she was told to put all her work on pause.

"You need to get rest for the big day," she emphasized.

"Simple day," Reese argued. Nothing was going to stress her out. Not this close to saying those two magical words. But they really weren't magical. If anything, her and Elliot's relationship showed her people can enjoy deep love, no fluff added. Though she wished she could turn back the clock and keep Amelia from getting hurt—even changing her own response toward Tracy, despite what she may have deserved—she knew the hardships they'd experienced would only serve to make them stronger.

After everyone settled in from the drive back from the airport, Elliot whisked her away with a promise to the family he'd have her back and in bed before nine.

Blanket thrown over his shoulder, lantern in one hand, Reese's hand in the other, he led her down the splintered wooden steps to the sandy shore. The moonlight bounced off the ocean's top.

"It's like having two moons."

He pulled the blanket around the two of them, her head against his beating heart.

Out of all the ways her last night as a single woman could have ended, this far surpassed any she'd ever dreamed up.

It was a breezy fifty degrees on January 10, 2019, on Saint Simons Island.

Reese stood behind a white sheet adorned with handmade vines, sprinkled with tiny white flowers. The sheet flowed down from a wooden trellis that would lead to the next, where Elliot would be, Rob by his side.

"You look beautiful," Reese told Amelia.

"Thank you for letting me pick out the dresses."

"They're perfect."

Amelia took a deep breath.

The violinist her mom hired began playing.

"That's my cue."

Dana pulled the sheet over enough to let Amelia through. "Here we go."

Reese stood behind her sister.

"Doing okay back there?"

"Mmmhmm," Reese replied.

"My turn."

Her mom pulled the curtain back, and Dana made her way down the runner, slow and steady.

"Your turn." Her mom smiled.

Reese adjusted the hem of the slender gown Amelia had picked out for her. It was much like her mom's, but new. Her hair was braided in a fish tail on the side, with two small curls in the front.

"You look amazing. I love you. Now go to your man."

This is really happening. This is really happening.

She'd imagined this moment more times than she could count, and now here she was—walking across a white runner, barefoot, feeling the squish of the cool sand beneath the cotton.

She looked straight at Elliot. *You sure know how to pull off a tux, Mr. Jacobson.* She watched his eye movement. *He's looking for his mom.*

He focused back to Reese and smiled the remainder of the time she walked toward him, and he wiped a tear from his eye.

She was sure others were crying too—but she dared not look away from him. Not yet.

He took her hands, and the minister began.

Amelia handed them both the twine-wrapped vows, and they took turns reading them aloud to one another. When it was time, she also gave them the rings.

"You may now kiss your bride."

Elliot pulled Reese into a maddening kiss, sending her heart into outer space.

He leaned into her ear. "There's more where that came from."

Reese burst into laughter.

They turned toward their tiny audience, and the minister spoke up. "Let's now celebrate the marriage of Mr. and Mrs. Elliot and Reese Jacobson."

CHAPTER 65

Each person shared sweet words during the toast.

When it was Elliot's turn, Reese made sure to have a tissue in hand.

"Your lover's a poet. Want the whole box?" Dana snickered.

There were no mics involved.

He only turned to Reese and spoke from his heart. "This toast is to the woman who changed my life the year 2018. Laughter had been a stranger to me, but Reese reintroduced us. Friends made themselves scarce—she became one. True love was unknown to me—she lived true love in the way she put others first. What we have is not a common thing. I know this. I will hold on to you, my wonderful, smart, smoking-hot wife—Reese Jacobson—until the day I take my final breath."

Everyone swooned and hollered, but Reese was all puddles.

He held her hips and pressed his lips into hers.

She whispered in his ear this time. "I don't think I can top that."

She gripped the tissue and shut her eyes, trying to focus

her thoughts into a cohesive strand of sentences. "Of all the days I never saw coming, my first glance at Elliot told me something more existed. He left my stomach in knots, had me spying through windows on more than one occasion—and had me downright smitten. Everything about him makes me speechless—even now." Her eyes popped open. "I'm all yours, Mr. Jacobson."

Dana hit play on the stereo she'd set up. "Dance, people!"

Journal entry: January 30th, 2019

My family's been back home in Kentucky for seventeen days now.

I'm sinking my feet in this new one quite well.

After much consideration, my husband has decided to hire me as his full-time editor and assistant. I almost didn't pass the interview—but I threw all morals out the French doors and bribed my sexy employer with kisses and a tray of sushi.

It worked.

I must say, trying to focus on correcting his grammatical errors is challenging. Sure, he's fairly practiced by now—but my biggest issue is when he sits on the balcony in his pajama pants, writing as if his life depended on it.

I mean—who can focus on work with a view like him?

But really—I am proud of the man.

He's finishing the series he put on hold during the holidays. I've never seen him happier except for the moments he talks about his mom. She called recently, to apologize—but it doesn't instantly heal the hurt. I can see it in his eyes. But I have a feeling in the deepest recesses of my gut—hope is not far away. Reconciliation is powerful. It's Amelia who taught us this. And speaking of her—

Amelia's even thinking about taking after her brother to write her own stories. I think it's a great idea. What did I do to deserve this life?

They said I was someone special, but I still can't see it; I only felt like a stumbler and a fumbler—but I'm not wasting any more time fretting about the mess. Fresh starts come because we need them. Not because we don't.

Timer's going off. Free time over. Time to make my freakishly handsome boss a cup of tea and get back to work.

ACKNOWLEDGMENTS

It felt like I wrote this book alone—but upon reflection, I realized this is just not true. All who come to mind—the seed sowers, the waterers—in the writing of this story are found here. Thank you from the bottom of my heart. I'll start by thanking my best friend Jesus, for helping me to finally finish something. He and mom know the nature of my struggle with finishing things. A special never-ending bear hug will be prescribed to my husband who—without his help, this book would not be. You helped feed, entertain, and do homework with the kids while I pushed through the uphill mud of writing this story to completion. Your investment in all the ways reach further than feeble words can muster. Angie—what can I say but thank you for walking with me through the doubts of half written manuscripts. For cheering me on and refueling me with hope. Thank you, Bettie, for being a consistent encouragement in my writing endeavors, since day one. Thank you, Aunt Marlena, for investing in my love of words as a young child. Your kindness was an eternal seed. Thank you, Aunt Leigh Ann, for your kind words and support over the years. Thank you, Aunt Nita, for asking about my writing and sending articles of interest my way. Knowing someone cares is immeasurable. Jennifer—your enthusiasm for the book helped me immensely. Thank you, Janna for all the times you checked in with me to see how I was doing. This went such a long way. Thank you, Sean, for letting me bounce book ideas off you over a year ago. Thank you, mom and dad, for supporting me in my dream. Lastly, thank you to all the writers who have been so generous with wisdom and knowledge in this book-writing process. You have changed my life.

ABOUT THE AUTHOR

M. E. Weyerbacher is a published poet, winning historical essayist, and full-time writer fueled by imagination and strong coffee. Stay informed of her next romance novel by signing up at:

https://meghanweyerbacher.com/romance-readers/

Email: meg@thebloggingwriter.com

facebook.com/MEWeyerbacher

twitter.com/MegWeyerbacher

instagram.com/MegWeyerbacher

goodreads.com/MegWeyerbacher

28494832R00188

Made in the USA
Columbia, SC
12 October 2018